Robert Michael Ba

The World of Ice

Robert Michael Ballantyne

The World of Ice

1st Edition | ISBN: 978-3-73409-334-0

Place of Publication: Frankfurt am Main, Germany

Year of Publication: 2019

Outlook Verlag GmbH, Germany.

Reproduction of the original.

THE

WORLD OF ICE

OR

**The Whaling Cruise
of "The Dolphin"**

AND

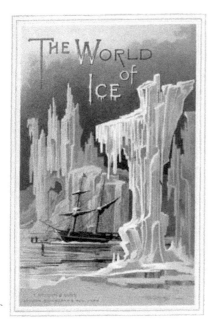

The Adventures of Her Crew
in the Polar Regions

By

Robert Michael Ballantyne

Author of "The Dog Crusoe and his Master," "The Young Fur-Traders," "The Gorilla-Hunters," "Ungava," "The Coral Island," &c.

1893

PREFACE.

Dear Reader, most people prefer a short to a long preface. Permit me, therefore, to cut this one short, by simply expressing an earnest hope that my book may afford you much profit and amusement.

R.M. BALLANTYNE.

CONTENTS.

CHAPTER I.

Some of the "dramatis personæ" introduced—Retrospective glances—Causes of future effects—Our hero's early life at sea—A pirate—A terrible fight and its consequences—Buzzby's helm lashed amidships—A whaling-cruise begun.

Nobody ever caught John Buzzby asleep by any chance whatever. No weasel was ever half so sensitive on that point as he was. Wherever he happened to be (and in the course of his adventurous life he had been to nearly all parts of the known world) he was the first awake in the morning and the last asleep at night; he always answered promptly to the first call; and was never known by any man living to have been seen with his eyes shut, except when he winked, and that operation he performed less frequently than other men.

John Buzzby was an old salt—a regular true-blue Jack tar of the old school, who had been born and bred at sea; had visited foreign ports innumerable; had weathered more storms than he could count, and had witnessed more strange sights than he could remember. He was tough, and sturdy, and grizzled, and broad, and square, and massive —a first-rate specimen of a John Bull, and according to himself, "always kept his weather-eye open." This remark of his was apt to create confusion in the minds of his hearers; for John meant the expression to be understood figuratively, while, in point of fact, he almost always kept one of his literal eyes open and the other partially closed, but as he reversed the order of arrangement frequently, he might have been said to keep his lee-eye as much open as the weather one. This peculiarity gave to his countenance an expression of earnest thoughtfulness mingled with humour. Buzzby was fond of being thought old, and he looked much older than he really was. Men guessed his age at fifty-five, but they were ten years out in their reckoning; for John had numbered only forty-five summers, and was as tough and muscular as ever he had been—although not quite so elastic.

John Buzzby stood on the pier of the sea-port town of Grayton watching the active operations of the crew of a whaling-ship which was on the point of starting for the ice-bound seas of the Frozen Regions, and making sundry remarks to a stout, fair-haired boy of fifteen, who stood by his side gazing at the ship with an expression of deep sadness.

"She's a trim-built craft and a good sea-boat, I'll be bound, Master Fred," observed the sailor; "but she's too small by half, accordin' to my notions, and I *have* seen a few whalers in my day. Them bow-timbers, too, are scarce thick enough for goin' bump agin the ice o' Davis' Straits. Howsom'iver, I've seen worse craft drivin' a good trade in the Polar Seas."

"She's a first-rate craft in all respects; and you have too high an opinion of your own judgment," replied the youth indignantly. "Do you suppose that my father, who is an older man than yourself and as good a sailor, would buy a ship, and fit her out, and go off to the whale-fishery in her, if he did not think her a good one?"

"Ah! Master Fred, you're a chip of the old block—neck or nothing—carry on all sail till you tear the masts out of her! Reef the t'gallant sails of your temper, boy, and don't run foul of an old man who has been all but a wet-nurse to ye—taught ye to walk, and swim, and pull an oar, and build ships, and has hauled ye out o' the sea when ye fell in—from the time ye could barely stump along on two legs, lookin' like as if ye was more nor half-seas-over."

"Well, Buzzby," replied the boy, laughing, "if you've been all that to me, I think you *have* been a *wet*-nurse too! But why do you run down my father's ship? Do you think I'm going to stand that? No! not even from you, old boy."

"Hallo! youngster," shouted a voice from the deck of the vessel in question, "run up and tell your father we're all ready, and if he don't make haste he'll lose the tide, so he will, and that'll make us have to start on a Friday, it will, an' that'll not do for me, nohow it won't; so make sail and look sharp about it, do—won't you?"

"What a tongue he's got!" remarked Buzzby. "Before I'd go to sea with a first mate who jawed like that I'd be a landsman. Don't ever you git to talk too much, Master Fred, wotever ye do. My maxim is—and it has served me through life, uncommon—'Keep your weather-eye open and your tongue housed 'xcept when you've got occasion to use it.' If that fellow'd use his eyes more and his tongue less, he'd see your father comin' down the road there, right before the wind, with his old sister in tow."

"How I wish he would have let me go with him!" muttered Fred to himself sorrowfully.

"No chance now, I'm afeard," remarked his companion. "The gov'nor's as stiff as a nor'-wester. Nothin' in the world can turn him once he's made up his mind but a regular sou'-easter. Now, if you had been *my* son, and yonder tight craft *my* ship, I would have said, 'Come at once.' But your father knows best, lad; and you're a wise son to obey orders cheerfully, without question. That's another o' my maxims, 'Obey orders, an' ax no questions.'"

Frederick Ellice, senior, who now approached, whispering words of consolation into the ear of his weeping sister, might, perhaps, have just numbered fifty years. He was a fine, big, bold, hearty Englishman, with a bald head, grizzled locks, a loud but not harsh voice, a rather quick temper, and a kind, earnest, enthusiastic heart. Like Buzzby, he had spent nearly all his life at sea, and had become so thoroughly accustomed to walking on an unstable foundation that he felt quite uncomfortable on solid ground, and never remained more than a few months at a time on shore. He was a man of good education and gentlemanly manners, and had worked his way up in the merchant service step by step until he obtained the command of a West India trader.

A few years previous to the period in which our tale opens, an event occurred which altered the course of Captain Ellice's life, and for a long period plunged him into the deepest affliction. This was the loss of his wife at sea under peculiarly distressing circumstances.

At the age of thirty Captain Ellice had married a pretty blue-eyed girl, who resolutely refused to become a sailor's bride unless she should be permitted to accompany her husband to sea. This was without much difficulty agreed to, and forthwith Alice Bremner became Mrs. Ellice, and went to sea. It was during her third voyage to the West Indies that our hero Fred was born, and it was during this and succeeding voyages that Buzzby became "all but a wet-nurse" to him.

Mrs. Ellice was a loving, gentle, seriously-minded woman. She devoted herself, heart and soul to the training of her boy, and spent many a pleasant hour in that little, unsteady cabin in endeavouring to instil into his infant mind the blessed truths of Christianity, and in making the name of Jesus familiar to his ear. As Fred grew older his mother encouraged him to hold occasional intercourse with the sailors —for her husband's example taught her the value of a bold, manly spirit, and she knew that it was impossible for her to instil *that* into him —but she was careful to guard him from the evil that he might chance to learn from the men, by committing him to the tender care of Buzzby.

To do the men justice, however, this was almost unnecessary, for they felt that a mother's watchful eye was on the child, and no unguarded word fell from their lips while he was romping about the forecastle.

When it was time for Fred to go to school, Mrs. Ellice gave up her roving life and settled in her native town of Grayton, where she resided with her widowed sister, Amelia Bright, and her niece Isobel. Here Fred received the rudiments of an excellent education at a private academy. At the age of twelve, however, Master Fred became restive, and during one of his father's periodical visits home, begged to be taken to sea. Captain Ellice agreed; Mrs. Ellice insisted on accompanying them; and in a few weeks they were once again on their old home, the ocean, and Fred was enjoying his native air in company with his friend Buzzby, who stuck to the old ship like one of her own stout timbers.

But this was destined to be a disastrous voyage. One evening, after crossing the line, they descried a suspicious-looking schooner to windward, bearing down upon them under a cloud of canvas.

"What do you think of her, Buzzby?" inquired Captain Ellice, handing his glass to the seaman.

Buzzby gazed in silence and with compressed lips for some time; then he returned the glass, at the same time muttering the word, "Pirate."

"I thought so," said the captain in a deep, unsteady voice. "There is but one course for us, Buzzby," he continued, glancing towards his wife, who, all unconscious of their danger, sat near the taffrail employed with her needle; "these fellows show no mercy, because they expect none either from God or man. We must fight to the last. Go, prepare the men and get out the arms. I'll tell my wife."

Buzzby went forward; but the captain's heart failed him, and he took two or three rapid, hesitating turns on the quarter-deck ere he could make up his mind to speak.

"Alice," he said at length abruptly, "yonder vessel is a pirate."

Mrs. Ellice looked up in surprise, and her face grew pale as her eye met the troubled gaze of her husband.

"Are you quite sure, Frederick?"

"Yes, quite. Would God that I were left alone to—but—nay, do not be alarmed; perhaps I am wrong, it may be a—a clipper-built trading-vessel. If not, Alice, we must make some show of fighting, and try to frighten them. Meanwhile you must go below."

The captain spoke encouragingly as he led his wife to the cabin; but his candid countenance spoke too truthfully, and she felt that his look of anxious concern bade her fear the worst.

Pressing her fervently to his heart, Captain Ellice sprang on deck.

By this time the news had spread through the ship, and the crew, consisting of upwards of thirty men, were conversing earnestly in knots of four or five while they sharpened and buckled on cutlasses, or loaded pistols and carbines.

"Send the men aft, Mr. Thompson," said the captain, as he paced the deck to and fro, casting his eyes occasionally on the schooner, which was rapidly nearing the vessel. "Take another pull at these main-topsail-halyards, and send the steward down below for my sword and pistols. Let the men look sharp; we've no time to lose, and hot work is before us."

"I will go for your sword, father," cried Fred, who had just come on deck.

"Boy, boy, you must go below; you can be of no use here."

"But, father, you know that I'm not *afraid*."

"I know that, boy—I know it well; but you're too young to fight—you're not strong enough. Besides, you must comfort and cheer your mother; she may want you."

"I'm old enough and strong enough to load and fire a pistol, father; and I heard one of the men say we would need all the hands on board, and more if we had them. Besides, it was my mother who told me what was going on, and sent me on deck to *help you, to fight*."

A momentary gleam of pride lit up the countenance of the captain as he said hastily, "You may stay, then," and turned towards the men, who now stood assembled on the quarter-deck.

Addressing the crew in his own blunt, vigorous style, he said, "Lads, yon rascally schooner is a pirate, as you all know well enough. I need not ask you if you are ready to fight; I see by your looks you are. But that's not enough—you must make up your minds to fight *well*. You know that pirates give no quarter. I see the decks are swarming with men. If you don't go at them like bull-dogs, you'll walk the plank before sunset every man of you. Now, go forward, and double-shot your muskets and pistols, and stick as many of the latter into your belts as they will hold. Mr. Thompson, let the gunner double-shot the four big guns, and load the little carronade with musket-balls to the muzzle. If they do try to board us, they'll get a warm reception."

'There goes a shot, sir," said Buzzby, pointing towards the piratical schooner, from the side of which a white cloud burst, and a round shot ricochetted over the sea, passing close ahead of the ship.

'Ay, that's a request for us to lay-to," said the captain bitterly, "but we won't. Keep her away a point."

"Ay, ay, sir," sung out the man at the wheel. A second and a third shot were fired, but passed unheeded, and the captain, fully expecting that the next would be fired into them, ordered the men below.

"We can't afford to lose a man, Mr. Thompson; send them all down."

"Please, sir, may I remain?" said Buzzby, touching his hat.

"Obey orders," answered the captain sternly. The sailor went below with a sulky fling.

For nearly an hour the two vessels cut through the water before a steady breeze, during which time the fast-sailing schooner gradually overhauled the heavy West Indiaman, until she approached within speaking distance. Still Captain Ellice paid no attention to her, but stood with compressed lips beside the man at the wheel, gazing alternately at the sails of his vessel and at the windward horizon, where he fancied he saw indications that led him to hope the breeze would fail ere long.

As the schooner drew nearer, a man leaped on the hammock-nettings, and, putting a trumpet to his mouth, sang out lustily, "Ship ahoy! where are you from, and what's your cargo?"

Captain Ellice made no reply, but ordered four of his men on deck to point one of the stern-chasers.

Again the voice came harshly across the waves, as if in passion, "Heave to, or I'll sink you." At the same moment the black flag was run up to the peak, and a shot passed between the main and fore masts.

"Stand by to point this gun," said the captain in a subdued voice.

"Ay, ay, sir!"

"Fetch a red-hot iron; luff, luff a little—a little more steady—so." At the last word there was a puff and a roar, and an iron messenger flew towards the schooner. The gun had been fired more as a reply of defiance to the pirate than with the hope of doing him any damage; but the shot had been well aimed—it cut the schooner's main-sail-yard in two and brought it rattling down on deck. Instantly the pirate yawed and delivered a broadside; but in the confusion on deck the guns were badly aimed, and none took effect. The time lost in this manoeuvre, added to the crippled condition of the schooner, enabled the West Indiaman to gain considerably on her antagonist; but the pirate kept up a well-directed fire with his bow-chasers, and many of the shots struck the hull and cut the rigging seriously. As the sun descended towards the horizon the wind fell gradually, and ceased at length altogether, so that both vessels lay rolling on the swell with their sails flapping idly against the masts.

"They're a-gittin' out the boats, sir," remarked John Buzzby, who, unable to restrain himself any longer, had crept upon deck at the risk of another reprimand; "and, if my eyes be'n't deceiving me, there's a sail on the horizon to wind'ard—leastways, the direction which *wos* wind'ard afore it fell calm."

"She's bringing a breeze along with her," remarked the captain, "but I fear the boats will come up before it reaches us. There are three in the water and manned already. There they come. Now, then, call up all hands."

In a few seconds the crew of the West Indiaman were at their stations ready for action, and Captain Ellice, with Fred at his elbow, stood beside one of the stern-chasers. Meanwhile, the boats of the pirate, five in number, pulled away in different directions, evidently with the intention of attacking the ship at different points. They were full of men armed to the teeth. While they rowed towards the ship the schooner resumed its fire, and one ball cut away the spanker-boom and slightly wounded two of the men with splinters. The guns of the ship were now brought to bear on the boats, but without effect, although the shot plunged into the water all round them. As they drew nearer a brisk fire of musketry was opened on them, and the occasional falling of an oar and confusion on board showed that the shots told. The pirates replied vigorously, but without effect, as the men of the ship were sheltered by the bulwarks.

"Pass the word to load and reserve fire," said the captain; "and hand me a musket, Fred. Load again as fast as I fire." So saying, the captain took aim and fired at the steersman of the largest boat, which pulled towards the stern. "Another, Fred—"

At this moment a withering volley was poured upon the boat, and a savage yell of agony followed, while the rowers who remained unhurt paused for an instant as if paralyzed. Next instant they recovered, and another stroke would have brought them almost alongside, when Captain Ellice pointed the little carronade and fired. There was a terrific crash; the gun recoiled violently to the other side of the deck; and the pirate boat sank, leaving the sea covered with dead and wounded men. A number, however, who seemed to bear charmed lives, seized their cutlasses with their teeth, and swam boldly for the ship. This incident, unfortunately, attracted too much of the attention of the crew, and ere they could prevent it another boat reached the bow of the ship, the crew of which sprang up the side like cats, formed on the forecastle, and poured a volley upon the men.

"Follow me, lads!" shouted the captain, as he sprang forward like a tiger. The first man he reached fell by a ball from his pistol; in another moment the opposing parties met in a hand-to-hand conflict. Meanwhile Fred, having been deeply impressed with the effect of the shot from the little carronade, succeeded in raising and reloading it. He had scarcely accomplished this when one of the boats reached the larboard quarter, and two of the men sprang up the side. Fred observed them, and felled the first with a handspike before he reached the deck; but the pirate who instantly followed would have killed him had he not been observed by the second mate, who had prevented several of the men from joining in the *mêlée* on the forecastle in order to meet such an emergency as this. Rushing to the rescue with his party, he drove the pirates back into the boat, which was immediately pulled towards the bow, where the other two boats were now grappling and discharging their crews on the forecastle. Although the men of the West Indiaman fought with desperate courage, they could not stand before the increasing numbers of pirates who now crowded the fore part of the ship in a dense mass. Gradually they were beaten back, and at length were brought to bay on the quarter-deck.

"Help, father!" cried Fred, pushing through the struggling crowd, "here's the carronade ready loaded."

"Ha! boy, well done!" cried the captain, seizing the gun, and, with the help of Buzzby, who never left his side, dragging it forward. "Clear the way, lads!"

In a moment the little cannon was pointed to the centre of the mass of men, and fired. One awful shriek of agony rose above the din of the fight, as a wide gap was cut through the crowd; but this only seemed to render the survivors more furious. With a savage yell they charged the quarter-deck, but were hurled back again and again by the captain and a few chosen men who stood around him. At length one of the pirates, who had been all along conspicuous for his strength and daring, stepped deliberately up, and pointing a pistol at the captain's breast, fired. Captain Ellice fell, and at the same moment a ball laid the pirate low; another charge was made; Fred rushed forward to protect his father, but was thrown down and trodden under foot in the rush, and in two minutes more the ship was in possession of the pirates.

Being filled with rage at the opposition they had met with, these villains proceeded, as they said, to make short work of the crew, while several of them sprang into the cabin, where they discovered Mrs. Ellice almost dead with terror. Dragging her violently on deck, they were about to cast her into the sea, when Buzzby, who stood with his hands bound, suddenly burst his bonds and sprang towards her. A blow from the butt of a pistol, however, stretched him insensible on the deck.

"Where is my husband? my boy?" screamed Mrs. Ellice wildly.

"They've gone before you, or they'll soon follow," said a savage fiercely, as he raised her in his powerful arms and hurled her overboard. A loud shriek was followed by a heavy plunge. At the same moment two of the men raised the captain, intending to throw him overboard also, when a loud boom arrested their attention, and a cannon-shot ploughed up the sea close in front of their bows.

While the fight was raging, no one had observed the fact that the breeze had freshened, and a large man-of-war, with American colours, at her peak, was now within gunshot of the ship. No sooner did the pirates make this discovery than they rushed to their boats, with the intention of pulling to their schooner; but those who had been left in charge, seeing the approach of the man-of-war, and feeling that there was no chance of escape for their comrades, or, as is more than probable, being utterly indifferent about them, crowded all sail and slipped away, and it was now hull-down on the horizon to leeward. The men in the boats rowed after her with the energy of despair; but the Americans gave chase, and we need scarcely add that, in a very short time, all were captured.

When the man-of-war rejoined the West Indiaman, the night had set in and a stiff breeze had arisen, so that the long and laborious search that was made for the body of poor Mrs. Ellice proved utterly fruitless. Captain Ellice, whose wound was very severe, was struck down as if by a thunderbolt, and for a long time his life was despaired of. During his illness Fred nursed him with the utmost tenderness, and in seeking

16

to comfort his father, found some relief to his own stricken heart.

Months passed away. Captain Ellice was conveyed to the residence of his sister in Grayton, and, under her care, and the nursing of his little niece Isobel, he recovered his wonted health and strength. To the eyes of men Captain Ellice and his son were themselves again; but those who judge of men's hearts by their outward appearance and expressions, in nine cases out of ten judge very wide of the mark indeed. Both had undergone a great change. The brilliancy and glitter of this world had been completely and rudely dispelled, and both had been led to inquire whether there was not something better to live for than mere present advantage and happiness—something that would stand by them in those hours of sickness and sorrow which must inevitably, sooner or later, come upon all men. Both sought, and discovered what they sought, in the *Bible*, the only book in all the world where the jewel of great price is to be found.

But Captain Ellice could not be induced to resume the command of his old ship, or voyage again to the West Indies. He determined to change the scene of his future labours and sail to the Frozen Seas, where the aspect of every object, even the ocean itself, would be very unlikely to recall the circumstances of his loss.

Some time after his recovery, Captain Ellice purchased a brig and fitted her out as a whaler, determined to try his fortune in the Northern Seas. Fred pleaded hard to be taken out, but his father felt that he had more need to go to school than to sea; so he refused, and Fred, after sighing very deeply once or twice, gave in with a good grace. Buzzby, too, who stuck to his old commander like a leech, was equally anxious to go; but Buzzby, in a sudden and unaccountable fit of tenderness, had, just two months before, married a wife, who might be appropriately described as "fat, fair, and forty," and Buzzby's wife absolutely forbade him to go. Alas! Buzzby was no longer his own master. At the age of forty-five he became—as he himself expressed it —an abject slave, and he would as soon have tried to steer in a slipper-bath right in the teeth of an equinoctial hurricane, as have opposed the will of his wife. He used to sigh gruffly when spoken to on this subject, and compare himself to a Dutch galliot that made more leeway than headway, even with a wind on the quarter. "Once," he would remark, "I was clipper-built, and could sail right in the wind's eye; but ever since I tuck this craft in tow, I've gone to leeward like a tub. In fact, I find there's only one way of going ahead with my Poll, and that is right before the wind! I used to yaw about a good deal at first, but she tuck that out o' me in a day or two. If I put the helm only so much as one stroke to starboard, she guv' a tug at the tow-rope that brought the wind dead aft again; so I've gi'n it up, and lashed the tiller right amid-ships."

So Buzzby did not accompany his old commander; he did not even so much as suggest the possibility of it; but he shook his head with great solemnity, as he stood with Fred, and Mrs. Bright, and Isobel, at the end of the pier, gazing at the brig, with one eye very much screwed up, and a wistful expression in the other, while the graceful craft spread out her canvas and bent over to the breeze.

CHAPTER II.

Departure of the "Pole Star" for the Frozen Seas—Sage reflections of Mrs. Bright, and sagacious remarks of Buzzby—Anxieties, fears, surmises, and resolutions—Isabel—A search proposed—Departure of the "Dolphin" for the Far North.

Digressions are bad at the best, and we feel some regret that we should have been compelled to begin our book with one; but they are necessary evils sometimes, so we must ask our reader's forgiveness, and beg him, or her, to remember that we are still at the commencement of our story, standing at the end of the pier, and watching the departure of the *Pole Star* whale-ship, which is now a scarcely distinguishable speck on the horizon.

As it disappeared Buzzby gave a grunt, Fred and Isobel uttered a sigh in unison, and Mrs. Bright resumed the fit of weeping which for some time she had unconsciously suspended.

"I fear we shall never see him again," sobbed Mrs. Bright, as she took Isobel by the hand and sauntered slowly home, accompanied by Fred and Buzzby, the latter of whom seemed to regard himself in the light of a shaggy Newfoundland or mastiff, who had been left to protect the family. "We are always hearing of whale-ships being lost, and, somehow or other, we *never* hear of the crews being saved, as one reads of when ships are wrecked in the usual way on the seashore."

Isobel squeezed her mother's hand, and looked up in her face with an expression that said plainly, "Don't cry so, mamma; I'm *sure* he will come back," but she could not find words to express herself, so she glanced towards the mastiff for help.

Buzzby felt that it devolved upon him to afford consolation under the circumstances; but Mrs. Bright's mind was of that peculiar stamp which repels advances in the way of consolation unconsciously, and Buzzby was puzzled. He screwed up first the right eye and then the left, and smote his thigh repeatedly; and assuredly, if contorting his visage could have comforted Mrs. Bright, she would have returned home a happy woman, for he made faces at her violently for full five minutes. But it did her no good, perhaps because she didn't see him, her eyes

20

being suffused with tears.

"Ah! yes," resumed Mrs. Bright, with another burst, "I *know* they will never come back, and your silence shows that you think so too. And to think of their taking two years' provisions with them *in case of accidents!*—doesn't that prove that there are going *to be* accidents? And didn't I hear one of the sailors say that she was a crack ship, A number one? I don't know what he meant by A number one, but if she's a cracked ship I *know* she will never come back; and although I told my dear brother of it, and advised him not to go, he only laughed at me, which was very unkind, I'm sure."

Here Mrs. Bright's feelings overcame her again.

"Why, aunt," said Fred, scarce able to restrain a laugh, despite the sadness that lay at his heart, "when the sailor said it was a crack ship, he meant that it was a good one, a first-rate one."

"Then why did he not say what he meant? But you are talking nonsense, boy. Do you think that I will believe a man means to say a thing is good when he calls it cracked? and I'm sure nobody would say a cracked tea-pot was as good as a whole one. But tell me, Buzzby, do you think they ever *will* come back?"

"Why, ma'am, in coorse I do," replied Buzzby, vehemently; "for why, if they don't, they're the first that ever, went out o' this port in my day as didn't. They've a good ship and lots o' grub, and it's like to be a good season; and Captain Ellice has, for the most part, good luck; and they've started with a fair wind, and kep' clear of a Friday, and what more could ye wish? I only wish as I was aboard along with them, that's all."

Buzzby delivered himself of this oration with the left eye shut and screwed up, and the right one open. Having concluded, he shut and screwed up the right eye, and opened the left—he reversed the engine, so to speak, as if he wished to back out from the scene of his triumph and leave the course clear for others to speak. But his words were thrown away on Mrs. Bright, who was emphatically a weak-minded woman, and never exercised her reason at all, except in a spasmodic, galvanic sort of way, when she sought to defend or to advocate some unreasonable conclusion of some sort, at which her own weak mind had arrived somehow. So she shook her head, and sobbed good-bye to Buzzby, as she ascended the sloping avenue that led to her pretty cottage on the green hill that overlooked the harbour and the sea beyond.

As for John Buzzby, having been absent from home full half-an-hour beyond his usual dinner-hour, he felt that, for a man who had lashed his helm amid-ships, he was yawing alarmingly out of his course; so he spread all the canvas he could carry, and steered right before the wind towards the village, where, in a little whitewashed, low-roofed, one-doored, and two little-windowed cottage, his spouse (and dinner) awaited him.

To make a long story short, three years passed away, but the *Pole Star* did not return, and no news of her could be got from the various whale-ships that visited the port of Grayton. Towards the end of the second year Buzzby began to shake his head despondingly; and as the third drew to a close, the expression of gloom never left his honest, weather-beaten face. Mrs. Bright, too, whose anxiety at first was only half genuine, now became seriously alarmed, and the fate of the missing brig began to be the talk of the neighbourhood. Meanwhile, Fred Ellice and Isobel grew and improved in mind and body; but anxiety as to his father's fate rendered the former quite unable to pursue his studies, and he determined at last to procure a passage in a whale-ship, and go out in search of the brig.

It happened that the principal merchant and shipowner in the town, Mr. Singleton by name, was an intimate friend and old school-fellow of Captain Ellice, so Fred went boldly to him and proposed that a vessel should be fitted out immediately, and sent off to search for his father's brig. Mr. Singleton smiled at the request, and pointed out the utter impossibility of his agreeing to it; but he revived Fred's sinking hopes by saying that he was about to send out a whaler to the Northern Seas at any rate, and that he would give orders to the captain to devote a *portion* of his time to the search, and, moreover, agreed to let Fred go as a passenger in company with his own son Tom.

Now, Tom Singleton had been Fred's bosom friend and companion during his first year at school; but during the last two years he had been sent to the Edinburgh University to prosecute his medical studies, and the two friends had only met at rare intervals. It was with unbounded delight, therefore, that he found his old companion, now a youth of twenty, was to go out as surgeon of the ship, and he could scarce contain himself as he ran down to Buzzby's cottage to tell him the good news, and ask him to join.

Of course Buzzby was ready to go, and, what was of far greater importance in the matter, his wife threw no obstacle in the way. On the contrary, she undid the lashings of the helm with her own hand, and told her wondering partner, with a good-humoured but firm smile, to steer where he chose, and she would content herself with the society of the two young Buzzbys (both miniature fac-similes of their father) till he came back.

Once again a whale-ship prepared to sail from the port of Grayton, and once again Mrs. Bright and Isobel stood on the pier to see her depart. Isobel was about thirteen now, and as pretty a girl, according to Buzzby, as you could meet with in any part of Britain. Her eyes were blue and her hair nut-brown, and her charms of face and figure were enhanced immeasurably by an air of modesty and earnestness that went straight home to your heart, and caused you to adore her at once. Buzzby doated on her as if she were his only child, and felt a secret pride in being in some indefinable way her protector. Buzzby philosophized about her, too, after a strange fashion. "You see," he would say to Fred, "it's not that her figurehead is cut altogether after a parfect pattern—by no means, for I've seen pictur's and statues that wos better—but she carries her head a little down, d'ye see, Master Fred? and there's where it is; that's the way I gauges the worth o' young women, jist accordin' as they carry their chins up or down. If their brows come well for'ard, and they seems to be lookin' at the ground they walk on, I knows their brains is firm stuff, and in good workin' order; but when I sees them carryin' their noses high out o' the water, as if they wos afeard o' catchin' sight o' their own feet, and their chins elevated, so that a little boy standin' in front o' them couldn't see their faces nohow, I make pretty sure that t'other end is filled with a sort o' *mush* that's fit only to think o'dress and dancing."

On the present occasion Isobel's eyes were red and swollen, and by no means improved by weeping. Mrs. Bright, too, although three years had done little to alter her character, seemed to be less demonstrative and much more sincere than usual in her grief at parting from Fred.

In a few minutes all was ready. Young Singleton and Buzzby having hastily but earnestly bade Mrs. Bright and her daughter farewell, leaped on board. Fred lingered for a moment.

"Once more, dear aunt," said he, "farewell. With God's blessing we shall come back soon.—Write to me, darling Isobel, won't you? to Upernavik, on the coast of Greenland. If none of our ships are bound in that direction, write by way of Denmark. Old Mr. Singleton will tell you how to address your letter; and see that it be a long one."

"Now then, youngster, jump aboard," shouted the captain; "look sharp!"

23

"Ay, ay," returned Fred, and in another moment he was on the quarterdeck, by the side of his friend Tom.

The ship, loosed from her moorings, spread her canvas, and plunged forward on her adventurous voyage.

But this time she does not grow smaller as she advances before the freshening breeze, for you and I, reader, have embarked in her, and the land now fades in the distance, until it sinks from view on the distant horizon, while nothing meets our gaze but the vault of the bright blue sky above, and the plane of the dark blue sea below.

CHAPTER III.

The voyage—The "Dolphin" and her crew—Ice ahead—Polar scenes —Masthead observations—The first whale—Great excitement.

And now we have fairly got into blue water—the sailor's delight, the landsman's dread,—

"The sea! the sea! the open sea;
The blue, the fresh, the everfree."

"It's my opinion," remarked Buzzby to Singleton one day, as they stood at the weather gangway watching the foam that spread from the vessel's bow as she breasted the waves of the Atlantic gallantly—it's my opinion that our skipper is made o' the right stuff. He's entered quite into the spirit of the thing, and I heard him say to the first mate yesterday he'd made up his mind to run right up into Baffin's Bay and make inquiries for Captain Ellice first, before goin' to his usual whalin'-ground. Now that's wot I call doin' the right thing; for, ye see, he runs no small risk o' getting beset in the ice, and losing the fishin' altogether by so doin'."

"He's a fine fellow," said Singleton; "I like him better every day, and I feel convinced he will do his utmost to discover the whereabouts of our missing friend; but I fear much that our chances are small, for, although we know the spot which Captain Ellice intended to visit, we cannot tell to what part of the frozen ocean ice and currents may have carried him."

"True," replied Buzzby, giving to his left eye and cheek just that peculiar amount of screw which indicated intense sagacity and penetration; "but I've a notion that, if they are to be found, Captain Guy is the man to find 'em."

"I hope it may turn out as you say. Have you ever been in these seas before, Buzzby?"

"No, sir—never; but I've got a half-brother wot has bin in the Greenland whale-fishery, and I've bin in the South Sea line myself."

"What line was that, Buzzby?" inquired David Summers, a sturdy boy of about fifteen, who acted as assistant steward, and was, in fact, a nautical maid-of-all-work. "Was it a log-line, or a bow-line, or a cod-line, or a bit of the equator, eh?"

The old salt deigned no reply to this passing sally, but continued his converse with Singleton.

"I could give ye many a long yarn about the South Seas," said Buzzby, gazing abstractedly down into the deep. "One time when I was about fifty miles to the sou'-west o' Cape Horn, I—"

"Dinner's ready, sir," said a thin, tall, active man, stepping smartly up to Singleton, and touching his cap.

"We must talk over that some other time, Buzzby. The captain loves punctuality." So saying, the young surgeon sprang down the companion ladder, leaving the old salt to smoke his pipe in solitude.

And here we may pause a few seconds to describe our ship and her crew.

The *Dolphin* was a tight, new, barque-rigged vessel of about three hundred tons burden, built expressly for the northern whale-fishery, and carried a crew of forty-five men. Ships that have to battle with the ice require to be much more powerfully built than those that sail in unencumbered seas. The *Dolphin* united strength with capacity and buoyancy. The under part of her hull and sides were strengthened with double timbers, and fortified externally with plates of iron, while, internally, stanchions and crossbeams were so arranged as to cause pressure on any part to be supported by the whole structure; and on her bows, where shocks from the ice might be expected to be most frequent and severe, extra planking, of immense strength and thickness, was secured. In other respects, the vessel was fitted up much in the same manner as ordinary merchantmen. The only other peculiarity about her worthy of notice was the crow's-nest, a sort of barrel-shaped structure fastened to the fore-mast-head, in which, when at the whaling-ground, a man is stationed to look out for whales. The chief men in the ship were Captain Guy, a vigorous, earnest, practical American; Mr. Bolton, the first mate, a stout, burly, off-hand Englishman; and Mr. Saunders, the second mate, a sedate, broad-shouldered, raw-boned Scot, whose opinion of himself was unbounded, whose power of argument was extraordinary, not to say exasperating, and who stood six feet three in his stockings. Mivins, the steward, was, as we have already remarked, a tall, thin, active young man, of a brisk, lively disposition, and was somewhat of a butt among the men, but being in a position of power and trust, he was respected.

The young surgeon, Tom Singleton, whom we have yet scarcely introduced to the reader, was a tall, slim, but firmly-knit youth, with a kind, gentle disposition. He was always open, straightforward, and polite. He never indulged in broad humour, though he enjoyed it much, seldom ventured on a witticism, was rather shy in the company of his companions, and spoke little; but for a quiet, pleasant *tête-à-tête* there was not a man in the ship equal to Tom Singleton. His countenance was Spanish-looking and handsome, his hair black, short, and curling, and his budding moustache was soft and dark as the eyebrow of an Andalusian belle.

It would be unpardonable, in this catalogue, to omit the cook, David Mizzle. He was round, and fat, and oily, as one of his own "duff" puddings. To look at him you could not help suspecting that he purloined and ate at least half of the salt pork he cooked, and his sly, dimpling laugh, in which every feature participated, from the point of his broad chin to the top of his bald head, rather tended to favour this supposition. Mizzle was prematurely bald—being quite a young man—and when questioned on the subject, he usually attributed it to the fact of his having been so long employed about the cooking coppers, that the excessive heat to which he was exposed had stewed all the hair off his head! The crew was made up of stout, active men in the prime of life, nearly all of whom had been more or less accustomed to the whale-fishing, and some of the harpooners were giants in muscular development and breadth of shoulder, if not in height.

Chief among these harpooners was Amos Parr, a short, thick-set, powerful man of about thirty-five, who had been at sea since he was a little boy, and had served in the fisheries of both the Northern and Southern Seas. No one knew what country had the honour of producing him—indeed, he was ignorant of that point himself; for, although he had vivid recollections of his childhood having been spent among green hills, and trees, and streamlets, he was sent to sea with a strange captain before he was old enough to care about the name of his native land. Afterwards he ran away from his ship, and so lost all chance of ever discovering who he was; but, as he sometimes remarked, he didn't much care who he was, so long as he was *himself*, so it didn't matter. From a slight peculiarity in his accent, and other qualities, it was surmised that he must be an Irishman—a supposition which he rather encouraged, being partial to the sons, and particularly partial to the daughters, of the Emerald Isle, one of which last he had married just six months before setting out on this whaling expedition.

Such were the *Dolphin* and her crew, and merrily they bowled along over the broad Atlantic with favouring winds, and without meeting with anything worthy of note until they neared the coast of Greenland.

One fine morning, just as the party in the cabin had finished breakfast, and were dallying with the last few morsels of the repast, as men who have more leisure than they desire are wont to do, there was a sudden shock felt, and a slight tremor passed through the ship as if something had struck her.

"Ha!" exclaimed Captain Guy, finishing his cup of chocolate, "there goes the first bump."

"Ice ahead, sir," said the first mate, looking down the skylight.

"Is there much?" asked the captain, rising and taking down a small telescope from the hook on which it usually hung.

"Not much, sir—only a stream; but there is an ice-blink right ahead all along the horizon."

"How's her head, Mr. Bolton?"

"Nor'-west and by north, sir."

Before this brief conversation came to a close, Fred Ellice and Tom Singleton sprang up the companion ladder, and stood on the deck gazing ahead with feelings of the deepest interest. Both youths were well read in the history of Polar Seas and Regions; they were well acquainted, by name at least, with floes, and bergs, and hummocks of ice, but neither of them had seen such in reality. These objects were associated in their young minds with all that was romantic and wild, hyperborean and polar, brilliant and sparkling, and light and white— emphatically *white*. To behold ice actually floating on the salt sea was an incident of note in their existence; and certainly the impressions of their first day in the ice remained sharp, vivid, and prominent, long after scenes of a much more striking nature had faded from the tablets of their memories.

At first the prospect that met their ardent gaze was not calculated to excite excessive admiration. There were only a few masses of low ice floating about in various directions. The wind was steady, but light, and seemed as if it would speedily fall altogether. Gradually the *blink* on the horizon (as the light haze always distinguishable above ice, or snow-covered land, is called) resolved itself into a long white line of ice, which seemed to grow larger as the ship neared it, and in about two hours more they were fairly in the midst of the pack, which was fortunately loose enough to admit of the vessel being navigated through the channels of open water. Soon after, the sun broke out in cloudless splendour, and the wind fell entirely, leaving the ocean in a dead calm.

"Let's go to the fore-top, Tom," said Fred, seizing his friend by the arm and hastening to the shrouds.

In a few seconds they were seated alone on the little platform at the top of the fore-mast, just where it is connected with the fore-top-mast, and from this elevated position they gazed in silent delight upon the fairy-like scene.

Those who have never stood at the mast-head of a ship at sea in a dead calm cannot comprehend the feeling of intense solitude that fills the mind in such a position. There is nothing analogous to it on land. To stand on the summit of a tower and look down on the busy multitude below is not the same, for there the sounds are quite different in *tone*, and signs of life are visible all over the distant country, while cries from afar reach the ear, as well as those from below. But from the mast-head you hear only the few subdued sounds under your feet—all beyond is silence; you behold only the small, oval-shaped platform that is your *world*—beyond lies the calm desolate ocean. On deck you cannot realize this feeling, for there sails and yards tower above you, and masts, and boats, and cordage intercept your view; but from above you *take in* the intense minuteness of your home at a single glance—you stand aside, as it were, and in some measure comprehend the insignificance of the *thing* to which you have committed your life.

The scene witnessed by our friends at the masthead of the *Dolphin* on this occasion was surpassingly beautiful. Far as the eye could stretch the sea was covered with islands and fields of ice of every conceivable shape. Some rose in little peaks and pinnacles, some floated in the form of arches and domes, some were broken and rugged like the ruins of old border strongholds, while others were flat and level like fields of white marble; and so calm was it, that the ocean in which they floated seemed like a groundwork of polished steel, in which the sun shone with dazzling brilliancy. The tops of the icy islets were pure white, and the sides of the higher ones of a delicate blue colour, which gave to the scene a transparent lightness that rendered it pre-eminently fairy-like.

"It far surpasses anything I ever conceived," ejaculated Singleton after a long silence. "No wonder that authors speak of scenes being ndescribable. Does it not seem like a dream, Fred?"

"Tom," replied Fred earnestly, "I've been trying to fancy myself in another world, and I have almost succeeded. When I look long and ntently at the ice, I get almost to believe that these are streets, and palaces, and cathedrals. I never felt so strong a desire to have wings that I might fly from one island to another, and go floating in and out and round about those blue caves and sparkling pinnacles."

"It's a curious fancy, Fred, but not unnatural."

"Tom," said Fred after another long silence, "has not the thought occurred to you that God made it all?"

"Some such thought did cross my mind, Fred, for a moment, but it soon passed away. Is it not very strange that the idea of the Creator is so seldom and so slightly connected with his works in our minds?"

Again there was a long silence. Both youths had a desire to continue the conversation, and yet each felt an unaccountable reluctance to renew it. Neither of them distinctly understood that the natural heart is enmity against God, and that, until he is converted by the Holy Spirit, man neither loves to think of his Maker nor to speak of him.

While they sat thus musing, a breeze dimmed the surface of the sea, and the Dolphin, which had hitherto lain motionless in one of the numerous canals, began slowly to advance between the islands of ice. The breeze freshened, and rendered it impossible to avoid an occasional collision with the floating masses; but the good ship was well armed for the fight, and, although she quivered under the blows, and once or twice recoiled, she pushed her way through the pack gallantly. In the course of an hour or two they were once more in comparatively clear water.

Suddenly there came a cry from the crow's-nest—"There she blows!"

Instantly every man in the ship sprang to his feet as if he had received an electric shock.

"Where away?" shouted the captain.

"On the lee-bow, sir," replied the look-out.

From a state of comparative quiet and repose the ship was now thrown into a condition of the utmost animation, and, apparently, unmeaning, confusion. The sight of a whale acted on the spirits of the men like wild-fire.

"There she blows!" sang out the man at the masthead again.

31

"Are we keeping right for her?" asked the captain.

"Keep her away a bit; steady!" replied the lookout.

"Steady it is!" answered the man at the wheel.

"Call all hands and get the boats out, Mr. Bolton," said the captain.

"All hands ahoy!" shouted the mate in a tempestuous voice, while the men rushed to their respective stations.

"Boat-steerers, get your boats ready."

"Ay, ay, sir."

"There go flukes," cried the look-out, as the whale dived and tossed its flukes—that is, its tail—in the air, not more than a mile on the lee-bow; "she's heading right for the ship."

"Down with the helm!" roared the captain. "Mr. Bolton, brace up the mizzen-top-sail! Hoist and swing the boats! Lower away!"

In another moment three boats struck the water, and their respective crews tumbled tumultuously into them. Fred and Singleton sprang into the stern-sheets of the captain's boat just as it pushed off, and, in less than five minutes, the three boats were bounding over the sea in the direction of the whale like race-horses. Every man did his best, and the tough oars bent like hoops as each boat's crew strove to outstrip the others.

CHAPTER IV.

The chase and the battle—The chances and dangers of whaling war—
Buzzby dives for his life and saves it—So does the whale and loses it
—An anxious night, which terminates happily, though with a heavy
loss.

The chase was not a long one, for, while the boats were rowing swiftly towards the whale, the whale was, all unconsciously, swimming towards the boats.

"Give way now, lads, give way," said the captain in a suppressed voice; "bend your backs, boys, and don't let the mate beat us."

The three boats flew over the sea, as the men strained their muscles to the utmost, and for some time they kept almost in line, being pretty equally matched; but gradually the captain shot ahead, and it became evident that his harpooner, Amos Parr, was to have the honour of harpooning the first whale. Amos pulled the bow-oar, and behind him was the tub with the line coiled away, and the harpoon bent on to it. Being an experienced whaleman, he evinced no sign of excitement, save in the brilliancy of his dark eye and a very slight flush on his bronzed face. They had now neared the whale and ceased rowing for a moment, lest they should miss it when down.

"There she goes!" cried Fred in a tone of intense excitement, as he caught sight of the whale not more than fifty yards ahead of the boat.

"Now, boys," cried the captain, in a hoarse whisper, "spring hard—lay back hard, I say—*stand up!*"

At the last word Amos-Parr sprang to his feet and seized the harpoon, the boat ran right on to the whale's back, and in an instant Parr sent two irons to the hitches into the fish.

"Stern all!" The men backed their oars with all their might, in order to avoid the flukes of the wounded monster of the deep, as it plunged down headlong into the sea, taking the line out perpendicularly like lightning. This was a moment of great danger. The friction of the line as it passed the loggerhead was so great that Parr had to keep constantly pouring water on it to prevent its catching fire. A hitch in the line at that time, as it flew out of the tub, or any accidental entanglement, would have dragged the boat and crew right down: many such fatal accidents occur to whalers, and many a poor fellow has had a foot or an arm torn off, or been dragged overboard and drowned, in consequence of getting entangled. One of the men stood ready with a small hatchet to cut the line in a moment, if necessary; for whales sometimes run out all that is in a boat at the first plunge, and should none of the other boats be at hand to lend a second line to attach to the one nearly expended, there is nothing for it but to cut. On the present occasion, however, none of these accidents befell the men of the captain's boat. The line ran all clear, and long before it was exhausted the whale ceased to descend, and the *slack* was hauled rapidly in.

Meanwhile the other boats pulled up to the scene of action, and prepared to strike the instant the fish should rise to the surface. It appeared, suddenly, not twenty yards from the mate's boat, where Buzzby, who was harpooner, stood in the bow ready to give it the iron.

"Spring, lads, spring!" shouted the mate, as the whale spouted into the air a thick stream of water. The boat dashed up, and Buzzby planted his harpoon vigorously. Instantly the broad flukes of the tail were tossed into the air, and, for a single second, spread like a canopy over Buzzby's head. There was no escape. The quick eye of the whaleman saw at a glance that the effort to back out was hopeless. He bent his head, and the next moment was deep down in the waves. Just as he disappeared the flukes descended on the spot which he had left, and cut the bow of the boat completely away, sending the stern high into the air with a violence that tossed men, and oars, and shattered planks, and cordage, flying over the monster's back into the seething caldron of foam around it. It was apparently a scene of the most complete and instantaneous destruction, yet, strange to say, not a man was lost. A few seconds after, the white foam of the sea was dotted with black heads as the men rose one by one to the surface, and struck out for floating oars and pieces of the wrecked boat.

"They're lost!" cried Fred Ellice in a voice of horror.

"Not a bit of it, youngster; they're safe enough, I'll warrant," replied the captain, as his own boat flew past the spot, towed by the whale.—"Pay out, Amos Parr; give him line, or he'll tear the bows out of us."

"Ay, ay, sir," sang out Amos, as he sat coolly pouring water on the loggerhead round which a coil of the rope was whizzing like lightning; "all right. The mate's men are all safe, sir; I counted them as we shot past, and I seed Buzzby come up last of all, blowin' like a grampus; and small wonder, considerin' the dive he took."

"Take another turn of the coil, Amos, and hold on," said the captain.

The harpooner obeyed, and away they went after the whale like a rocket, with a tremendous strain on the line and a bank of white foam gurgling up to the edge of the gunwale, that every moment threatened to fill the boat and sink her. Such a catastrophe is of not unfrequent occurrence, when whalemen thus towed by a whale are tempted to hold on too long; and many instances have happened of boats and their crews being in this way dragged under water and lost. Fortunately the whale dashed horizontally through the water, so that the boat was able to hold on and follow, and in a short time the creature paused and rose for air. Again the men bent to their oars, and the rope was hauled in until they came quite close to the fish. This time a harpoon was thrown and a deep lance-thrust given which penetrated to the vital parts of its huge carcass, as was evidenced by the blood which it spouted and the convulsive lashing of its tremendous tail.

While the captain's crew were thus engaged, Saunders, the second mate, observing from the ship the accident to the first mate's boat, sent off a party of men to the rescue, thus setting free the third boat, which was steered by a strapping fellow named Peter Grim, to follow up the chase. Peter Grim was the ship's carpenter, and he took after his name. He was, as the sailors expressed it, a "grim customer," being burnt by the sun to a deep rich brown colour, besides being covered nearly up to the eyes with a thick coal-black beard and moustache, which completely concealed every part of his visage except his prominent nose and dark, fiery-looking eyes. He was an immense man, the largest in the ship, probably, if we except the Scotch second mate Saunders, to whom he was about equal in all respects—except argument. Like most big men, he was peaceable and good-humoured.

"Look alive now, lads," said Grim, as the men pulled towards the whale; "we'll get a chance yet, we shall, if you give way like tigers. Split your sides, boys—do—that's it. Ah! there she goes right down. Pull away now, and be ready when she rises."

As he spoke the whale suddenly *sounded*—that is, went perpendicularly down, as it had done when first struck—and continued to descend until most of the line in the captain's boat was run out.

"Hoist an oar!" cried Amos Parr, as he saw the coil diminishing. Grim observed the signal of distress, and encouraged his men to use their utmost exertions. "Another oar!—another!" shouted Parr, as the whale continued its headlong descent.

"Stand by to cut the line," said Captain Guy with compressed lips. "No! hold on, hold on!"

At this moment, having drawn down more than a thousand fathoms of rope, the whale slackened its speed, and Parr, taking another coil round the loggerhead, held on until the boat was almost dragged under water. Then the line became loose, and the slack was hauled in rapidly. Meanwhile Grim's boat had reached the spot, and the men now lay on their oars at some distance ahead, ready to pull the instant the whale should show itself. Up it came, not twenty yards ahead. One short, energetic pull, and the second boat sent a harpoon deep into it, while Grim sprang to the bow and thrust a lance with deadly force deep into the carcass. The monster sent up a stream of mingled blood, oil, and water, and whirled its huge tail so violently that the sound could be heard a mile off. Before it dived again, the captain's boat came up, and succeeded in making fast another harpoon, while several additional lance-thrusts were given with effect, and it seemed as if the battle were about to terminate, when suddenly the whale struck the sea with a clap like thunder, and darted away once more like a rocket to windward, tearing the two boats after it as if they had been egg-shells.

Meanwhile a change had come over the scene. The sun had set, red and lowering, behind a bank of dark clouds, and there was every appearance of stormy weather; but as yet it was nearly calm, and the ship was unable to beat up against the light breeze in the wake of the two boats, which were soon far away on the horizon. Then a furious gust arose and passed away, a dark cloud covered the sky as night fell, and soon boats and whale were utterly lost to view.

"Wae's me!" cried the big Scotch mate, as he ran up and down the quarter-deck wringing his hands, "what *is* to be done noo?"

Saunders spoke a mongrel kind of language—a mixture of Scotch and English—in which, although the Scotch words were sparsely scattered, the Scotch accent was very strong.

"How's her head?"

"Nor'-nor'-west, sir."

"Keep her there, then. Maybe, if the wind holds stiddy, we may overhaul them before it's quite dark."

Although Saunders was really in a state of the utmost consternation at this unexpected termination to the whale-hunt, and expressed the agitation of his feelings pretty freely, he was too thorough a seaman to neglect anything that was necessary to be done under the circumstances. He took the exact bearings of the point at which the boats had disappeared, and during the night, which turned out gusty and threatening, kept making short tacks, while lanterns were hung at the mast-heads, and a huge torch, or rather a small bonfire, of tarred materials was slung at the end of a spar and thrust out over the stern of the ship. But for many hours there was no sign of the boats, and the crew of the *Dolphin* began to entertain the most gloomy forebodings regarding them.

At length, towards morning, a small speck of light was noticed on the weather-beam. It flickered for a moment, and then disappeared.

"Did ye see yon?" said Saunders to Mivins in an agitated whisper, laying his huge hand on the shoulder of that worthy. "Down your helm" (to the steersman).

"Ay, ay, sir!"

"Stiddy!"

"Steady it is, sir."

Mivins's face, which for some hours had worn an expression of deep anxiety, relaxed into a bland smile, and he smote his thigh powerfully, as he exclaimed, "That's them, sir, *and* no mistake! What's your opinion, Mr. Saunders?"

The second mate peered earnestly in the direction in which the light had been seen; and Mivins, turning in the same direction, screwed up his visage into a knot of earnest attention so complicated and intense, that it seemed as if no human power could evermore unravel it.

"There it goes again!" cried Saunders, as the light flashed distinctly over the sea.

"Down helm; back fore-top-sails!" he shouted, springing forward; "lower away the boat there!"

In a few seconds the ship was hove to, and a boat, with a lantern fixed to an oar, was plunging over the swell in the direction of the light. Sooner than was expected they came up with it, and a hurrah in the distance told that all was right.

"Here we are, thank God," cried Captain Guy, "safe and sound. We don't require assistance, Mr. Saunders; pull for the ship."

A short pull sufficed to bring the three boats alongside, and in a few seconds more the crew were congratulating their comrades with that mingled feeling of deep heartiness and a disposition to jest which is characteristic of men who are used to danger, and think lightly of it after it is over.

"We've lost our fish, however," remarked Captain Guy, as he passed the crew on his way to the cabin; "but we must hope for better luck next time."

"Well, well," said one of the men, wringing the water out of his wet clothes as he walked forward, "we got a good laugh at Peter Grim, if we got nothin' else by our trip."

"How was that, Jack?"

"Why, ye see, jist before the whale gave in, it sent up a spout o' blood and oil as thick as the main-mast, and, as luck would have it, down it came slap on the head of Grim, drenchin' him from head to foot, and makin' him as red as a lobster."

"'Ow did you lose the fish, sir?" inquired Mivins, as our hero sprang up the side, followed by Singleton.

"Lost him as men lose money in railway speculations now-a-days. We sank him, and that was the last of it After he had towed us I don't know how far—out of sight of the ship at any rate—he suddenly stopped, and we pulled up and gave him some tremendous digs with the lances, until he spouted jets of blood, and we made sure of him, when all at once down he went head-foremost like a cannon ball, and took all the line out of both boats, so we had to cut, and he never came up again. At least, if he did it became so dark that we never saw him. Then we pulled to where we thought the ship was, and, after rowing nearly all night, caught sight of your lights; and here we are, dead tired, wet to the skin, and minus about two miles of whale-line and three harpoons."

CHAPTER V.

*Miscellaneous reflections—The coast of Greenland—Upernavik—
News of the "Pole Star"—Midnight-day—Scientific facts and fairy-like
scenes—Tom Singleton's opinion of poor old women—In danger of a
squeeze—Escape.*

In pursuance of his original intention, Captain Guy now proceeded
through Davis' Straits into Baffin's Bay, at the head of which he
intended to search for the vessel of his friend Captain Ellice, and
afterwards prosecute the whale-fishery. Off the coast of Greenland
many whalers were seen actively engaged in warfare with the giants of
the Polar Seas, and to several of these Captain Guy spoke, in the faint
hope of gleaning some information as to the fate of the *Pole Star*, but
without success. It was now apparent to the crew of the *Dolphin* that
they were engaged as much on a searching as a whaling expedition;
and the fact that the commander of the lost vessel was the father of
"young Mr. Fred," as they styled our hero, induced them to take a deep
interest in the success of their undertaking.

This interest was further increased by the graphic account that honest
John Buzzby gave of the death of poor Mrs. Ellice, and the
enthusiastic way in which he spoke of his old captain. Fred, too, had,
by his frank, affable manner and somewhat reckless disposition,
rendered himself a general favourite with the men, and had particularly
recommended himself to Mivins the steward (who was possessed of
an intensely romantic spirit), by stating once or twice very emphatically
that he (Fred) meant to land on the coast of Baffin's Bay, should the
captain fail to find his father, and continue the search on foot and
alone. There was no doubt whatever that poor Fred was in earnest,
and had made up his mind to die in the search rather than not find him.
He little knew the terrible nature of the country in which for a time his
lot was to be cast, and the hopelessness of such an undertaking as he
meditated. With boyish inconsiderateness he thought not of how his
object was to be accomplished; he cared not what impossibilities lay in
the way; but, with manly determination, he made up his mind to quit
the ship and search for his father through the length and breadth of the
land. Let not the reader smile at what he may perhaps style a childish

piece of enthusiasm. Many a youth at his age has dreamed of attempting as great if not greater impossibilities. All honour, we say, to the boy who *dreams* impossibilities, and greater honour to him who, like Fred, *resolves to attempt them!* James Watt stared at an iron tea-kettle till his eyes were dim, and meditated the monstrous impossibility of making that kettle work like a horse; and men might (perhaps did) smile at James Watt *then*, but do men smile at James Watt *now?*— now that thousands of iron kettles are dashing like dreadful comets over the length and breadth of the land, not to mention the sea, with long tails of men and women and children behind them!

"That's 'ow it is, sir," Mivins used to say, when spoken to by Fred on the subject; "I've never bin in cold countries myself, sir, but I've bin in 'ot, and I knows that with a stout pair o' legs and a will to work, a man can work 'is way hanywhere. Of course there's not much of a pop'lation in them parts, I've heerd; but there's Heskimos, and where one man can live so can another, and what one man can do so can another—that's bin my hexperience, and I'm not ashamed to hown it, I'm not, though I *do* say it as shouldn't, and I honour you, sir, for your filleral detarmination to find your father, sir, and—"

"Steward!" shouted the captain down the cabin skylight.

"Yes, sir!"

"Bring me the chart."

"Yes, sir," and Mivins disappeared like a Jack-in-the-box from the cabin just as Tom Singleton entered it.

"Here we are, Fred," he said, seizing a telescope that hung over the cabin door, "within sight of the Danish settlement of Upernavik; come on deck and see it."

Fred needed no second bidding. It was here that the captain had hinted there would, probably, be some information obtained regarding the *Pole Star*, and it was with feelings of no common interest that the two friends examined the low-roofed houses of this out-of-the-way settlement.

In an hour afterwards the captain and first mate with our young friends landed amid the clamorous greetings of the entire population, and proceeded to the residence of the governor, who received them with great kindness and hospitality; but the only information they could obtain was that, a year ago, Captain Ellice had been driven there in his brig by stress of weather, and after refitting and taking in a supply of provisions, had set sail for England.

Here the *Dolphin* laid in a supply of dried fish, and procured several dogs, besides an Esquimau interpreter and hunter, named Meetuck.

Leaving this little settlement, they stood out once more to sea, and threaded their way among the ice, with which they were now well acquainted in all its forms, from the mighty berg, or mountain of ice, to the wide field. They passed in succession one or two Esquimau settlements, the last of which, Yotlik, is the most northerly point of colonization. Beyond this all was *terra incognita*. Here inquiry was again made through the medium of the Esquimau interpreter who had been taken on board at Upernavik, and they learned that the brig in question had been last seen beset in the pack, and driving to the northward. Whether or not she had ever returned they could not tell.

A consultation was now held, and it was resolved to proceed north, as far as the ice would permit, towards Smith's Sound, and examine the coast carefully in that direction.

For several weeks past there had been gradually coming over the aspect of nature a change, to which we have not yet referred, and which filled Fred Ellice and his friend, the young surgeon, with surprise and admiration. This was the long-continued daylight, which now lasted the whole night round, and increased in intensity every day as they advanced north. They had, indeed, often heard and read of it before, but their minds had utterly failed to form a correct conception of the exquisite calmness and beauty of the *midnight-day* of the north.

Every one knows that, in consequence of the axis of the earth not being perpendicular to the plane of its orbit round the sun, the poles are alternately directed more or less *towards* that great luminary during one part of the year, and *away* from it during another part. So that far north the days during the one season grow longer and longer until at last there is *one long day* of many weeks' duration, in which the sun does not set at all; and during the other season there is *one long night*, in which the sun is never seen. It was approaching the height of the summer season when the *Dolphin* entered the Arctic Regions, and, although the sun descended below the horizon for a short time each night, there was scarcely any diminution of the light at all, and, as far as one's sensations were concerned, there was but one long continuous day, which grew brighter and brighter at midnight as they advanced.

"How thoroughly splendid this is!" remarked Tom Singleton to Fred one night, as they sat in their favourite outlook, the main-top, gazing down on the glassy sea, which was covered with snowy icebergs and floes, and bathed in the rays of the sun; "and how wonderful to think that the sun will only set for an hour or so, and then get up as splendid as ever!"

The evening was still as death. Not a sound broke upon the ear save the gentle cries of a few sea-birds that dipped ever and anon into the sea, as if to kiss it gently while asleep, and then circled slowly into the bright sky again. The sails of the ship, too, flapped very gently, and a spar creaked plaintively, as the vessel rose and fell on the gentle undulations that seemed to be the breathing of the ocean. But such sounds did not disturb the universal stillness of the hour; neither did the gambols of yonder group of seals and walruses that were at play round some fantastic blocks of ice; nor did the soft murmur of the swell that broke in surf at the foot of yonder iceberg, whose blue sides were seamed with a thousand watercourses, and whose jagged pinnacles rose up like needles of steel into the clear atmosphere.

There were many bergs in sight, of various shapes and sizes, at some distance from the ship, which caused much anxiety to the captain, although they were only a source of admiration to our young friends in the main-top.

"Tom," said Fred, breaking a long silence, "it may seem a strange idea to you, but, do you know, I cannot help fancying that heaven must be something like this."

"I'm not sure that that's such a strange idea, Fred, for it has two of the characteristics of heaven in it—peace and rest."

"True; that didn't strike me. Do you know, I wish that it were always calm like this, and that we had no wind at all."

Tom smiled. "Your voyage would be a long one if that were to happen. I daresay the Esquimaux would join with you in the wish, however, for their kayaks and oomiaks are better adapted for a calm than a stormy sea."

"Tom," said Fred, breaking another long silence, "you're very tiresome and stupid to-night, why don't you talk to me?"

"Because this delightful dreamy evening inclines me to think and be silent."

"Ah, Tom! that's your chief fault. You are always inclined to think too much and to talk too little. Now I, on the contrary, am always—"

"Inclined to talk too much and think too little—eh, Fred?"

"Bah! don't try to be funny, man; you haven't it in you. Did you ever see such a miserable set of creatures as the old Esquimau women are at Upernavik?"

"Why, what put *them*, into your head?" inquired Tom laughing.

"Yonder iceberg! Look at it! There's the nose and chin exactly of the extraordinary hag you gave your silk pocket-handkerchief to at parting Now, I never saw such a miserable old woman as that before, did you?"

Tom Singleton's whole demeanour changed, and his dark eyes brightened as the strongly-marked brows frowned over them, while he replied, "Yes, Fred, I have seen old women more miserable than that. I have seen women so old that their tottering limbs could scarcely support them, going about in the bitterest November winds, with clothing too scant to cover their wrinkled bodies, and so ragged and filthy that you would have shrunk from touching it—I have seen such groping about among heaps of filth that the very dogs looked at and turned away from as if in disgust."

Fred was inclined to laugh at his friend's sudden change of manner; but there was something in the young surgeon's character—perhaps its deep earnestness—that rendered it impossible, at least for his friends, to be jocular when he was disposed to be serious. Fred became grave as he spoke.

"Where have you seen such poor wretches, Tom?" he asked, with a look of interest.

"In the cities, the civilized cities of our own Christian land. If you have ever walked about the streets of some of these cities before the rest of the world was astir, at gray dawn, you must have seen them shivering along and scratching among the refuse cast out by the tenants of the neighbouring houses. O Fred, Fred! in my professional career, short though it has been, I have seen much of these poor old women, and many others whom the world never sees on the streets at all, experiencing a slow, lingering death by starvation, and fatigue, and cold. It is the foulest blot on our country that there is no sufficient provision for the *aged poor*."

"I have seen those old women too," replied Fred, "but I never thought very seriously about them before."

"That's it—that's just it; people don't *think*, otherwise this dreadful state

44

of things would not continue. Just listen *now*, for a moment, to what I have to say. But don't imagine that I'm standing up for the poor in general. I don't feel—perhaps I'm wrong," continued Tom thoughtfully—"perhaps I'm wrong—I hope not—but it's a fact, I don't feel much for the young and the sturdy poor, and I make it a rule *never* to give a farthing to *young* beggars, not even to little children, for I know full well that they are sent out to beg by idle, good-for-nothing parents. I stand up only for the *aged* poor, because, be they good or wicked, they *cannot* help themselves. If a man fell down in the street, struck with some dire disease that shrunk his muscles, unstrung his nerves, made his heart tremble, and his skin shrivel up, would you look upon him and then pass him by *without thinking?*"

"No," cried Fred in an emphatic tone, "I would not! I would stop and help him."

"Then, let me ask you," resumed Tom earnestly, "is there any difference between the weakness of muscle and the faintness of heart which is produced by disease, and that which is produced by old age, except that the latter is incurable? Have not these women feelings like other women? Think you that there are not amongst them those who have 'known better times'? They think of sons and daughters dead and gone, perhaps, just as other old women in better circumstances do. But they must not indulge such depressing thoughts; they must reserve all the energy, the stamina they have, to drag round the city—barefoot, it may be, and in the cold—to beg for food, and scratch up what they can find among the cinder heaps. They groan over past comforts and past times, perhaps, and think of the days when their limbs were strong and their cheeks were smooth; for they were not always 'hags.' And remember that *once* they had friends who loved them and cared for them, although they are old, unknown, and desolate now."

Tom paused and pressed his hand upon his flushed forehead.

"You may think it strange," he continued, "that I speak to you in this way about poor old women, but I *feel* deeply for their forlorn condition. The young can help themselves, more or less, and they have strength to stand their sorrows, with *hope*, blessed hope, to keep them up; but *poor* old men and old women cannot help themselves, and cannot stand their sorrows, and, as far as this life is concerned, they have *no hope,* except to die soon and easy, and, if possible, in summer time, when the wind is not so very cold and bitter."

"But how can this be put right, Tom?" asked Fred in a tone of deep commiseration. "Our being sorry for it and anxious about it (and you've made me sorry, I assure you) can do very little good, you know."

"I don't know, Fred," replied Tom, sinking into his usual quiet tone. "If every city and town in Great Britain would start a society, whose first resolution should be that they would not leave one poor *old* man or woman unprovided for, *that* would do it. Or if the Government would take it in hand *honestly*, that would do it."

"Call all hands, Mr. Bolton," cried the captain in a sharp voice. "Get out the ice-poles, and lower away the boats."

"Hallo! what's wrong?" said Fred, starting up.

"Getting too near the bergs, I suspect," remarked Tom. "I say, Fred, before we go on deck, will you promise to do what I ask you?"

"Well—yes, I will."

"Will you promise, then, all through your life, especially if you ever come to be rich or influential, to think *of* and *for* old men and women who are poor?"

"I will," answered Fred; "but I don't know that I'll ever be rich, or influential, or able to help them much."

"Of course you don't. But when a thought about them strikes you, will you always *think it out*, and, if possible, *act it out*, as God shall enable you?"

"Yes, Tom, I promise to do that as well as I can."

"That's right; thank you, my boy," said the young surgeon, as they descended the shrouds and leaped on deck.

Here they found the captain walking up and down rapidly, with an anxious expression of face. After taking a turn or two he stopped short, and gazed out astern.

"Set the stun'-sails, Mr. Bolton. The breeze will be up in a little, I think. Let the men pull with a will."

The order was given, and soon the ship was under a cloud of canvas, advancing slowly as the boats towed her between two large icebergs, which had been gradually drawing near to each other the whole afternoon.

"Is there any danger, Buzzby?" inquired Fred, as the sturdy sailor stood looking at the larger berg, with an ice-pole in his hands.

"Danger? ay, that there is, lad, more nor's agreeable, d'ye see. Here we are without a breath o' wind to get us on, right between two bergs as could crack us like a walnut. We can't get to starboard of 'em for the current, nor to larboard of 'em for the pack, as ye see, so we must go between them, neck or nothing."

The danger was indeed imminent. The two bergs were within a hundred yards of each other, and the smaller of the two, being more easily moved by the current probably, was setting down on the larger at a rate that bade fair to decide the fate of the *Dolphin* in a few minutes. The men rowed lustily, but their utmost exertions could move the ship but slowly. Aid was coming, however, direct from the hand of Him who is a refuge in the time of danger. A breeze was creeping over the calm sea right astern, and it was to meet this that the studding-sails had been set a-low and aloft, so that the wide-spreading canvas, projecting far to the right and left, had, to an inexperienced eye, the appearance of being out of all proportion to the little hull by which it was supported.

With breathless anxiety those on board stood watching the two bergs and the approaching breeze.

At last it came. A few cat's-paws ruffled the surface of the sea, distending the sails for a moment, then leaving them flat and loose as before. This, however, was sufficient; another such puff, and the ship was almost out of danger; but before it came the projecting summit of the smaller berg was overhanging the deck. At this critical moment the wind began to blow steadily, and soon the *Dolphin* was in the open water beyond. Five minutes after she had passed, the moving mountains struck with a noise louder than thunder; the summits and large portions of the sides fell with a succession of crashes like the roaring of artillery, just above the spot where the ship had lain not a quarter of an hour before; and the vessel, for some time after, rocked violently to and fro in the surges that the plunge of the falling masses had raised.

CHAPTER VI.

The gale—Anchored to a berg which proves to be a treacherous one—Dangers of the "pack"—Beset in the ice—Mivins shows an inquiring mind—Walruses—Gale freshens—Chains and cables—Holding on for life—An unexpected discovery—A "nip" and its terrible consequences—Yoked to an iceberg.

The narrow escape related in the last chapter was but the prelude to a night of troubles. Fortunately, as we have before mentioned, night did not now add darkness to their difficulties. Soon after passing the bergs, a stiff breeze sprang up off shore, between which and the *Dolphin* there was a thick belt of loose ice, or sludge, while outside, the pack was in motion, and presented a terrible scene of crashing and grinding masses under the influence of the breeze, which soon freshened to a gale.

'Keep her away two points," said Captain Guy to the man at the wheel; "we'll make fast to yonder berg, Mr. Bolton. If this gale carries us into the pack, we shall be swept far out of our course, if, indeed, we escape being nipped and sent to the bottom."

Being *nipped* is one of the numberless dangers to which Arctic navigators are exposed. Should a vessel get between two moving fields or floes of ice, there is a chance, especially in stormy weather, of the ice being forced together and squeezing in the sides of the ship; this is called nipping.

"Ah!" remarked Buzzby, as he stood with folded arms by the capstan, "many and many a good ship has been sent to the bottom by that same. I've see'd a brig, with my own two eyes, squeezed together a'most flat by two big floes of ice, and after doin' it they jist separated agin and let her go plump down to the bottom. Before she was nipped, the crew saved themselves by jumpin' on to the ice, and they wos picked up by our ship that wos in company."

"There's no dependin' on the ice, by no means," remarked Amos Parr; "for I've see'd the self-same sort of thing that ye mention happen to a small steamer in Davis' Straits, only instead o' crushin' it flat, the ice lifted it right high and dry out o' the water, and then let it down again, without more ado, as sound as iver."

"Get out the warps and ice-anchors there!" cried the captain.

In a moment the men were in the boats and busy heaving and planting ice-anchors, but it was not until several hours had been spent in this tedious process that they succeeded in making fast to the berg. They had barely accomplished this when the berg gave indications of breaking up, so they cast off again in great haste, and not long afterwards a mass of ice, many tons in weight, fell from the edge of the berg close to where they had been moored.

The captain now beat up for the land in the hope of finding anchoring-ground. At first the ice presented an impenetrable barrier, but at length a lead of open water was found, through which they passed to within a few hundred yards of the shore, which at this spot showed a front of high precipitous cliffs.

"Stand by to let go the anchor!" shouted the captain.

"Ay, ay, sir."

"Down your helm! Let go!"

Down went the anchor to the music of the rattling chain-cable—a sound which had not been heard since the good ship left the shores of Old England.

"If we were only a few yards farther in, sir," remarked the first-mate, "we should be better. I'm afraid of the stream of ice coming round yonder point."

"So am I," replied the captain; "but we can scarcely manage it, I fear, on account of the shore ice. Get out a boat, Mr. Saunders, and try to fix an anchor. We may warp in a few yards."

The anchor was fixed, and the men strained at the capstan with a will, but, notwithstanding their utmost efforts, they could not penetrate the shore ice. Meanwhile the wind increased, and snow began to fall in large flakes. The tide, too, as it receded, brought a stream of ice round the point ahead of them, which bore right down on their bows. At first the concussions were slight, and the bow of the ship turned the floes aside; but heavier masses soon came down, and at last one fixed itself on the cable, and caused the anchor to drag with a harsh, grating sound.

Fred Ellice, who stood beside the second mate near the companion hatch, looked inquiringly at him.

"Ah! that's bad," said Saunders, shaking his head slowly; "I dinna like that sound. If we're carried out into the pack there, dear knows where we'll turn up in the long run."

"Perhaps we'll turn bottom up, sir," suggested the fat cook as he passed at the moment with a tray of meat. Mizzle could not resist a joke—no matter how unsuitable the time or dreadful the consequences.

"Hold your tongue, sir!" exclaimed Saunders indignantly. "Attend to your business, and speak only when you're spoken to."

With some difficulty the mass of ice that had got foul of the cable was disengaged, but in a few moments another and a larger mass fixed upon it, and threatened to carry it away. In this extremity the captain ordered the anchor to be hove up; but this was not easily accomplished, and when at last it was hove up to the bow both flukes were found to have been broken off, and the shank was polished bright with rubbing on the rocks.

Ice now came rolling down in great quantities and with irresistible force, and at last the ship was whirled into the much-dreaded pack, where she became firmly embedded, and drifted along with it before the gale into the unknown regions of the North all that night. To add to their distress and danger a thick fog overspread the sea, so that they could not tell whither the ice was carrying them, and to warp out of it was impossible. There was nothing for it therefore but to drive before the gale, and take advantage of the first opening in the ice that should afford them a chance of escape.

Towards evening of the following day the gale abated, and the sun shone out bright and clear; but the pack remained close as ever, drifting steadily towards the north.

"We're far beyond the most northerly sea that has ever yet been reached," remarked Captain Guy to Fred and Singleton, as he leaned on the weather bulwarks, and gazed wistfully over the fields of ice in which they were embedded.

"I beg your pardon for differing, Captain Guy, but I think that Captain Parry was farther north than this when he attempted to reach the Pole," remarked Saunders, with the air of a man who was prepared to defend his position to the last.

"Very possibly, Mr. Saunders; but I think we are at least farther north in *this* direction than any one has yet been; at least I make it out so by the chart."

"I'm no sure o' that," rejoined the second mate positively; "charts are not always to be depended on, and I've heard that whalers have been up hereabouts before now."

"Perhaps you are right, Mr. Saunders," replied the captain, smiling; "nevertheless, I shall take observations, and name the various headlands, until I find that others have been here before me.—Mivins, hand me the glass; it seems to me there's a water-sky to the northward."

"What is a water-sky, captain?" inquired Fred.

"It is a peculiar, dark appearance of the sky on the horizon, which indicates open water; just the reverse of that bright appearance which you have often seen in the distance, and which we call the ice-blink."

"We'll have open water soon," remarked the second mate authoritatively.

"Mr. Saunders," said Mivins, who, having just finished clearing away and washing up the *débris* and dishes of one meal, was enjoying in complete idleness the ten minutes of leisure that intervened between that and preparations for the next—"Mr. Saunders, sir, can you *h*inform me, sir, 'ow it is that the sea don't freeze at 'ome the same as it does *h*out 'ere?"

The countenance of the second mate brightened, for he prided himself not a little on his vast and varied stores of knowledge, and nothing pleased him so much as to be questioned, particularly on knotty subjects.

"Hem! yes, Mivins, I can tell 'ee that. Ye must know that before fresh water can freeze on the surface the whole volume of it must be cooled down to 40 degrees, and *salt* water must be cooled down to 45 degrees. Noo, frost requires to be very long continued and very sharp indeed before it can cool the deep sea from the top to the bottom, and until it is so cooled it canna freeze."

"Oh!" remarked Mivins, who only half understood the meaning of the explanation, "'ow very *h*odd. But can you tell me, Mr. Saunders, 'ow it is that them 'ere *h*icebergs is made? Them's wot I don't comprehend no'ow."

"Ay," replied Saunders, "there has been many a wiser head than yours, puzzled for a long time about icebergs. But if ye'll use yer eyes you'll see how they are formed. Do you see the high cliffs yonder away to the nor'-east? Weel, there are great masses o' ice that have been formed against them by the melting and freezing of the snows of many years. When these become too heavy to stick to the cliffs, they tumble into the sea and float away as icebergs. But the biggest bergs come from the foot of glaciers. You know what glaciers are, Mivins?"

"No, sir, I don't."

The second mate sighed. "They are immense accumulations of ice, Mivins, that have been formed by the freezings and meltings of the snows of hundreds of years. They cover the mountains of Norway and Switzerland, and many other places in this world, for miles and miles in extent, and sometimes they flow down and fill up whole valleys. I once saw one in Norway that filled up a valley eight miles long, two miles broad, and seven or eight' hundred feet deep; and that was only a wee bit of it, for I was told by men who had travelled over it that it covered the mountains of the interior, and made them a level field of ice, with a surface like rough, hard snow, for more than twenty miles in extent."

"You don't say so, sir!" said Mivins in surprise. "And don't they *never* melt?"

"No, never. What they lose in summer they more than gain in winter. Moreover, they are always in motion; but they move so slow that you may look at them ever so closely and so long, you'll not be able to observe the motion—just like the hour hand of a watch—but we know it by observing the changes from year to year. There are immense glaciers here in the Arctic Regions, and the lumps which they are constantly shedding off into the sea are the icebergs that one sees and hears so much about."

Mivins seemed deeply impressed with this explanation, and would probably have continued the conversation much longer, had he not been interrupted by the voice of his mischievous satellite, Davie Summers, who touched his forelock and said, "Please, Mr. Mivins, shall I lay the table-cloth? or would it be better to slump dinner with tea this afternoon?"

Mivins started. "Ha! caught me napping! Down below, you young dog!"

The boy dived instantly, followed, first by a dish-clout, rolled tightly up and well aimed, and afterwards by his active-limbed superior. Both reached the region of smells, cruets, and crockery at the same moment, and each set energetically to work at their never-ending duties.

Soon after this the ice suddenly loosened, and the crew succeeded, after a few hours' hard labour, in warping the *Dolphin* once more out of the pack; but scarcely had this been accomplished when another storm, which had been gradually gathering, burst upon them, and compelled them once more to seek the shelter of the land.

Numerous walruses rolled about in the bays here, and they approached much nearer to the vessel than they had yet done, affording those on board a good view of their huge, uncouth visages, as they shook their shaggy fronts and ploughed up the waves with their tusks. These enormous creatures are the elephants of the Arctic Ocean. Their aspect is particularly grim and fierce, and being nearly equal to elephants in bulk they are not less terrible than they appear. In form they somewhat resemble seals, having barrel-shaped bodies, with round, or rather square, blunt heads and shaggy bristling moustaches, and two long ivory tusks which curve downwards instead of upwards, serving the purpose frequently of hooks, by means of which and their fore-flippers they can pull themselves up on the rocks and icebergs. Indeed, they are sometimes found at a considerable height up the sides of steep cliffs, basking in the sun.

Fred was anxious to procure the skull of one of these monstrous animals, but the threatening appearance of the weather rendered any attempt to secure one at that time impossible. A dark sinister scowl overhung the blink under the cloud-bank to the southward, and the dovkies which had enlivened their progress hitherto forsook the channel, as if they distrusted the weather. Captain Guy made every possible preparation to meet the coming storm, by warping down under the shelter of a ledge of rock, to which he made fast with two good hawsers, while everything was made snug on board.

"We are going to catch it, I fear," said Fred, glancing at the black clouds that hurried across the sky to the northward, while he walked the deck with his friend, Tom Singleton.

"I suspect so," replied Tom, "and it does not raise my spirits to see Saunders shaking his huge visage so portentously. Do you know, I have a great belief in that fellow. He seems to know everything and to have gone through every sort of experience, and I notice that most of his prognostications come to pass."

"So they do, Tom," said Fred; "but I wish he would put a better face on things till they *do* come to pass. His looks are enough to frighten one."

"I think we shall require another line out, Mr. Saunders," remarked the captain, as the gale freshened, and the two hawsers were drawn straight and rigid like bars of iron; "send ashore and make a whale-line fast immediately."

The second mate obeyed with a grunt that seemed to insinuate that *he* would have had one out long ago. In a few minutes it was fast; and not a moment too soon, for immediately after it blew a perfect hurricane. Heavier and heavier it came, and the ice began to drift more wildly than ever. The captain had just given orders to make fast another line, when the sharp, twanging snap of a cord was heard. The six-inch hawser had parted, and they were swinging by the two others, with the gale roaring like a lion through the spars and rigging. Half a minute more and "twang, twang!" came another report, and the whale-line was gone. Only one rope now held them to the land, and prevented them being swept into the turmoil of ice, and wind, and water, from which the rocky ledge protected them. The hawser was a good one—a new ten-inch rope. It sang like the deep tones of an organ, loud above the rattle of the rigging and the shrouds; but that was its death-song. It gave way with the noise of a cannon, and in the smoke that followed its recoil they were dragged out by the wild ice, and driven hither and thither at its mercy.

With some difficulty the ship was warped into a place of comparative security in the rushing drift, but it was soon thrown loose again, and severely squeezed by the rolling masses. Then an attempt was made to set the sails and beat up for the land; but the rudder was almost unmanageable owing to the ice, and nothing could be made of it, so they were compelled to go right before the wind under close-reefed top-sails, in order to keep some command of the ship. All hands were on deck watching in silence the ice ahead of them, which presented a most formidable aspect.

Away to the north the strait could be seen growing narrower, with heavy ice-tables grinding up and clogging it from cliff to cliff on either side. About seven in the evening they were close upon the piling masses, to enter into which seemed certain destruction.

"Stand by to let go the anchor!" cried the captain, in the desperate hope of being able to wind the ship.

"What's that ahead of us?" exclaimed the first mate suddenly.

"Ship on the starboard bow, right in-shore!" roared the look-out.

The attention of the crew was for a moment called from their own critical situation towards the strange vessel which now came into view, having been previously concealed from them by a large grounded berg.

"Can you make her out, Mr. Bolton?"

"Yes, sir; I think she's a large brig, but she seems much chafed, and there's no name left on the stern, if ever there was one."

As he spoke, the driving snow and fog cleared up partially, and the brig was seen not three hundred yards from them, drifting slowly into the loose ice. There was evidently no one on board; and although one or two of the sails were loose, they hung in shreds from the yards. Scarcely had this been noted when the *Dolphin* struck against a large mass of ice, and quivered under the violence of the shock.

"Let go!" shouted the captain.

Down went the heaviest anchor they had, and for two minutes the chain flew out at the hawse-hole.

"Hold on!"

The chain was checked, but the strain was awful. A mass of ice, hundreds of tons weight, was tearing down towards the bow. There was no hope of resisting it. Time was not even afforded to attach a buoy or log to the cable, so it was let slip, and thus the *Dolphin's* best bower was lost for ever.

But there was no time to think of or regret this, for the ship was now driving down with the gale, scraping against a lee of ice which was seldom less than thirty feet thick. Almost at the same moment the strange vessel was whirled close to them, not more than fifty yards distant, between two driving masses of thick ice.

"What if it should be my father's brig?" whispered Fred Ellice, as he grasped Singleton's arm and turned to him a face of ashy paleness.

"No fear of that, lad," said Buzzby, who stood near the larboard gangway and had overheard the remark. "I'd know your father's brig among a thousand—"

As he spoke, the two masses of ice closed, and the brig was nipped between them. For a few seconds she seemed to tremble like a living creature, and every timber creaked. Then she was turned slowly on one side, until the crew of the *Dolphin* could see down into her hold, where the beams were giving way and cracking up as matches might be crushed in the grasp of a strong hand. Then the larboard bow was observed to yield as if it were made of soft clay, the starboard bow was pressed out, and the ice was forced into the forecastle. Scarcely three minutes had passed since the nip commenced; in one minute more the brig went down, and the ice was rolling wildly, as if in triumph, over the spot where she had disappeared.

The fate of this vessel, which might so soon be their own, threw a momentary gloom over the crew of the *Dolphin*, but their position left them no time for thought. One upturned mass rose above the gunwale, smashed in the bulwarks, and deposited half a ton of ice on deck. Scarcely had this danger passed when a new enemy appeared in sight ahead. Directly in their way, just beyond the line of floe-ice against which they were alternately thumping and grinding, lay a group of bergs. There was no possibility of avoiding them, and the only question was, whether they were to be dashed to pieces on their hard blue sides, or, perchance, in some providential nook to find a refuge from the storm.

"There's an open lead between them and the floe-ice," exclaimed Bolton in a hopeful tone of voice, seizing an ice-pole and leaping on the gunwale.

"Look alive, men, with your poles," cried the captain, "and shove with a will!"

The "Ay, ay, sir," of the men was uttered with a heartiness that showed how powerfully this gleam of hope acted on their spirits; but a new damp was cast over them when, on gaining the open passage, they discovered that the bergs were not at rest, but were bearing down on the floe-ice with slow but awful momentum, and threatening to crush the ship between the two. Just then a low berg came driving up from the southward, dashing the spray over its sides, and with its forehead ploughing up the smaller ice as if in scorn. A happy thought flashed across the captain's mind.

"Down the quarter boat," he cried.

In an instant it struck the water, and four men were on the thwarts.

"Cast an ice-anchor on that berg."

Peter Grim obeyed the order, and, with a swing that Hercules would have envied, planted it securely. In another moment the ship was following in the wake of this novel tug! It was a moment of great danger, for the bergs encroached on their narrow canal as they advanced, obliging them to brace the yards to clear the impending ice-walls, and they shaved the large berg so closely that the port quarter-boat would have been crushed if it had not been taken from the davits. Five minutes of such travelling brought them abreast of a grounded berg, to which they resolved to make fast. The order was given to cast off the rope. Away went their white tug on his race to the far north, and the ship swung round in safety under the lee of the berg, where the crew acknowledged with gratitude their merciful deliverance from imminent danger.

CHAPTER VII.

New characters introduced—An old game under novel circumstances —Remarkable appearances in the sky—O'Riley meets with a mishap.

Dumps was a remarkably grave and sly character, and Poker was a wag—an incorrigible wag—in every sense of the term. Moreover, although they had an occasional fight, Dumps and Poker were excellent friends, and great favourites with the crew.

We have not yet introduced these individuals to our reader, but as they will act a conspicuous part in the history of the *Dolphin's* adventurous career in the Arctic Regions, we think it right now to present them.

While at Upernavik, Captain Guy had purchased a team of six good, tough Esquimau dogs, being desirous of taking them to England, and there presenting them to several of his friends who were anxious to possess specimens of those animals. Two of these dogs stood out conspicuous from their fellows, not only in regard to personal appearance, but also in reference to peculiarities of character. One was pure white, with a lively expression of countenance, a large shaggy body, two erect, sharp-pointed ears, and a short projection that once had been a tail. Owing to some cause unknown, however, his tail had been cut or bitten off, and nothing save the stump remained. But this stump did as much duty as if it had been fifty tails in one. It was never at rest for a moment, and its owner evidently believed that wagging it was the true and only way to touch the heart of man; therefore the dog wagged it, so to speak, doggedly. In consequence of this animal's thieving propensities, which led him to be constantly *poking* into every hole and corner of the ship in search of something to steal, he was named *Poker*. Poker had three jet-black spots in his white visage—one was the point of his nose, the other two were his eyes.

Poker's bosom friend, Dumps, was so named because he had the sulkiest expression of countenance that ever fell to the lot of a dog. Hopelessly incurable melancholy seemed to have taken possession of his mind, for he never by any chance smiled—and dogs do smile, you know, just as evidently as human beings do, although not exactly with heir mouths. Dumps never romped either, being old, but he sat and allowed his friend Poker to romp round him with a sort of sulky satisfaction, as if he experienced the greatest enjoyment his nature was capable of in witnessing the antics of his youthful companion—for Poker was young. The prevailing colour of Dumps's shaggy hide was a dirty brown, with black spots, two of which had fixed themselves rather awkwardly round his eyes, like a pair of spectacles. Dumps, also, was a thief, and, indeed, so were all his brethren. Dumps and Poker were both of them larger and stronger, and in every way better, than their comrades; and they afterwards were the sturdy, steady, unflinching leaders of the team during many a toilsome journey over the frozen sea.

One magnificent afternoon, a few days after the escape of the *Dolphin* just related, Dumps and Poker lay side by side in the lee-scuppers, calmly sleeping off the effects of a surfeit produced by the eating of a large piece of pork, for which the cook had searched in vain for three-quarters of an hour, and of which he at last found the bare bone sticking in the hole of the larboard pump.

'Bad luck to them dogs," exclaimed David Mizzle, stroking his chin as he surveyed the bone. "If I could only find out, now, which of ye it was, I'd have ye slaughtered right off, and cooked for the mess, I would."

'It was Dumps as did it, I'll bet you a month's pay," said Peter Grim, as he sat on the end of the windlass refilling his pipe, which he had just smoked out.

'Not a bit of it," remarked Amos Parr, who was squatted on the deck busily engaged in constructing a rope mat, while several of the men sat round him engaged in mending sails, or stitching canvas slippers, etc.—"not a bit of it, Grim; Dumps is too honest by half to do sich a thing. 'Twas Poker as did it, I can see by the roll of his eye below the skin. The blackguard's only shammin' sleep."

On hearing his name mentioned, Poker gently opened his right eye, but did not move. Dumps, on the contrary, lay as if he heard not the base aspersion on his character.

"What'll ye bet it was Dumps as did it?" cried Davie Summers, who passed at the moment with a dish of some sort of edible towards the galley or cooking-house on deck.

"I'll *bet* you over the 'ead, I will, if you don't mind your business," said Mivins.

"You'd *better* not," retorted Davie with a grin. "It's as much as your situation's worth to lay a finger on me."

"That's it, youngster, give it 'im," cried several of the men, while the bo confronted his superior, taking good care, however, to keep the foremast between them.

"What do you mean, you young rascal?" cried Mivins with a frown.

"Mean!" said Davie, "why, I mean that if you touch me I'll resign office; and if I do that, you'll have to go out, for every one knows you can't ge on without me."

"I say, Mivins," cried Tom Green, the carpenter's mate, "if you were asked to say, '*H*old on *h*ard to this *h*andspike *h*ere, my *h*earties,' how would ye go about it?"

"He'd 'it you a pretty 'ard crack *h*over the 'ead with it, 'e would," remarked one of the men, throwing a ball of yarn at Davie, who stood listening to the conversation with a broad grin.

In stepping back to avoid the blow, the lad trod on Dumps's paw, and instantly there came from the throat of that excellent dog a roar of anguish that caused Poker to leap, as the cook expressed it, nearly out of his own skin. Dogs are by nature extremely sympathetic and remarkably inquisitive; and no sooner was Dumps's yell heard than it was vigorously responded to by every dog in the ship, as the whole pack rushed each from his respective sleeping-place and looked round in amazement.

"Hallo! what's wrong there for'ard?" inquired Saunders, who had been pacing the quarter-deck with slow giant strides, arguing mentally with himself in default of a better adversary.

"Only trod on Dumps's paw, sir," said Mivins, as he hurried aft; "the men are sky-larking."

"Sky-larking, are you?" said Saunders, going forward. "Weel, lads, you've had a lot o' hard work of late, ye may go' and take a run on the ice."

Instantly the men, like boys set free from school, sprang up, tumbled over the side, and were scampering over the ice like madmen.

"Pitch over the ball—the football!" they cried. In a second the ball was tossed over the ship's side, and a vigorous game was begun.

For two days past the *Dolphin* had been sailing with difficulty through large fields of ice, sometimes driving against narrow necks and tongues that interrupted her passage from one lead or canal to another; at other times boring with difficulty through compact masses of sludge; or occasionally, when unable to advance farther, making fast to a large berg or a field. They were compelled to proceed north, however, in consequence of the pack having become fixed towards, the south, and thus rendering retreat impossible in that direction until the ice should be again set in motion. Captain Guy, however, saw, by the steady advance of the larger bergs, that the current of the ocean in that place flowed southward, and trusted that in a short time the ice which had been forced into the strait by the late gales would be released, and open up a passage. Meanwhile he pushed along the coast, examining every bay and inlet in the hope of discovering some trace of the *Pole Star* or her crew.

On the day about which we are writing, the ship was beset by large fields, the snow-white surfaces of which extended north and south to the horizon, while on the east the cliffs rose in dark, frowning precipices from the midst of the glaciers that encumber them all the year round.

It was a lovely Arctic day. The sun shone with unclouded splendour, and the bright air, which trembled with that liquidity of appearance that one occasionally sees in very hot weather under peculiar circumstances, was vocal with the wild music of thousands of gulls, and auks, and other sea-birds, which clustered on the neighbouring cliffs and flew overhead in clouds. All round the pure surfaces of the ice-fields were broken by the shadows which the hummocks and bergs cast over them, and by the pools of clear water which shone like crystals in their hollows, while the beautiful beryl blue of the larger bergs gave a delicate colouring to the dazzling scene. Words cannot describe the intense *glitter* that characterized everything. Every point seemed a diamond, every edge sent forth a gleam of light, and many of the masses reflected the rich prismatic colours of the rainbow. It seemed as if the sun himself had been multiplied in order to add to the excessive brilliancy, for he was surrounded by *parhelia*, or *sun-dogs,* as the men called them. This peculiarity in the sun's appearance was very striking. The great orb of day was about ten degrees above the horizon, and a horizontal line of white passed completely through it, extending to a considerable distance on either hand, while around it were two distinct halos, or circles of light. On the inner halo were situated the mock-suns, which were four in number—one above and one below the sun, and one on each side of him.

Not a breath of wind stirred the little flag that drooped from the mizzen-peak, and the clamorous, ceaseless-cries of sea-birds, added to the merry shouts and laughter of the men as they followed the restless football, rendered the whole a scene of life, as it was emphatically one of beauty.

"Ain't it glorious?" panted Davie Summers vehemently as he stopped exhausted in a headlong race beside one of his comrades, while the ball was kicked hopelessly beyond his reach by a comparatively fresh member of the party.

"Ah! then, it bates the owld country intirely, it does," replied O'Riley, wiping the perspiration from his forehead.

It is needless to say that O'Riley was an Irishman. We have not mentioned him until now, because up to this time he had not done anything to distinguish himself beyond his messmates; but on this particular day O'Riley's star was in the ascendant, and fortune seemed to have singled him out as an object of her special attention. He was a short man, and a broad man, and a particularly *rugged* man—so to speak. He was all angles and corners. His hair stuck about his head in violently rigid and entangled tufts, rendering it a matter of wonder how anything in the shape of a hat could stick on. His brow was a countless mass of ever-varying wrinkles, which gave to his sly visage an aspect of humorous anxiety that was highly diverting—and all the more diverting when you came to know that the man had not a spark of anxiety in his composition, though he often said he had. His dress, like that of most Jack tars, was naturally rugged, and he contrived to make it more so than usual.

"An' it's hot, too, it is," he continued, applying his kerchief again to his pate "If it warn't for the ice we stand on, we'd be melted down, I do belave, like bits o' whale blubber."

"Wot a jolly game football is, ain't it?" said Davie seating himself on a hummock, and still panting hard.

"Ay, boy, that's jist what it is. The only objiction I have agin it is, that it makes ye a'most kick the left leg clane off yer body."

"Why don't you kick with your right leg, then, stupid, like other people?" inquired Summers.

"Why don't I, is it? Troth, then, I don't know for sartin. Me father lost his left leg at the great battle o' the Nile, and I've sometimes thought that had somethin' to do wid it. But then me mother was lame o' the *right* leg intirely, and wint about wid a crutch, so I can't make out how it was, d'ye see?"

"Look out, Pat," exclaimed Summers, starting up, "here comes the ball."

As he spoke, the football came skimming over the ice towards the spot on which they stood, with about thirty of the men running at full speed and shouting like maniacs after it.

"That's your sort, my hearties! another like that and it's home! Pitch into it, Mivins. You're the boy for me! Now then, Grim, trip him up! Hallo! Buzzby, you bluff-bowed Dutchman, luff! luff! or I'll stave in your ribs! Mind your eye, Mizzle! there's Green, he'll be into your larboard quarter in no time. Hurrah! Mivins, up in the air with it. Kick, boy, kick like a spanker-boom in a hurricane!"

Such were a few of the expressions that showered like hail round the men as they rushed hither and thither after the ball. And here we may remark that the crew of the *Dolphin* played football in a somewhat different style from the way in which that noble game is played by boys in England. Sides, indeed, were chosen, and boundaries were marked out, but very little, if any, attention was paid to such secondary matters! To kick the ball, and keep on kicking it in front of his companions, was the ambition of each man; and so long as he could get a kick at it that caused it to fly from the ground like a cannon-shot, little regard was had by any one to the direction in which it was propelled. But, of course, in this effort to get a kick, the men soon became scattered over the field, and ever and anon the ball would fall between two men, who rushed at it simultaneously from opposite directions. The inevitable result was a collision, by which both men were suddenly and violently arrested in their career. But generally the shock resulted in one of the men being sent staggering backwards, and the other getting the *kick*. When the two were pretty equally matched, both were usually, as they expressed it, "brought up all standing," in which case a short scuffle ensued, as each endeavoured to trip up the heels of his adversary. To prevent undue violence in such struggles, a rule was laid down that hands were not to be used on any account. They might use their feet, legs, shoulders, and elbows, but not their hands.

In such rough play the men were more equally matched than might have been expected, for the want of weight among the smaller men was often more than counterbalanced by their activity, and frequently a sturdy little fellow launched himself so vigorously against a heavy tar as to send him rolling head over heels on the ice. This was not always the case, however, and few ventured to come into collision with Peter Grim, whose activity was on a par with his immense size. Buzzby contented himself with galloping on the outskirts of the fight, and putting in a kick when fortune sent the ball in his way. In this species of warfare he was supported by the fat cook, whose oily carcass could neither stand the shocks nor keep up with the pace of his messmates. Mizzle was a particularly energetic man in his way, however, and frequently kicked with such goodwill that he missed the ball altogether, and the tremendous swing of his leg lifted him from the ice and laid him sprawling on his back.

"Look out ahead!" shouted Green, the carpenter's mate; "there's a sail bearing down on your larboard bow."

Mivins, who had the ball before him at the moment, saw his own satellite, Davie, coming down towards him with vicious intentions. He quietly pushed the ball before him for a few yards, then kicked it far over the boy's head, and followed it up like an antelope. Mivins depended for success on his almost superhuman activity. His tall, slight frame could not stand the shocks of his comrades, but no one could equal or come near to him in speed, and he was quite an adept at dodging a *charge*, and allowing his opponent to rush far past the ball by the force of his own momentum. Such a charge did Peter Grim make at him at this moment.

"Starboard hard!" yelled Davie Summers, as he observed his master's danger.

"Starboard it is!" replied Mivins, and leaping aside to avoid the shock, he allowed Grim to pass. Grim knew his man, however, and had held himself in hand, so that in a moment he pulled up and was following close on his heels.

"It's an ill wind that blows no good," cried one of the crew, towards whose foot the ball rolled, as he quietly kicked it into the centre of the mass of men. Grim and Mivins turned back, and for a time looked on at the general *mêlée* that ensued. It seemed as though the ball must inevitably be crushed among them as they struggled and kicked hither and thither for five minutes, in their vain efforts to get a kick; and during those few exciting moments many tremendous kicks, aimed at the ball, took effect upon shins, and many shouts of glee terminated in yells of anguish.

"It can't last much longer!" screamed the cook, his face streaming with perspiration and beaming with glee, as he danced round the outside of he circle. "There it goes!"

As he spoke, the ball flew out of the circle like a shell from a mortar. Unfortunately it went directly over Mizzle's head. Before he could wink he went down before them, and the rushing mass of men passed over him like a mountain torrent over a blade of grass.

Meanwhile Mivins ran ahead of the others, and gave the ball a kick that nearly burst it, and down it came exactly between O'Riley and Grim, who chanced to be far ahead of the others. Grim dashed at it. "Och! ye big villain," muttered the Irishman to himself, as he put down his head and rushed against the carpenter like a battering-ram.

Big though he was, Grim staggered back from the impetuous shock, and O'Riley following up his advantage, kicked the ball in a side direction, away from every one except Buzzby, who happened to have been steering rather wildly over the field of ice. Buzzby, on being brought thus unexpectedly within reach of the ball, braced up his energies for a kick; but seeing O'Riley coming down towards him like a runaway locomotive, he pulled up, saying quietly to himself, "Ye may take it all yer own way, lad; I'm too old a bird to go for to make my carcass a buffer for a madcap like you to run agin."

Jack Mivins, however, was troubled by no such qualms. He happened to be about the same distance from the ball as O'Riley, and ran like a deer to reach it first. A pool of water lay in his path, however, and the necessity of going round it enabled the Irishman to gain on him a little, so that it became evident that both would come up at the same moment, and a collision be inevitable.

"Hold yer wind, Paddy," shouted the men, who paused for a moment to watch the result of the race. "Mind your timbers, Mivins! Back your top-sails, O'Riley; mind how he yaws!"

Then there was a momentary silence of breathless expectation. The two men seemed about to meet with a shock that would annihilate both, when Mivins bounded to one side like an indiarubber ball. O'Riley shot past him like a rocket, and the next instant went head foremost into the pool of water.

This unexpected termination to the affair converted the intended huzzah of the men into a yell of mingled laughter and consternation as they hastened in a body to the spot; but before they reached it, O'Riley's head and shoulders reappeared, and when they came up he was standing on the margin of the pool blowing like a walrus.

"Oh! then, but it *is* cowld!" he exclaimed, wringing the water from his garments. "Och! where's the ball? give me a kick or I'll freeze! so I will."

As he spoke the drenched Irishman seized the ball from Mivins's hands and gave it a kick that sent it high into the air. He was too wet and heavy to follow it up, however, so he ambled off towards the ship as vigorously as his clothes would allow him, followed by the whole crew.

CHAPTER VIII.

Fred and the doctor go on an excursion in which, among other strange things, they meet with red snow and a white bear, and Fred makes his first essay as a sportsman.

But where were Fred Ellice and Tom Singleton all this time? the reader will probably ask.

Long before the game at football was suggested they had obtained leave of absence from the captain, and, loaded with game-bag, a botanical box and geological hammer, and a musket, were off along the coast on a semi-scientific cruise. Young Singleton carried the botanical box and hammer, being an enthusiastic geologist and botanist, while Fred carried the game-bag and musket.

"You see, Tom," he said as they stumbled along over the loose ice towards the ice-belt that lined the cliffs—"you see, I'm a great dab at ornithology, especially when I've got a gun on my shoulder. When I haven't a gun, strange to say, I don't feel half so enthusiastic about birds!"

"That's a very peculiar style of regarding the science. Don't you think it would be worth while communicating your views on the subject to one of the scientific bodies when we get home again. They might elect you a member, Fred."

"Well, perhaps I shall," replied Fred gravely; "but I say, to be serious, I'm really going to screw up my energies as much as possible, and make coloured drawings of all the birds I can get hold of in the Arctic Regions. At least, I would like to try."

Fred finished his remark with a sigh, for just then the object for which he had gone out to those regions occurred to him; and although the natural buoyancy and hopefulness of his feelings enabled him generally to throw off anxiety in regard to his father's fate, and join in the laugh, and jest, and game as heartily as any one on board, there were times when his heart failed him, and he almost despaired of ever seeing his father again, and these feelings of despondency had been more frequent since the day on which he witnessed the sudden and utter destruction of the strange brig.

"Don't let your spirits down, Fred," said Tom, whose hopeful and earnest disposition often reanimated his friend's drooping spirits; "it will only unfit you for doing any good service. Besides, I think we have no cause yet to despair. We know that your father came up this inlet, or strait, or whatever it is, and he had a good stock of provisions with him, according to the account we got at Upernavik, and it is not more than a year since he was there. Many and many a whaler and discovery ship has wintered more than a year in these regions. And then, consider the immense amount of animal life all round us. They might have laid up provisions for many months long before winter set in."

"I know all that," replied Fred, with a shake of his head; "but think of yon brig that we saw go down in about ten minutes."

"Well, so I do think of it. No doubt the brig was lost very suddenly, but there was ample time, had there been any one on board, to have leaped upon the ice, and they might have got to land by jumping from one piece to another. Such things have happened before frequently. To say truth, at every point of land we turn, I feel a sort of expectation amounting almost to certainty that we shall find your father and his party travelling southward on their way to the Danish settlements."

"Perhaps you are right. God grant that it may be so!"

As he spoke, they reached the fixed ice which ran along the foot of the precipices for some distance like a road of hard white marble. Many large rocks lay scattered over it, some of them several tons in weight, and one or two balanced in a very remarkable way on the edge of the cliffs.

"There's a curious-looking gull I should like to shoot," exclaimed Fred, pointing to a bird that hovered over his head, and throwing forward the muzzle of his gun.

"Fire away, then," said his friend, stepping back a pace.

Fred, being unaccustomed to the use of fire-arms, took a wavering aim and fired.

"What a bother! I've missed it!"

"Try again," remarked Tom with a quiet smile, as the whole cliff vomited forth an innumerable host of birds, whose cries were perfectly deafening.

"It's my opinion," said Fred with a comical grin, "that if I shut my eyes and point upwards I can't help hitting something; but I particularly want yon fellow, because he's beautifully marked. Ah! I see him sitting on a ock yonder, so here goes once more."

Fred now proceeded towards the coveted bird in the fashion that is known by the name of *stalking*—that is, creeping as close up to your game as possible, so as to get a good shot; and it said much for his patience and his future success the careful manner in which, on this occasion, he wound himself in and out among the rocks and blocks of ce on the shore in the hope of obtaining that sea-gull. At last he succeeded in getting to within about fifteen yards of it, and then, resting his musket on a lump of ice, and taking an aim so long and steadily that his companion began to fancy he must have gone to sleep, he fired, and blew the gull to atoms! There was scarcely so much as a shred of it to be found.

Fred bore his disappointment and discomfiture manfully. He formed a resolution then and there to become a good shot, and although he did not succeed exactly in becoming so that day, he nevertheless managed to put several fine specimens of gulls and an auk into his bag. The last bird amused him much, being a creature with a dumpy little body and a beak of preposterously large size and comical aspect. There were also a great number of eider-ducks flying about, but they failed to procure a specimen.

Singleton was equally successful in his scientific researches. He found several beautifully green mosses, one species of which was studded with pale yellow flowers, and in one place, where a stream trickled down the steep sides of the cliffs, he discovered a flower-growth which was rich in variety of colouring. Amid several kinds of tufted grasses were seen growing a small purple flower and the white star of the chickweed; The sight of all this richness of vegetation growing in a little spot close beside the snow, and amid such cold Arctic scenery, would have delighted a much less enthusiastic spirit than that of our young surgeon. He went quite into raptures with it, and stuffed his botanical box with mosses and rocks until it could hold no more, and became a burden that cost him a few sighs before he got back to the ship.

The rocks were found to consist chiefly of red sandstone. There was also a good deal of green-stone and gneiss, and some of the spires of these that shot up to a considerable height were particularly striking and picturesque objects.

But the great sight of the day's excursion was that which unexpectedly greeted their eyes on rounding a cape towards which they had been walking for several hours. On passing this point they stopped with an exclamation of amazement. Before them lay a scene such as the

Arctic Regions alone can produce.

In front lay a vast reach of the strait, which at this place opened up abruptly and stretched away northward, laden with floes, and fields, and hummocks, and bergs of every shade and size, to the horizon, where the appearance of the sky indicated open water. Ponds of various sizes and sheets of water whose dimensions entitled them to be styled lakes spangled the white surface of the floes; and around these were sporting innumerable flocks of wild-fowl, many of which, being pure white, glanced like snow-flakes in the sunshine. Far off to the west the ice came down with heavy uniformity to the water's edge. On the right there was an array of cliffs whose frowning grandeur filled them with awe. They varied from twelve to fifteen hundred feet in height, and some of the precipices descended sheer down seven or eight hundred feet into the sea, over which they cast a dark shadow.

Just at the feet of our young discoverers—for such we may truly call them—a deep bay or valley trended away to the right, a large portion of which was filled with the spur of a glacier, whose surface was covered with *pink snow!* One can imagine with what feelings the two youths gazed on this beautiful sight. It seemed as if that valley, instead of forming a portion of the sterile region beyond the Arctic Circle, were one of the sunniest regions of the south, for a warm glow rested on the bosom of the snow, as if the sun were shedding upon it his rosiest hues. A little farther to the north the red snow ceased, or only occurred here and there in patches; and beyond it there appeared another gorge in the cliffs, within which rose a tall column of rock, so straight and cylindrical that it seemed to be a production of art. The whole of the back country was one great rolling distance of glacier, and, wherever a crevice or gorge in the riven cliffs afforded an opportunity, this ocean of land-ice sent down spurs into the sea, the extremities of which were constantly shedding off huge bergs into the water.

"What a scene!" exclaimed Tom Singleton, when he found words to express his admiration. "I did not think that our world contained so grand a sight. It surpasses my wildest dreams of fairy-land."

"Fairy-land!" ejaculated Fred, with a slight look of contempt; "do you know since I came to this part of the world, I've come to the conclusion that fairy tales are all stuff, and very inferior stuff too! Why, this reality is a thousand million times grander than anything that was ever invented. But what surprises me most is the red snow. What can be the cause of it?"

"I don't know," replied Singleton, "it has long been a matter of dispute among learned men. But we must examine it for ourselves, so come along."

The remarkable colour of the snow referred to, although a matter of dispute at the period of the *Dolphin's* visit to the Arctic Seas, is generally admitted now to be the result of a curious and extremely minute vegetable growth, which spreads not only over its surface, but penetrates into it sometimes to a depth of several feet. The earlier navigators who discovered it, and first told the astonished world that the substance which they had been accustomed to associate with the idea of the purest and most radiant whiteness had been seen by them lying *red* upon the ground, attributed the phenomenon to innumerable multitudes of minute creatures belonging to the order *Radiata*; but the discovery of red snow among the central Alps of Europe, and in the Pyrenees, and on the mountains of Norway, where *marine* animalcula could not exist, effectually overturned this idea. The colouring matter has now been ascertained to result from plants belonging to the order called *Algae*, which have a remarkable degree of vitality, and possess the power, to an amazing extent, of growing and spreading with rapidity even over such an ungenial soil as the Arctic snow.

While Singleton was examining the red snow, and vainly endeavouring to ascertain the nature of the minute specks of matter by which it was coloured, Fred continued to gaze with a look of increasing earnestness towards the tall column, around which a bank of fog was spreading, and partially concealing it from view. At length he attracted the attention of his companion towards it.

"I say, I'm half inclined to believe that yon is no work of nature, but a monument set up to attract the attention of ships. Don't you think so?"

Singleton regarded the object in question for some time. "I don't think so, Fred; it is larger than you suppose, for the fog-bank deceives us. But let us go and see; it cannot be far off."

As they drew near to the tall rock, Fred's hopes began to fade, and soon were utterly quenched by the fog clearing away, and showing that the column was indeed of nature's own constructing. It was a single, solitary shaft of green limestone, which stood on the brink of a deep ravine, and was marked by the slaty limestone that once encased it. The length of the column was apparently about five hundred feet, and the pedestal of sandstone on which it stood was itself upwards of two hundred feet high.

This magnificent column seemed the flag-staff of a gigantic crystal fortress, which was suddenly revealed by the clearing away of the fog-bank to the north. It was the face of the great glacier of the interior, which here presented an unbroken perpendicular front—a sweep of solid glassy wall, which rose three hundred feet above the water-level, with an unknown depth below it. The sun glittered on the crags and peaks and battlements of this ice fortress, as if the mysterious inhabitants of the Far North had lit up their fires and planted their artillery to resist further invasion.

The effect upon the minds of the two youths, who were probably the first to gaze upon those wondrous visions of the Icy Regions, was tremendous. For a long time neither of them could utter a word, and it would be idle to attempt to transcribe the language in which, at length, their excited feelings sought to escape. It was not until their backs had been for some time turned on the scene, and the cape near the valley of red snow had completely shut it out from view, that they could condescend to converse again in their ordinary tones on ordinary subjects.

As they hastened back over the ice-belt at the foot of the cliffs, a loud boom rang out in the distance and rolled in solemn echoes along the shore.

"There goes a gun," exclaimed Tom Singleton, hastily pulling out his watch. "Hallo! do you know what time it is?"

"Pretty late, I suppose. It was afternoon, I know, when we started, and we must have been out a good while now. What time is it?"

"Just two o'clock in the morning!"

"What! do you mean to say it was *yesterday* when we started, and that we've been walking all night, and got into *to-morrow morning* without knowing it?"

"Even so, Fred. We have overshot our time, and the captain is signalling us to make haste. He said that he would not fire unless there seemed some prospect of the ice moving, so we had better run, unless we wish to be left behind; come along."

They had not proceeded more than half-a-mile when a Polar bear walked leisurely out from behind a lump of ice, where it had been regaling itself on a dead seal, and sauntered slowly out towards the icebergs seaward, not a hundred yards in advance of them.

"Hallo! look there! what a monster!" shouted Fred, as he cocked his musket and sprang forward. "What'll you do, Tom, you've no gun?"

"Never mind, I'll do what I can with the hammer. Only make sure you don't miss. Don't fire till you are quite close to him."

They were running after the bear at top speed while they thus conversed in hasty and broken sentences, when suddenly they came to a yawning crack in the ice, about thirty feet wide, and a mile long on either hand, with the rising tide boiling at the bottom of it. Bruin's pursuers came to an abrupt halt.

"Now, isn't that disgusting?"

Probably it was, and the expression of chagrin on Fred's countenance as he said so evidently showed that he meant it; but there is no doubt that this interruption to their hunt was extremely fortunate, for to attack a Polar bear with a musket charged only with small shot, and a geological hammer, would have been about as safe and successful an operation as trying to stop a locomotive with one's hand. Neither of them had yet had experience of the enormous strength of this white monarch of the Frozen Regions and his tenacity of life, although both were reckless enough to rush at him with any arms they chanced to have.

"Give him a long shot—quick!" cried Singleton.

Fred fired instantly; and the bear stopped, and looked round, as much as to say, "Did you speak, gentlemen?" Then, not receiving a reply, he walked away with dignified indifference, and disappeared among the ice-hummocks.

An hour afterwards the two wanderers were seated at a comfortable breakfast in the cabin of the *Dolphin*, relating their adventures to the captain and mates, and, although unwittingly, to Mivins, who generally managed so to place himself, while engaged in the mysterious operations of his little pantry, that most of the cabin talk reached his ear, and travelled thence through his mouth to the forecastle. The captain was fully aware of this fact, but he winked at it, for there was nothing but friendly feeling on board the ship, and no secrets. When, however, matters of serious import had to be discussed, the cabin door was closed, and Mivins turned to expend himself on Davie Summers, who, in the capacity of a listener, was absolutely necessary to the comfortable existence of the worthy steward.

Having exhausted their appetites and their information, Fred and Tom were told that, during their absence, a bear and two seals had been shot by Meetuck, the Esquimau interpreter, whom they had taken on board at Upernavik; and they were further informed that the ice was in motion to the westward, and that there was every probability of their being released by the falling tide. Having duly and silently weighed these facts for a few minutes, they simultaneously, and as if by a common impulse, yawned, and retired to bed.

CHAPTER IX.

The "Dolphin" gets beset in the ice—Preparations for wintering in the ice—Captain Guy's code of laws.

An accident now befell the *Dolphin* which effectually decided the fate of the ship and her crew, at least for that winter. This was her getting aground near the ravine of the giant flagstaff before mentioned, and being finally beset by ice, from which all efforts on the part of the men to extricate her proved abortive, and in which she was ultimately frozen in, hard and fast.

The first sight the crew obtained of the red snow filled them with unbounded amazement, and a few of the more superstitious amongst them with awe approaching to fear. But soon their attention was attracted from this by the wonderful column.

"Och, then! may I niver!" exclaimed O'Riley, the moment he caught sight of it, "if there ben't the north pole at long last—*sure* enough!"

The laugh that greeted this remark was almost immediately checked, partly from the feelings of solemnity inspired by the magnificent view which opened up to them, and partly from a suspicion on the part of the more ignorant among the men that there might be some truth in O'Riley's statement after all.

But their attention and energies were speedily called to the dangerous position of the ship, which unexpectedly took the ground in a bay where the water proved to be unusually shallow, and before they could warp her off the ice closed round her in compact, immovable masses. At first Captain Guy was not seriously alarmed by this untoward event, although he felt a little chagrin in consequence of the detention, for the summer was rapidly advancing, and it behoved him to return to Baffin's Bay and prosecute the whale-fishing as energetically as possible; but when day after day passed, and the ice round the ship still remained immovable, he became alarmed, and sought by every means in his power to extricate himself.

His position was rendered all the more aggravating by the fact that, a week after he was beset, the main body of the ice in the strait opened up and drifted to the southward, leaving a comparatively clear sea through which he could have pushed his way without much difficulty in any direction; but the solid masses in which they lay embedded were fast to the ground for about fifty yards beyond the vessel, seaward, and until these should be floated away there was no chance of escape.

"Get up some powder and canisters, Mr. Bolton," he exclaimed, one morning after breakfast, "I'll try what can be done by blasting the ice. The highest spring tide will occur to-morrow, and if the ship don't move then we shall—"

He did not finish the sentence, but turned on his heel and walked forward, where he found Buzzby and some of the men preparing the ice-saws.

"Ay, ay," muttered the mate, as he went below to give the necessary directions, "you don't need to conclude your speech, captain. If we don't get out to-morrow, we're locked up for one winter, at least, if not more."

"Ay, and ye'll no get oot to-morrow," remarked Saunders, with a shake of his head as he looked up from the log-book in which he was making an entry. "We're hard and fast, so we'll just have to make the best o't."

Saunders was right, as the efforts of the next day proved. The ice lay around the vessel in solid masses, as we have said, and with each of the last three tides these masses had been slightly moved. Saws and ice chisels, therefore, had been in constant operation, and the men worked with the utmost energy, night and day, taking it by turns, and having double allowance of hot coffee served out to them. We may mention here that the *Dolphin* carried no spirits, except what was needed for medicinal purposes, and for fuel to several small cooking lamps that had been recently invented. It had now been proved by many voyagers of experience that in cold countries, as well as hot, men work harder, and endure the extremity of hardship better, without strong drink than with it, and the *Dolphin's* crew were engaged on the distinct understanding that coffee, and tea, and chocolate were to be substituted for rum, and that spirits were never to be given to any one on board, except in cases of extreme necessity.

But, to return—although the men worked as only those can who toil for liberation from long imprisonment, no impression worth mentioning could be made on the ice. At length the attempt to rend it by means of gunpowder was made.

A jar containing about thirty pounds of powder was sunk in a hole in an immense block of ice which lay close against the stern of the ship.

Mivins, being light of foot, was set to fire the train. He did so, and ran—ran so fast that he missed his footing in leaping over a chasm, and had well-nigh fallen into the water below. There was a whiz and a loud report, and the enormous mass of ice heaved upwards in the centre, and fell back in huge fragments. So far the result was satisfactory, and the men were immediately set to sink several charges in various directions around the vessel, to be in readiness for the highest tide, which was soon expected. Warps and hawsers were also got out and fixed to the seaward masses, ready to heave on them at a moment's notice; the ship was lightened as much as possible by lifting her stores upon the ice; and the whole crew—captain, mates, and all—worked and heaved like horses, until the perspiration streamed from their faces, while Mizzle kept supplying them with a constant deluge of hot coffee. Fred and the young surgeon, too, worked like the rest, with their coats off, handkerchiefs bound round their heads, and shirt-sleeves tucked up to their shoulders.

At last the tide rose—inch by inch, and slowly, as if it grudged to give them even a chance of escape.

Mivins grew impatient and unbelieving under it. "I don't think it'll rise another hinch," he remarked to O'Riley, who stood near him.

"Niver fear, boy. The capting knows a sight better than you do, and *he* says it'll rise a fut yit."

"Does he?" asked Grim, who was also beginning to despond.

"Ov coorse he does. Sure he towld me in a confidintial way, just before he wint to turn in last night—if it wasn't yisturday forenoon, for it's meself as niver knows an hour o' the day since the sun became dissipated, and tuck to sitting up all night in this fashion."

"Shut up yer tatie-trap and open yer weather-eye," muttered Buzzby, who had charge of the gang; "there'll be time enough to speak after we're off."

Gradually, as the tide rose, the ice and the ship moved, and it became evident that the latter was almost afloat, though the former seemed to be only partly raised from the ground. The men were at their several posts ready for instant action, and gazing in anxious expectation at the captain, who stood, watch in hand, ready to give the word.

"Now, then, fire!" he said in a low voice.

In a moment the ice round the ship was rent, and upheaved, as if some leviathan of the deep were rising from beneath it, and the vessel swung slowly round. A loud cheer burst from the men.

"Now, lads, heave with a will!" roared the captain.

Round went the capstan, the windlass clanked, and the ship forged slowly ahead, as the warps and hawsers became rigid. At that moment a heavy block of ice, which had been overbalanced by the motion of the vessel, fell with a crash on the rudder, splitting off a large portion of it, and drawing the iron bolts that held it completely out of the stern-post.

"Never mind; heave away—for your lives!" cried the captain. "Jump on board, all of you!"

The few men who had until now remained on the ice scrambled up the side. There was a sheet of ice right ahead which the ship could not clear, but which she was pushing out to sea in advance of her. Suddenly this took the ground and remained motionless.

"Out there with ice-chisels! Sink a hole like lightning! Prepare a canister, Mr. Bolton—quick!" shouted the captain in desperation, as he sprang over the side and assisted to cut into the unwieldy obstruction. The charge was soon fixed and fired, but it only split the block in two and left it motionless as before. A few minutes after the ship again grounded; the ice settled round her; the spring tide was lost, and they were not delivered.

Those who know the bitterness of repeated disappointment and of hope deferred, may judge of the feelings with which the crew of the *Dolphin* now regarded their position. Little, indeed, was said, but the grave looks of most of the men, and the absence of the usual laugh, and jest, and disposition to skylark, which, on almost all other occasions characterized them, showed too plainly how heavily the prospect of a winter in the Arctic Regions weighed upon their spirits. They continued their exertions to free the ship, however, for several days after the high tide, and did not finally give in until all reasonable hope of moving her was utterly annihilated. Before this, however, a reaction began to take place; the prospects of the coming winter were discussed; and some of the more sanguine looked even beyond the winter, and began to consider how they would contrive to get the ship out of her position into deep water again.

Fred Ellice, too, thought of his father, and this abrupt check to the search, and his spirits sank again as his hopes decayed. But poor Fred, like the others, at last discovered that it was of no use to repine, and that it was best to face his sorrows and difficulties "like a man!"

Alas! poor human nature; how difficult do we find it to face sorrows and difficulties *cheerfully*, even when we do conscientiously try! Well would it be for all of us could we submit to such, not only because they are inevitable, but because they are the will of God—of him who has asserted in his own Word that "he afflicteth not the children of men willingly."

Among so many men there were all shades of character, and the fact that they were doomed to a year's imprisonment in the Frozen Regions was received in very different ways. Some looked grave and thought of it seriously; others laughed and treated it lightly; a few grumbled and spoke profanely; but most of them became quickly reconciled, and in a week or two nearly all forgot the past and the future in the duties, and cares, and amusements of the present. Captain Guy and his officers, however, and a few of the more sedate men, among whom were Buzzby and Peter Grim, looked forward with much anxiety, knowing full well the dangers and trials that lay before them.

It is true the ship was provisioned for more than a year, but most of the provisions were salt, and Tom Singleton could have told them, had they required to be told, that without fresh provisions they stood a poor chance of escaping that dire disease scurvy, before which have fallen so many gallant tars whom nothing in the shape of dangers or difficulties could subdue. There were, indeed, myriads of wild-fowl flying about the ship, on which the men feasted and grew fat every day; and the muskets of Meetuck and those who accompanied him seldom failed to supply the ship with an abundance of the flesh of seals, walruses, and Polar bears, portions of all of which creatures were considered very good indeed by the men, and particularly by the dogs, which grew so fat that they began to acquire a very disreputable waddle in their gait as they walked the deck for exercise, which they seldom did, by the way, being passionately fond of sleep! But birds, and perchance beasts, might be expected to take themselves off when the winter arrived, and leave the crew without fresh food.

Then, although the *Dolphin* was supplied with every necessary for a whaling-expedition, and with many luxuries besides, she was ill provided with the supplies that men deem absolutely indispensable for a winter in the Arctic Regions, where the cold is so bitterly intense that, after a prolonged sojourn, men's minds become almost entirely engrossed by two clamant demands of nature—food and heat. They had only a small quantity of coal on board, and nothing except a few extra spars that could be used as a substitute, while the bleak shores afforded neither shrub nor tree of any kind. Meanwhile, they had a sufficiency of everything they required for at least two or three months to come, and for the rest, as Grim said, they had "stout hearts and strong arms."

As soon as it became apparent that they were to winter in the bay, which the captain named the Bay of Mercy, all further attempt to extricate the ship was abandoned, and every preparation for spending the winter was begun and carried out vigorously. It was now that Captain Guy's qualities as a leader began to be displayed. He knew, from long experience and observation, that in order to keep up the *morale* of any body of men it was absolutely necessary to maintain the strictest discipline. Indeed, this rule is so universal in its application, that many men find it advantageous to impose strict rules on themselves in the regulation of their time and affairs, in order to keep their own spirits under command. One of the captain's first resolves therefore was, to call the men together and address them on this subject; and he seized the occasion of the first Sabbath morning they spent in the Bay of Mercy, when the crew were assembled for prayers on the quarter-deck, to speak to them.

Hitherto we have not mentioned the Sabbath day in this story, because, while at sea, and while struggling with the ice, there was little to mark it from other days, except the cessation of unnecessary labour, and the reading of prayers to those who chose to attend; but as necessary labour preponderated at all times, and the reading of prayers occupied scarce half-an-hour, there was little *perceptible* difference between the Sabbath and any other day. We would not be understood to speak lightly of this difference. Little though it was in point of time and appearance, it was immeasurably great in *fact*, as it involved the great principle that the day of rest ought to be observed, and that the Creator should be honoured in a special manner on that day.

On the Sabbath in question—and it was an exceedingly bright, peaceful one—Captain Guy, having read part of the Church of England service as usual, stood up, and in an earnest, firm tone said:—

"My lads, I consider it my duty to say a few plain words to you in reference to our present situation and prospects. I feel that the responsibility of having brought you here rests very much upon myself, and I deem it my solemn duty, in more than the ordinary sense, to do all I can to get you out of the ice again. You know as well as I do that this is impossible at the present time, and that we are compelled to spend a winter here. Some of you know what that means, but the most of you know it only by hearsay, and that's much the same as knowing nothing about it at all. Before the winter is done your energies and endurance will probably be taxed to the uttermost. I think it right to be candid with you. The life before you will not be child's play, but I assure you that it may be mingled with much that will be pleasant and hearty if you choose to set about it in the right way. Well, then, to be short about it. There is no chance whatever of our getting through the winter in this ship comfortably, or even safely, unless the strictest discipline is maintained aboard. I know, for I've been in similar circumstances before, that when cold and hunger, and, it may be, sickness press upon us—should it please the Almighty to send these on us in great severity—you will feel duty to be irksome, and you'll think it useless, and perhaps be tempted to mutiny. Now, I ask you solemnly, while your minds are clear from all prejudices, each individually to sign a written code of laws, and a written promise that you will obey the same, and help me to enforce them even with the punishment of *death*, if need be. Now, lads, will you agree to that?"

"Agreed! agreed!" cried the men at once, and in a tone of prompt decision that convinced their leader he had their entire confidence—a matter of the highest importance in the critical circumstances in which they were placed.

"Well, then, I'll read the rules. They are few, but sufficiently comprehensive:—

"1st. Prayers shall be read every morning before breakfast, unless circumstances render it impossible to do so."

The captain laid down the paper, and looked earnestly at the men.

"My lads, I have never felt so strongly as I now do the absolute need we have of the blessing and guidance of the Almighty, and I am persuaded that it is our duty as well as our interest to begin, not only the Sabbath, but *every* day with prayer.

"2nd. The ordinary duties of the ship shall be carried on, the watches regularly set and relieved, regular hours observed, and the details of duty attended to in the usual way, as when in harbour.

"3rd. The officers shall take watch and watch about as heretofore, except when required to do otherwise. The log-books, and meteorological observations, etc., shall be carried on as usual.

"4th. The captain shall have supreme and absolute command as when at sea; but he, on his part, promises that, should any peculiar circumstance arise in which the safety of the crew or ship shall be implicated, he will, if the men are so disposed, call a council of the whole crew, in which case the decision of the majority shall become law, but the minority, in that event, shall have it in their option to separate from the majority and carry along with them their share of the general provisions.

"5th. Disobedience to orders shall be punishable according to the decision of a council to be appointed specially for the purpose of framing a criminal code, hereafter to be submitted for the approval of the crew."

The rules above laid down were signed by every man in the ship. Several of them could not write, but these affixed a cross (x) at the foot of the page, against which their names were written by the captain in presence of witnesses, which answered the same purpose. And from that time, until events occurred which rendered all such rules unnecessary, the work of the ship went on pleasantly and well.

CHAPTER X.

Beginning of winter—Meetuck effects a remarkable change in the men's appearance—Mossing, and working, and plans for a winter campaign.

In August the first frost came and formed "young ice" on the sea, but this lasted only for a brief hour or two, and was broken up by the tide and melted. By the 10th of September the young ice cemented the floes of last year's ice together, and soon rendered the ice round the ship immovable. Hummocks clustered round several rocky islets in the neighbourhood, and the rising and falling of the tide covered the sides of the rocks with bright crystals. All the feathered tribes took their departure for less rigorous climes, with the exception of a small white bird about the size of a sparrow, called the snow-bird, which is the last to leave the icy North. Then a tremendous storm arose, and the sea became choked up with icebergs and floes, which the frost soon locked together into a solid mass. Towards the close of the storm snow fell in great abundance, and when the mariners ventured again to put their heads up the opened hatchways, the decks were knee-deep, the drift to windward was almost level with the bulwarks, every yard was edged with white, every rope and cord had a light side and a dark, every point and truck had a white button on it, and every hole, corner, crack, and crevice was choked up.

The land and the sea were also clothed with this spotless garment, which is indeed a strikingly appropriate emblem of purity, and the only dark objects visible in the landscape were those precipices which were too steep for the snow to lie on, the towering form of the giant flagstaff, and the leaden clouds that rolled angrily across the sky. But these leaden clouds soon rolled off, leaving a blue wintry sky and a bright sun behind.

The storm blew itself out early in the morning, and at breakfast-time on that day, when the sun was just struggling with the last of the clouds, Captain Guy remarked to his friends who were seated round the cabin table, "Well, gentlemen, we must begin hard work to-day."

"Hard work, captain!" exclaimed Fred Ellice, pausing for a second or two in the hard work of chewing a piece of hard salt junk; "why, what do you call the work we've been engaged in for the last few weeks?"

"Play, my lad; that was only play—just to bring our hands in, before setting to work in earnest!—What do you think of the health of the men, doctor?"

"Never was better; but I fear the hospital will soon fill if you carry out your threat in regard to work."

"No fear," remarked the second mate; "the more work the better health is my experience. Busy men have no time to git seek."

"No doubt of it, sir," said the first mate, bolting a large mouthful of pork. "Nothing so good for 'em as work."

"There are two against you, doctor," said the captain.

"Then it's two to two," cried Fred, as he finished breakfast; "for I quite agree with Tom, and with that excellent proverb which says, 'All work and no play makes Jack a dull boy.'"

The captain shook his head as he said, "Of all the nuisances I ever met with in a ship a semi-passenger is the worst. I think, Fred, I must get you bound apprentice and give you regular work to do, you good-for-nothing."

We need scarcely say that the captain jested, for Fred was possessed of a spirit that cannot rest, so to speak, unless at work. He was able to do almost anything *after a fashion*, and was never idle for a moment. Even when his hands chanced to be unemployed, his brows were knitted, busily planning what to do next.

"Well now, gentlemen," resumed the captain, "let us consider the order of business. The first thing that must be done now is to unstow the hold and deposit its contents on the small island astern of us, which we shall call Store Island, for brevity's sake. Get a tent pitched there, Mr. Bolton, and bank it up with snow. You can leave Grim to superintend the unloading.—Then, Mr. Saunders, do you go and set a gang of men to cut a canal through the young ice from the ship to the island. Fortunately the floes there are wide enough apart to let our quarter-boats float between them. The unshipping won't take long. Tell Buzzby to take a dozen men with him and collect moss; we'll need a large quantity for fuel, and if another storm like this comes it'll be hard work to get down to it. Send Meetuck to me when you go on deck; I shall talk to him as to our prospects of finding deer hereabouts, and arrange a hunt.—Doctor, you may either join the hunting-party, or post up the observations, etc., which have accumulated of late."

"Thank you, captain," said Singleton; "I'll accept the latter duty, the more willingly that I wish to have a careful examination of my botanical specimens."

"And what am I to do, captain?" inquired Fred.

"What you please, lad."

"Then I'll go and take care of Meetuck; he's apt to get into mischief when left—"

At this moment a tremendous shout of laughter, long continued, came from the deck, and a sound as if numbers of men dancing overhead was heard.

The party in the cabin seized their caps and sprang up the companion ladder, where they beheld a scene that accounted for the laughter, and induced them to join in it. At first sight it seemed as if thirty Polar bears had boarded the vessel, and were executing a dance of triumph before proceeding to make a meal of the crew; but on closer inspection it became apparent that the men had undergone a strange transformation, and were capering with delight at the ridiculous appearance they presented. They were clad from head to foot in Esquimau costume, and now bore as strong a resemblance to Polar bears as man could attain to.

Meetuck was the pattern and the chief instrument in effecting this change. At Upernavik Captain Guy had been induced to purchase a large number of fox-skins, deer-skins, seal-skins, and other furs, as a speculation, and had them tightly packed and stowed away in the hold, little imagining the purpose they were ultimately destined to serve. Meetuck had come on board in a mongrel sort of worn-out seal-skin dress; but the instant the cold weather set in he drew from a bundle which he had brought with him a dress made of the fur of the Arctic fox, some of the skins being white and the others blue. It consisted of a loose coat, somewhat in the form of a shirt, with a large hood to it, and a short elongation behind like the commencement of a tail. The boots were made of white bear-skin, which, at the end of the foot, were made to terminate with the claws of the animal; and they were so long that they came up the thigh under the coat, or "jumper," as the men called it, and thus served instead of trousers. He also wore fur mittens, with a bag for the fingers, and a separate little bag for the thumb. The hair on these garments was long and soft, and worn outside, so that when a man enveloped himself in them, and put up the hood, which well-nigh concealed the face, he became very much like a bear or some such creature standing on its hind legs.

Meetuck was a short, fat, burly little fellow by nature; but when he put on his winter dress he became such a round, soft, squat, hairy, and comical-looking creature, that no one could look at him without laughing, and the shout with which he was received on deck the first time he made his appearance in his new costume was loud and prolonged. But Meetuck was as good-humoured an Esquimau as ever speared a walrus or lanced a Polar bear. He joined in the laugh, and cut a caper or two to show that he entered into the spirit of the joke.

When the ship was set fast, and the thermometer fell pretty low, the men found that their ordinary dreadnoughts and pea-jackets, etc., were not a sufficient protection against the cold, and it occurred to the captain that his furs might now be turned to good account. Sailors are proverbially good needle-men of a rough kind. Meetuck showed them how to set about their work. Each man made his own garments, and in less than a week they were completed. It is true, the boots perplexed them a little, and the less ingenious among the men made very rare and curious-looking foot-gear for themselves; but they succeeded after a fashion, and at last the whole crew appeared on deck in their new habiliments, as we have already mentioned, capering among the snow like bears, to their own entire satisfaction and to the intense delight of Meetuck, who now came to regard the white men as brothers—so true is it that "the tailor makes the man!"

"'Ow 'orribly 'eavy it is, hain't it?" gasped Mivins, after dancing round the main-hatch till he was nearly exhausted.

"Heavy!" cried Buzzby, whose appearance was such that you would have hesitated to say whether his breadth or length was greater —"heavy, d'ye say? It must be your sperrits wot's heavy, then, for I feel as light as a feather myself."

"O morther! then may I niver sleep on a bed made o' sich feathers!" cried O'Riley, capering up to Green, the carpenter's mate, and throwing a mass of snow in his face. The frost rendered it impossible to form the snow into balls, but the men made up for this by throwing it about each other's eyes and ears in handfuls.

"What d'ye mean by insultin' my mate?—take that!" said Peter Grim, giving the Irishman a twirl that tumbled him on the deck.

"Oh, bad manners to ye!" spluttered O'Riley, as he rose and ran away; "why don't ye hit a man o' yer own size?"

"'Deed, then, it must be because there's not one o' my own size to hit," remarked the carpenter with a broad grin.

This was true. Grim's colossal proportions were increased so much by his hairy dress that he seemed to have spread out into the dimensions of two large men rolled into one. But O'Riley was not to be overturned with impunity. Skulking round behind the crew, who were laughing at Grim's joke, he came upon the giant in the rear, and seizing the short tail of his jumper, pulled him violently down on the deck.

"Ah, then, give it him, boys!" cried O'Riley, pushing the carpenter flat down, and obliterating his black beard and his whole visage in a mass of snow. Several of the wilder spirits among the men leaped on the prostrate Grim, and nearly smothered him before he could gather himself up for a struggle; then they fled in all directions while their victim regained his feet, and rushed wildly after them. At last he caught O'Riley, and grasping him by the two shoulders gave him a heave that was intended and "calc'lated," as Amos Parr afterwards remarked, "to pitch him over the foretop-sail-yard!" But an Irishman is not easily overcome. O'Riley suddenly straightened himself and held his arms up over his head, and the violent heave, which, according to Parr, was to have sent him to such an uncomfortable elevation, only pulled the jumper completely off his body, and left him free to laugh in the face of his big friend, and run away.

At this point the captain deemed it prudent to interfere.

"Come, come, my lads!" he cried, "enough o' this. That's not the morning work, is it? I'm glad to find that your new dresses," he added with a significant smile, "make you fond of rough work in the snow; there's plenty of it before us.—Come down below with me, Meetuck; I wish to talk with you."

As the captain descended to the cabin the men gave a final cheer, and in ten minutes they were working laboriously at their various duties.

DARING LEAP AT FULL SPEED

Buzzby and his party were the first ready and off to cut moss. They drew a sledge after them towards the red-snow valley, which was not more than two miles distant from the ship. This "mossing," as it was termed, was by no means a pleasant duty. Before the winter became severe, the moss could be cut out from the beds of the snow streams wlth comparative ease; but now the mixed turf of willows, heaths, grasses, and moss was frozen solid, and had to be quarried with crowbars and carried to the ship like so much stone. However, it was prosecuted vigorously, and a sufficient quantity was soon procured to pack on the deck of the ship, and around its sides, so as to keep out the cold. At the same time, the operation of discharging the stores was carried on briskly; and Fred, in company with Meetuck, O'Riley, and Joseph West, started with the dog-sledge on a hunting-expedition.

In order to enable the reader better to understand the condition of the *Dolphin* and her crew, we will detail the several arrangements that were made at this time and during the succeeding fortnight. As a measure of precaution, the ship, by means of blasting, sawing, and warping, was with great labour got into deeper water, where one night's frost set her fast with a sheet of ice three inches thick round her. In a few weeks this ice became several feet thick; and the snow drifted up her hull so much that it seemed as if she were resting on the land, and had taken final leave of her native element. Strong hawsers were then secured to Store Island, in order to guard againstthe possibility of her being carried away by any sudden disruption of the ice. The disposition of the masts, yards, and sails was next determined on. The top-gallant-masts were struck, the lower yards got down to the housings. The top-sail-yards, gaff, and jib-boom, however, were left in their places. The topsails and courses were kept bent to the yards, the sheets being unrove and the clews tucked in. The rest of the binding-sails were stowed on deck to prevent their thawing during winter; and the spare spars were lashed over the ship's sides, to leave a clear space for taking exercise in bad weather.

The stores, in order to relieve the strain on the ship, were removed to Store Island, and snugly housed under the tent erected there, and then a thick bank of snow was heaped up round it. After this was accomplished, all the boats were hauled up beside the tent, and covered with snow, except the two quarter-boats, which were left hanging at the davits all winter. When the thermometer fell below zero, it was found that the vapours below, and the breath of the men, condensed on the beams of the lower deck and in the cabin near the hatchway. It was therefore resolved to convert some sheet-iron, which they fortunately possessed, into pipes, which, being conducted from the cooking-stove through the length of the ship, served in some degree to raise the temperature and ventilate the cabins. A regular daily allowance of coal was served out, and four steady men appointed to attend to the fire in regular watches, for the double purpose of seeing that none of the fuel should be wasted and of guarding against fire. They had likewise charge of the fire-pumps and buckets, and two tanks of water, all of which were kept in the hatchway in constant readiness in case of accidents. In addition to this, a fire-brigade was formed, with Joseph West, a steady, quiet, active young seaman, as its captain, and their stations in the event of fire were fixed beforehand; also, a hole was kept constantly open in the ice alongside to insure at all times a sufficient supply of water.

Strict regulations as to cleanliness and the daily airing of the hammocks were laid down, and adhered to throughout the winter. A regular allowance of provisions was appointed to each man, so that they should not run the risk of starving before the return of the wild-fowl in spring. But those provisions were all salt, and the captain trusted much to their hunting-expeditions for a supply of fresh food, without which there would be little hope of their continuing in a condition of good health. Coffee was served out at breakfast and cocoa at supper, besides being occasionally supplied at other times to men who had been engaged in exhausting work in extremely cold weather. Afterwards, when the dark season set in, and the crew were confined by the intense cold more than formerly within the ship, various schemes were set afoot for passing the time profitably and agreeably. Among others, a school was started by the captain for instructing such of the crew as chose to attend in reading, writing, and arithmetic, and in this hyperborean academy Fred Ellice acted as the writing master, and Tom Singleton as the accountant. The men were much amused at first at the idea of "goin' to school," and some of them looked rather shy at it; but O'Riley, after some consideration, came boldly forward and said, "Well, boys, bad luck to me if I don't think I'll be a scholard afther all. My old gran'mother used to tell me, whin I refused to go to the school that was kip be an owld man as tuck his fees out in murphies and potheen,—says she, 'Ah! ye spalpeen, ye'll niver be cliverer nor the pig, ye won't.' 'Ah, then, I hope not,' says I, 'for sure she's far the cliverest in the house, an' ye wouldn't have me to be cliverer than me own gran'mother, would ye?' says I. So I niver wint to school, and more be token, I can't sign me name, and if it was only to larn how to do that, I'll go and jine; indeed I will." So O'Riley joined, and before long every man in the ship was glad to join, in order to have something to do.

The doctor also, twice a-week, gave readings from Shakespeare, a copy of which he had fortunately brought with him. He also read extracts from the few other books they happened to have on board; and after a time, finding unexpectedly that he had a talent that way, he began to draw upon his memory and his imagination, and told long stories (which were facetiously called *lectures*) to the men, who listened to them with great delight. Then Fred started an illustrated newspaper once a-week, which was named the *Arctic Sun*, and which was in great favour during the whole course of its brief existence. It is true, only one copy was issued each morning of publication, because, besides supplying the greater proportion of the material himself, and executing the illustrations in a style that would have made Mr. Leech of the present day envious, he had to transcribe the various contributions he received from the men and others in a neat, legible hand. But this *one* copy was perused and re-perused, as no single copy of any paper extant—not excepting *The Times* or *Punch*—has ever yet been perused; and when it was returned to the editor, to be carefully placed in the archives of the *Dolphin*, it was emphatically the worse for wear. Besides all this, a theatre was set agoing, of which we shall have more to say hereafter.

In thus minutely recounting the various expedients which these banished men fell upon to pass the long dark hours of an Arctic winter, we may, perhaps, give the reader the impression that a great deal of thought and time were bestowed upon *amusement*, as if that were the chief end and object of their life in those regions. But we must remind him that though many more pages might be filled in recounting all the particulars, but a small portion of their time was, after all, taken up in this way; and it would have been well for them had they been able to find more to amuse them than they did, for the depressing influence of the long-continued darkness, and the want of a sufficiency of regular employment for so many months added to the rigorous nature of the climate in which they dwelt, well-nigh broke their spirits at last.

In order to secure warmth during winter, the deck of the ship was padded with moss about a foot deep, and down below the walls were lined with the same material. The floors were carefully plastered with common paste and covered with oakum a couple of inches deep, over which a carpet of canvas was spread. Every opening in the deck was fastened down and covered deeply over with moss, with the exception of one hatch, which was their only entrance, and this was kept constantly closed except when it was desirable to ventilate. Curtains were hung up in front of it to prevent draughts. A canvas awning was also spread over the deck from stem to stern, so that it was confidently hoped the *Dolphin* would prove a snug tenement even in the severest cold.

As has been said before, the snow-drift almost buried the hull of the ship, and as snow is a good *non-conductor* of heat, this further helped to keep up the temperature within. A staircase of snow was built up to the bulwarks on the larboard quarter, and on the starboard side an inclined plane of snow was sloped down to the ice to facilitate the launching of the sledges when they had to be pulled on deck.

Such were the chief arrangements and preparations that were made by our adventurers for spending the winter; but although we have described them at this point in our story, many of them were not completed until a much later period.

CHAPTER XI.

*A hunting-expedition, in the course of which the hunters meet with
many interesting, dangerous, peculiar, and remarkable experiences,
and make acquaintance with seals, walruses, deer, and rabbits.*

We must now return to Fred Ellice and his companions, Meetuck the
Esquimau, O'Riley, and Joseph West, whom we left while they were on
the point of starting on a hunting-expedition.

They took the direction of the ice-hummocks out to sea, and, seated
comfortably on a large sledge, were dragged by the team of dogs over
the ice at the rate of ten miles an hour.

"Well! did I iver expect to ride a carriage and six?" exclaimed O'Riley in
a state of great glee as the dogs dashed forward at full speed, while
Meetuck nourished his awful whip, making it crack like a pistol-shot
ever and anon.

The sledge on which they travelled was of the very curious and simple
construction peculiar to the Esquimaux, and was built by Peter Grim
under the direction of Meetuck. It consisted of two runners of about ten
feet in length, six inches high, two inches broad, and three feet apart.
They were made of tough hickory, slightly curved in front, and were
attached to each other by cross-bars. At the stern of the vehicle there
was a low back composed of two uprights and a single bar across. The
whole machine was fastened together by means of tough lashings of
raw seal-hide, so that, to all appearance, it was a rickety affair, ready
to fall to pieces. In reality, however, it was very strong. No metal nails
of any kind could have held in the keen frost—they would have
snapped like glass at the first jolt—but the sealskin fastenings yielded
to the rude shocks and twistings to which the sledge was subjected,
and seldom gave way, or if they did, were easily and speedily renewed
without the aid of any other implement than a knife.

But the whip was the most remarkable part of the equipage. The
handle was only sixteen inches in length, but the lash was twenty *feet*
long, made of the toughest seal-skin, and as thick as a man's wrist
near the handle, whence it tapered off to a fine point. The labour of
using such a formidable weapon is so great that Esquimaux usually,

when practicable, travel in couples, one sledge behind the other. The dogs of the last sledge follow mechanically and require no whip, and the riders change about so as to relieve each other. When travelling, the whip trails behind, and can be brought with a tremendous crack that makes the hair fly from the wretch that is struck; and Esquimaux are splendid *shots*, so to speak. They can hit any part of a dog with certainty, but usually rest satisfied with simply cracking the whip—a sound that produces an answering yell of terror, whether the lash takes effect or not.

Our hunters were clothed in their Esquimau garments, and cut the oddest imaginable figures. They had a soft, rotund, cuddled-up appearance, that was powerfully suggestive of comfort. The sledge carried one day's provisions, a couple of walrus harpoons with a sufficient quantity of rope, four muskets with the requisite ammunition, an Esquimau cooking-lamp, two stout spears, two tarpaulins to spread on the snow, and four blanket sleeping-bags. These last were six feet long, and just wide enough for a man to crawl into at night, feet first.

"What a jolly style of travelling, isn't it?" cried Fred, as the dogs sprang wildly forward, tearing the sledge behind them, Dumps and Poker leading and looking as lively as crickets.

"Well now, isn't it true that wits jump?—that's jist what I was sayin' to meself," remarked O'Riley, grinning from ear to ear as he pulled the fur-hood farther over his head, crossed his arms more firmly on his breast, and tried to double himself up as he sat there like an overgrown rat. "I wouldn't exchange it wid the Lord Mayor o' London and his coach an' six—so I wouldn't.—Arrah! have a care, Meetuck, ye baste, or ye'll have us kilt."

This last exclamation was caused by the reckless driver dashing over a piece of rough ice that nearly capsized the sledge. Meetuck did not answer, but he looked over his shoulder with a quiet smile on his oily countenance.

"Ah, then, ye may laugh," said O'Riley with menacing look, "but av ye break a bone o' me body I'll—"

Down went the dogs into a crack in the ice as he spoke, over went the sledge and hurled them all out upon the ice.

"Musha! but ye've done it!"

"Hallo, West! are you hurt?" cried Fred anxiously, as he observed the sailor fall heavily on the ice.

"Oh no, sir; all right, thank you," replied the man, rising alertly and limping to the sledge. "Only knocked the skin off my shin, sir."

West was a quiet, serious, polite man, an American by birth, who was much liked by the crew in consequence of a union of politeness and modesty with a disposition to work far beyond his strength. He was not very robust, however, and in powers of physical endurance scarcely fitted to engage in an Arctic expedition.

"An' don't ye think it's worth makin' inquiries about *me*?" cried O'Riley, who had been tossed into a crevice in the hummock, where he lay jammed and utterly unable to move.

Fred and the Esquimau laughed heartily while O'Riley extricated himself from his awkward position. Fortunately no damage was done, and in five minutes they were flying over the frozen sea as madly as ever in the direction of the point at the opposite side of Red-Snow Valley, where a cloud of frost-smoke indicated open water.

"Now, look you, Mr. Meetuck, av ye do that again ye'll better don't, let me tell ye. Sure the back o' me's brack entirely," said O'Riley, as he re-arranged himself with a look of comfort that belied his words. "Och, there ye go again," he cried, as the sledge suddenly fell about six inches from a higher level to a lower, where the floe had cracked, causing the teeth of the whole party to come together with a snap. "A man durs'n't spake for fear o' bitin' his tongue off."

"No fee," said Meetuck, looking over his shoulder with a broader smirk.

"No fee, ye lump of pork! it's a double fee I'll have to pay the dacter an ye go on like that."

No fee was Meetuck's best attempt at the words *no fear*. He had picked up a little English during his brief sojourn with the sailors, and already understood much of what was said to him; but words were as yet few, and his manner of pronouncing them peculiar.

"Holo! look! look!" cried the Esquimau, suddenly checking the dogs and leaping off the sledge.

"Eh! what! where?" ejaculated Fred, seizing his musket.

"I think I see something, sir," said West, shading his eyes with his hand, and gazing earnestly in the direction indicated by Meetuck.

"So do I, be the mortial," said O'Riley in a hoarse whisper. "I see the mountains and the sky, I do, as plain as the nose on me face!"

"Hush! stop your nonsense, man," said Fred. "I see a deer, I'm certain of it."

Meetuck nodded violently to indicate that Fred was right.

"Well, what's to be done? Luckily we are well to leeward, and it has neither sighted nor scented us."

Meetuck replied by gestures and words to the effect that West and O'Riley should remain with the dogs, and keep them quiet under the shelter of a hummock, while he and Fred should go after the reindeer. Accordingly, away they went, making a pretty long detour in order to gain the shore, and come upon it under the shelter of the grounded floes, behind which they might approach without being seen. In hurrying along the coast they observed the footprints of a musk-ox, and also of several Arctic hares and foxes; which delighted them much, for hitherto they had seen none of these animals, and were beginning to be fearful lest they should not visit that part of the coast at all. Of course Fred knew not what sort of animals had made the tracks in question, but he was an adept at guessing, and the satisfied looks of his companion gave him reason to believe that he was correct in his surmises.

In half-an-hour they came within range, and Fred, after debating with himself for some time as to the propriety of taking the first shot, triumphed over himself, and stepping back a pace, motioned to the Esquimau to fire. But Meetuck was an innate gentleman, and modestly declined; so Fred advanced, took a good aim, and fired.

The deer bounded away, but stumbled as it went, showing that it was wounded.

"Ha! ha! Meetuck," exclaimed Fred, as he recharged in tremendous excitement (taking twice as long to load in consequence), "I've improved a little, you see, in my shoot—oh bother this—ramrod!—tut! tut! there, that's it."

Bang went Meetuck's musket at that moment, and the deer tumbled over upon the snow.

"Well done, old fellow!" cried Fred, springing forward. At the same instant a white hare darted across his path, at which he fired, without even putting the gun to his shoulder, and knocked it over, to his own intense amazement.

The three shots were the signal for the men to come up with the sledge, which they did at full gallop, O'Riley driving, and flourishing the long whip about in a way that soon entangled it hopelessly with the dogs' traces.

"Ah, then, ye've done it this time, ye have, sure enough. Musha! what a purty crature it is. Now, isn't it, West? Stop, then, won't ye (to the estive dogs); ye've broke my heart entirely, and the whip's tied up into ver so many knots. Arrah, Meetuck! ye may drive yer coach yerself for ne, you may; I've had more nor enough of it."

n a few minutes the deer and the hare were lashed to the sledge— which the Irishman asserted was a great improvement, inasmuch as :he carcass of the former made an excellent seat—and they were off again at full gallop over the floes. They travelled without further nterruption or mishap, until they drew near to the open water, when suddenly they came upon a deep fissure or crack in the ice about four feet wide, with water in the bottom. Here they came to a dead stop.

'Arrah! what's to be done now?" inquired O'Riley.

'Indeed I don't know," replied Fred, looking toward Meetuck for advice.

'Hup, cut-up ice, mush, hurroo!" said that fat individual. Fortunately he followed his advice with a practical illustration of its meaning. Seizing an axe, he ran to the nearest hummock, and chopping it down, rolled the heaviest pieces he could move into the chasm. The others followed his example, and in the course of an hour the place was bridged across, and the sledge passed over. But the dogs required a good deal of coaxing to get them to trust to this rude bridge, which their sagacity taught them was not to be depended on like the works of nature.

A quarter of an hour's drive brought them to a place where there was another crack of little more than two feet across. Meetuck stretched his neck and took a steady look at this as they approached it at full gallop. Being apparently satisfied with his scrutiny, he resumed his look of self-satisfied placidity.

"Look out, Meetuck—pull up!" cried Fred in some alarm; but the Esquimau paid no attention.

"O morther! we're gone now for iver," exclaimed O'Riley, shutting his eyes and clenching his teeth as he laid fast hold of the sides of the sledge.

The feet of the dogs went faster and faster until they pattered on the hard surface of the snow like rain. Round came the long whip, as O'Riley said, "like the shot of a young cannon," and the next moment they were across, skimming over the ice on the other side like the wind.

It happened that there had been a break in the ice at this point on the previous night, and the floes had been cemented by a sheet of ice only an inch thick. Upon this, to the consternation even of Meetuck himself they now passed, and in a moment, ere they were aware, they were passing over a smooth, black surface that undulated beneath them like the waves of the sea, and crackled fearfully. There was nothing for it but to go on. A moment's halt would have allowed the sledge to break through, and leave them struggling in the water. There was no time for remark. Each man held his breath. Meetuck sent the heavy lash with a tremendous crack over the backs of the whole team; but just as they neared the solid floe the left runner broke through. In a moment the men flung themselves horizontally upon their breasts, and scrambled over the smooth surface until they gained the white ice, while the sledge and the dogs nearest to it were sinking. One vigorous pull, however, by dogs and men together, dragged the sledge upon the solid floe, even before the things in it had got wet.

"Safe!" cried Fred, as he hauled on the sledge rope to drag it farther out of danger.

"So we are," replied O'Riley, breathing very hard; "and it's meself thought to have had a wet skin at this minute.—Come, West, lind a hand to fix the dogs, will ye?"

A few minutes sufficed to put all to rights and enable them to start afresh. Being now in the neighbourhood of dangerous ice, they advanced with a little more caution; the possibility of seals being in the neighbourhood also rendered them more circumspect. It was well that they were on the alert, for a band of seals were soon after descried in a pool of open water not far ahead, and one of them was lying on the ice.

There were no hummocks, however, in the neighbourhood to enable them to approach unseen; but the Esquimau was prepared for such a contingency. He had brought a small sledge, of about two feet in length by a foot and a half in breadth, which he now unfastened from the large sledge, and proceeded quietly to arrange it, to the surprise of his companions, who had not the least idea what he was about to do, and watched his proceedings with much interest.

"Is it to sail on the ice ye're goin', boy?" inquired O'Riley at last, when he saw Meetuck fix a couple of poles, about four feet long, into a hole in the little sledge, like two masts, and upon these spread a piece of canvas upwards of a yard square, with a small hole in the centre of it.

But Meetuck answered not. He fastened the canvas "sail" to a cross-yard above and below. Then placing a harpoon and coil of rope on the sledge, and taking up his musket, he made signs to the party to keep under the cover of a hummock, and, pushing the sledge before him, advanced towards the seals in a stooping posture, so as to be completely hid behind the bit of canvas.

"O the haythen! I see it now!" exclaimed O'Riley, his face puckering up with fun. "Ah, but it's a cliver trick, no doubt of it."

"What a capital dodge!" said Fred, crouching behind the hummock, and watching the movements of the Esquimau with deep interest.

"West, hand me the little telescope; you'll find it in the pack."

"Here it is, sir," said the man, pulling out a glass of about six inches long, and handing it to Fred.

"How many is there, an ye plaze?"

"Six, I think; yes—one, two, three—I can't make them out quite, but I think there are six, besides the one on the ice. Hist! there he sees him. Ah, Meetuck, he's too quick for you."

As he spoke the seal on the ice began to show symptoms of alarm. Meetuck had approached to within shot, but he did not fire; the wary Esquimau had caught sight of another object which a lump of ice had hitherto concealed from view. This was no less a creature than a walrus, who chanced at that time to come up to take a gulp of fresh air and lave his shaggy front in the brine, before going down again to the depths of his ocean home. Meetuck, therefore, allowed the seal to glide quietly into the sea, and advanced towards this new object of attack. At length he took a steady aim through the hole in the canvas screen, and fired. Instantly the seals dived, and at the same time the water round the walrus was lashed into foam and tinged with red. It was evidently badly wounded, for had it been only slightly hurt it would probably have dived.

Meetuck immediately seized his harpoon, and rushed towards the struggling monster; while Fred grasped a gun and O'Riley a harpoon, and ran to his assistance. West remained to keep back the dogs. As Meetuck gained the edge of the ice the walrus recovered partially, and tried, with savage fury, to reach his assailant, who planted the harpoon deep in its breast, and held on to the rope while the animal dived.

"Whereabouts is he?" cried O'Riley, as he came panting to the scene of action.

As he spoke the walrus ascended almost under his nose, with a loud bellow, and the Irishman started back in terror, as he surveyed at close quarters, for the first time, the colossal and horrible countenance of this elephant of the Northern Seas. O'Riley was no coward, but the suddenness of the apparition was too much for him, and we need not wonder that in his haste he darted the harpoon far over the animal's head into the sea beyond. Neither need we feel surprised that when Fred took aim at its forehead, the sight of its broad muzzle fringed with a bristling moustache, and defended by huge tusks, caused him to miss it altogether. But O'Riley recovered, hauled his harpoon back, and succeeded in planting it deep under the creature's left flipper; and Fred, reloading, lodged a ball in its head, which finished it. With great labour the four men, aided by the dogs, drew it out upon the ice.

This was a great prize, for walrus-flesh is not much inferior to beef, and would be an acceptable addition of fresh meat for the use of the *Dolphin's* crew; and there was no chance of it spoiling, for the frost was now severe enough to freeze every animal solid almost immediately after it was killed.

The body of this walrus was not less than eighteen feet long and eleven in circumference. It was more like an elephant in bulk and rotundity than any other creature. It partook very much of the form of a seal, having two large paw-like flippers, with which, when struggling for life, it had more than once nearly succeeded in getting upon the ice. Its upper face had a square, bluff aspect, and its broad muzzle and cheeks were completely covered by a coarse, quill-like beard of bristles, which gave to it a peculiarly ferocious appearance. The notion that the walrus resembles man is very much overrated. The square, bluff shape of the head already referred to destroys the resemblance to humanity when distant, and its colossal size does the same when near. Spine of the seals deserve this distinction more, their drooping shoulders and oval faces being strikingly like to those of man when at a distance. The white ivory tusks of this creature were carefully measured by Fred, and found to be thirty inches long.

The resemblance of the walrus to our domestic land-animals has obtained for it, among sailors, the names of the sea-horse and sea-cow; and the records of its ferocity when attacked are numerous. Its hide is nearly an inch thick, and is put to many useful purposes by the Esquimaux, who live to a great extent on the flesh of this creature. They cut up his hide into long lines to attach to the harpoons with which they catch himself, the said harpoons being pointed with his own tusks. This tough hide is not the only garment the walrus wears to protect him from the cold. He also wears under-flannels of thick fat and a top-coat of close hair, so that he can take a siesta on an iceberg without the least inconvenience. Talking of siestas, by the way, the walrus is sometimes "caught napping." Occasionally, when the weather is intensely cold, the hole through which he crawls upon the ice gets frozen over so solidly that, on waking, he finds it beyond even his enormous power to break it. In this extremity there is no alternative but to go to sleep again, and—die! which he does as comfortably as he can. The Polar bears, however, are quick to smell him out, and assembling round his carcass for a feast, they dispose of him, body and bones, without ceremony.

As it was impossible to drag this unwieldy animal to the ship that night, for the days had now shortened very considerably, the hunters hauled it towards the land, and having reached the secure ice, prepared to encamp for the night under the lee of a small iceberg.

CHAPTER XII.

A dangerous sleep interrupted—A night in a snow-hut, and an unpleasant visitor—Snowed up.

"Now, then," cried Fred, as they drew up on a level portion of the ice-floe, where the snow on its surface was so hard that the runners of the sledge scarce made an impression on it, "let us to work, lads, and get the tarpaulins spread. We shall have to sleep to-night under star-spangled bed-curtains."

"Troth," said O'Riley, gazing round towards the land, where the distant cliffs loomed black and heavy in the fading light, and out upon the floes and hummocks, where the frost-smoke from pools of open water on the horizon circled round the pinnacles of the icebergs—"troth, it's a cowld place intirely to go to wan's bed in, but that fat-faced Exqueemaw seems to be settin' about it quite coolly; so here goes!"

"It would be difficult to set about it otherwise than coolly with the thermometer forty-five below zero," remarked Fred, beating his hands together, and stamping his feet, while the breath issued from his mouth like dense clouds of steam, and fringed the edges of his hood and the breast of his jumper with hoar-frost.

"It's quite purty, it is," remarked O'Riley, in reference to this wreath of hoar-frost, which covered the upper parts of each of them; "it's jist like the ermine that kings and queens wear, so I'm towld, and it's chaper a long way."

"I don't know that," said Joseph West. "It has cost us a rough voyage and a winter in the Arctic Regions, if it doesn't cost us more yet, to put that ermine fringe on our jumpers. I can make nothing of this knot; try what you can do with it, messmate, will you?"

"Sorra wan o' me'll try it," cried O'Riley, suddenly leaping up and swinging both arms violently against his shoulders; "I've got two hands, I have, but niver a finger on them—leastwise I feel none, though it *is* some small degrae o' comfort to see them."

"My toes are much in the same condition," said West, stamping vigorously until he brought back the circulation.

"Dance, then, wid me," cried the Irishman, suiting his action to the word. "I've a mortial fear o' bein' bit wid the frost—for it's no joke, let me tell you. Didn't I see a whole ship's crew wance that wos wrecked in the Gulf o' St. Lawrence about the beginnin' o' winter, and before they got to a part o' the coast where there was a house belongin' to the fur-traders, ivery man-jack o' them was frost-bit more or less, they wor. Wan lost a thumb, and another the jint of a finger or two, and most o' them had two or three toes off, an' there wos wan poor fellow who lost the front half o' wan fut an' the heel o' the other, an' two inches o' the bone was stickin' out. Sure it's truth I'm tellin' ye, for I seed it wid me own two eyes, I did."

The earnest tones in which the last words were spoken convinced his comrades that O'Riley was telling the truth, so having a decided objection to be placed in similar circumstances, they danced and beat each other until they were quite in a glow.

"Why, what are you at there, Meetuck?" exclaimed Fred, pausing.

"Igloe make," replied the Esquimau.

"Ig—what?" inquired O'Riley.

"Oh, I see!" shouted Fred, "he's going to make a snow-hut—igloes they call them here. Capital!—I never thought of that. Come along; let's help him!"

Meetuck was indeed about to erect one of those curious dwellings of snow in which, for the greater part of the year, his primitive countrymen dwell. He had no taste for star-spangled bed-curtains, when solid walls, whiter than the purest dimity, were to be had for nothing. His first operation in the erection of this hut was to mark out a circle of about seven feet diameter. From the inside of this circle the snow was cut by means of a long knife in the form of slabs nearly a foot thick, and from two to three feet long, having a slight convexity on the outside. These slabs were then so cut and arranged that, when they were piled upon each other round the margin of the circle, they formed a dome-shaped structure like a bee-hive, which was six feet high inside, and remarkably solid. The slabs were cemented together with loose snow, and every accidental chink or crevice filled up with the same material. The natives sometimes insert a block of clear ice in the roof for a window, but this was dispensed with on the present occasion—first, because there was no light to let in; and, secondly, because if there had been, they didn't want it.

The building of the hut occupied only an hour, for the hunters were cold and hungry, and in their case the old proverb might have been paraphrased, "No *work*, no supper." A hole, just large enough to permit a man to creep through on his hands and knees, formed the door of this bee-hive. Attached to this hole, and cemented to it, was a low tunnel of about four feet in length. When finished, both ends of the tunnel were closed up with slabs of hard snow, which served the purpose of double doors, and effectually kept out the cold.

While this tunnel was approaching completion, Fred retired to a short distance, and sat down to rest a few minutes on a block of ice.

A great change had come over the scene during the time they were at work on the snow-hut. The night had settled down, and now the whole sky was lit up with the vivid and beautiful coruscations of the aurora borealis—that magnificent meteor of the North which, in some measure, makes up to the inhabitants for the absence of the sun. It spread over the whole extent of the sky in the form of an irregular arch, and was intensely brilliant. But the brilliancy varied, as the green ethereal fire waved mysteriously to and fro, or shot up long streamers toward the zenith. These streamers, or "merry dancers," as they are sometimes termed, were at times peculiarly bright. Their colour was most frequently yellowish white, sometimes greenish, and once or twice of a lilac tinge. The strength of the light was something greater than that of the moon in her quarter, and the stars were dimmed when the aurora passed over them as if they had been covered with a delicate gauze veil.

But that which struck our hero as being most remarkable was the magnitude and dazzling brightness of the host of stars that covered the black firmament. It seemed as if they were magnified in glory, and twinkled so much that the sky seemed, as it were, to tremble with light. A feeling of deep solemnity filled Fred's heart as he gazed upwards; and as he thought upon the Creator of these mysterious worlds, and remembered that he came to this little planet of ours to work out the miracle of our redemption, the words that he had often read in the Bible, "Lord, what is man, that thou art mindful of him?" came forcibly to his remembrance, and he felt the appropriateness of that sentiment which the sweet singer of Israel has expressed in the words, "Praise ye him, sun and moon; praise him, all ye stars of light."

There was a deep, solemn stillness all around—a stillness widely different from that peaceful composure which characterizes a calm day in an inhabited land. It was the death-like stillness of that most peculiar and dreary desolation which results from the total absence of animal existence. The silence was so oppressive that it was with a feeling of relief he listened to the low, distant voices of the men as they paused ever and anon in their busy task to note and remark on the progress of their work. In the intense cold of an Arctic night the sound of voices can be heard at a much greater distance than usual, and although the men were far off, and hummocks of ice intervened between them and Fred, their tones broke distinctly, though gently, on his ear. Yet these sounds did not interrupt the unusual stillness. They served rather to impress him more forcibly with the vastness of that tremendous solitude in the midst of which he stood.

Gradually his thoughts turned homeward, and he thought of the dear ones who circled round his own fireside, and perchance talked of him —of the various companions he had left behind, and the scenes of life and beauty where he used to wander. But such memories led him irresistibly to the Far North again; for in all home-scenes the figure of his father started up, and he was back again in an instant, searching toilsomely among the floes and icebergs of the Polar Seas. It was the invariable ending of poor Fred's meditations, and, however successful he might be in entering for a time into the spirit of fun that characterized most of the doings of his shipmates, and in following the bent of his own joyous nature, in the hours of solitude and in the dark night, when no one saw him, his mind ever reverted to the one engrossing subject, like the oscillating needle to the Pole.

As he continued to gaze up long and earnestly into the starry sky, his thoughts began to wander over the past and the present at random, and a cold shudder warned him that It was time to return to the hut. But the wandering thoughts and fancies seemed to chain him to the spot, so that he could not tear himself away. Then a dreamy feeling of rest and comfort began to steal over his senses, and he thought how pleasant it would be to lie down and slumber; but he knew that would be dangerous, so he determined not to do it.

Suddenly he felt himself touched, and heard a voice whispering in his ear. Then it sounded loud. "Hallo, sir! Mr. Ellice! Wake up, sir! d'ye hear me?" and he felt himself shaken so violently that his teeth rattled together. Opening his eyes reluctantly, he found that he was stretched at full length on the snow, and Joseph West was shaking him by the shoulder as if he meant to dislocate his arm.

"Hallo, West! is that you? Let me alone, man, I want to sleep." Fred sank down again instantly: that deadly sleep produced by cold, and from which those who indulge in it never awaken, was upon him.

"Sleep!" cried West frantically; "you'll die, sir, if you don't rouse up.—

Hallo! Meetuck! O'Riley! help! here.'

"I tell you," murmured Fred faintly, "I want to sleep—only a moment or two—ah! I see; is the hut finished? Well, well, go, leave me. I'll follow —in—a—"

His voice died away again, just as Meetuck and O'Riley came running up. The instant the former saw how matters stood, he raised Fred in his powerful arms, set him on his feet, and shook him with such vigour that it seemed as if every bone in his body must be forced out of joint.

"What mane ye by that, ye blubber-bag?" cried the Irishman wrathfully, doubling his mittened fists and advancing in a threatening manner towards the Esquimau; but seeing that the savage paid not the least attention to him, and kept on shaking Fred violently with a good-humoured smile on his countenance, he wisely desisted from interfering.

In a few minutes Fred was able to stand and look about him with a stupid expression, and immediately the Esquimau dragged and pushed and shook him along towards the snow-hut, into which he was finally thrust, though with some trouble, in consequence of the lowness of the tunnel. Here, by means of rubbing and chafing, with a little more buffeting, he was restored to some degree of heat, on seeing which, Meetuck uttered a quiet grunt and immediately set about preparing supper.

"I do believe I've been asleep," said Fred, rising and stretching himself vigorously as the bright flame of a tin lamp shot forth and shed a yellow lustre on the white walls.

"Aslaap is it! be me conscience an' ye have jist. Oh, then, may I niver indulge in the same sort o' slumber!"

"Why so?" asked Fred in some surprise.

"You fell asleep on the ice, sir," answered West, while he busied himself in spreading the tarpaulin and blanket-bags on the floor of the hut, "and you were very near frozen to death."

"Frozen, musha! I'm not too sure that he's melted yit!" said O'Riley, taking him by the arm and looking at him dubiously.

Fred laughed. "Oh yes; I'm melted now! But let's have supper, else I shall faint for hunger. Did I sleep many hours?"

"You slept only five minutes," said West, in some surprise at the question. "You were only gone about ten minutes altogether."

This was indeed the case. The intense desire for sleep which is produced in Arctic countries when the frost seizes hold of the frame soon confuses the faculties of those who come under its influence. As long as Fred had continued to walk and work he felt quite warm; but the instant he sat down on the lump of ice to rest, the frost acted on him. Being much exhausted, too, by labour and long fasting, he was more susceptible than he would otherwise have been to the influence of cold, so that it chilled him at once, and produced that deadly lethargy from which, but for the timely aid of his companions, he would never have recovered.

The arrangements for supping and spending the night made rapid progress, and, under the influence of fire and animal heat—for the dogs were taken in beside them—the igloe became comfortably warm. Yet the snow-walls did not melt, or become moist, the intense cold without being sufficient to counteract and protect them from the heat within. The fair roof, however, soon became very dingy, and the odour of melted fat rather powerful. But Arctic travellers are proof against such trifles.

The tarpaulin was spread over the floor, and a tin lamp, into which several fat portions of the walrus were put, was suspended from a stick thrust into the wall. Bound this lamp the hunters circled, each seated on his blanket-bag, and each attended to the duty which devolved upon him. Meetuck held a tin kettle over the flame till the snow with which it was filled melted and became cold water, and then gradually heated until it boiled; and all the while he employed himself in masticating a lump of raw walrus-flesh, much to the amusement of Fred, and to the disgust, real or pretended, of O'Riley. But the Irishman, and Fred too, and every man on board the *Dolphin*, came at last to *relish* raw meat, and to long for it! The Esquimaux prefer it raw in these parts of the world (although some travellers assert that in more southern latitudes they prefer cooked meat); and with good reason, for it is much more nourishing than cooked flesh, and learned, scientific men who have wintered in the Arctic Regions have distinctly stated that in those cold countries they found raw meat to be better for them than cooked meat, and they assure us that they at last came to *prefer* it! We would not have our readers to begin forthwith to dispense with the art of cookery, and cast Soyer to the dogs; but we would have them henceforth refuse to accept that common opinion and vulgar error that Esquimaux eat their food raw *because they are savages.* They do it because nature teaches them that, under the circumstances, it is best.

The duty that devolved upon O'Riley was to roast small steaks of the walrus, in which operation he was assisted by West; while Fred undertook to get out the biscuit-bag and pewter plates, and to infuse the coffee when the water should boil. It was a strange feast in a strange place, but it proved to be a delightful one, for hunger requires not to be tempted, and is not fastidious.

"Oh, but it's good, isn't it?" remarked O'Riley, smacking his lips, as he swallowed a savoury morsel of the walrus and tossed the remnant, a sinewy bit, to Dumps, who sat gazing sulkily at the flame of the lamp, having gorged himself long before the bipeds began supper.

"Arrah! ye won't take it, won't ye?—Here, Poker!"

Poker sprang forward, wagging the stump of his tail, and turned his head to one side, as if to say, "Well, what's up? Any fun going?"

"Here, take that, old boy; Dumps is sulky."

Poker took it at once, and a single snap caused it to vanish. He, too, had finished supper, and evidently ate the morsel to please the Irishman.

"Hand me the coffee, Meetuck," said Fred.—"The biscuit lies beside you, West; don't give in so soon, man."

"Thank you, sir; I have about done."

"Meetuck, ye haythen, try a bit o' the roast; do now, av it was only to plaze me."

Meetuck shook his head quietly, and, cutting a *fifteenth* lump off the mass of raw walrus that lay beside him, proceeded leisurely to devour it.

"The dogs is nothin' to him," muttered O'Riley. "Isn't it a curious thing, now, to think that we're all *at sea* a-eatin', and drinkin', and slaapin'— or goin' to slaap—jist as if we wor on the land, and the great ocean away down below us there, wid whales, and seals, and walruses, and mermaids, for what I know, a-swimmin' about jist under whare we sit, and maybe lookin' through the ice at us this very minute. Isn't it quare?"

"It is odd," said Fred, laughing, "and not a very pleasant idea. However, as there is at least twelve feet of solid ice between us and the company you mention, we don't need to care much."

"Ov coorse not," replied O'Riley, nodding his head approvingly as he lighted his pipe; "that's my mind intirely—in all cases o' danger, when ye don't need to be afeard, you needn't much care. It's a good chart to steer by, that same."

This last remark seemed to afford so much food for thought to the company that nothing further was said by any one until Fred rose and proposed to turn in. West had already crawled into his blanket-bag, and was stretched out like a mummy on the floor, and the sound of Meetuck's jaws still continued as he winked sleepily over the walrus-meat, when a scraping was heard outside the hut.

"Sure, it's the foxes; I'll go and look," whispered O'Riley, laying down his pipe and creeping to the mouth of the tunnel.

He came back, however, faster than he went, with a look of consternation, for the first object that confronted him on looking out was the enormous head of a Polar bear. To glance round for their fire-arms was the first impulse, but these had unfortunately been left on the sledge outside. What was to be done? They had nothing but their clasp-knives in the igloe. In this extremity Meetuck cut a large hole in the back of the hut, intending to creep out and procure one of the muskets; but the instant the opening was made the bear's head filled it up. With a savage yell O'Riley seized the lamp and dashed the flaming fat in the creature's face. It was a reckless deed, for it left them all in the dark; but the bear seemed to think himself insulted, for he instantly retreated, and when Meetuck emerged and laid hold of a gun he had disappeared.

They found, on issuing into the open air, that a stiff breeze was blowing, which, from the threatening appearance of the sky, promised to become a gale; but as there was no apprehension to be entertained in regard to the stability of the floe, they returned to the hut, taking care to carry in their arms along with them. Having patched up the hole, closed the doors, rekindled the lamp, and crept into their respective bags, they went to sleep; for, however much they might dread the return of Bruin, sleep was a necessity of nature that would not be denied.

Meanwhile the gale freshened into a hurricane, and was accompanied with heavy snow, and when they attempted to move next morning, they found it impossible to face it for a single moment. There was no alternative, therefore, but to await the termination of the gale, which lasted two days, and kept them close prisoners all the time. It was very wearisome, doubtless, but they had to submit, and sought to console themselves and pass the time as pleasantly as possible by sleeping, and eating, and drinking coffee.

CHAPTER XIII.

Journey resumed—The hunters meet with bears and have a great fight, in which the dogs are sufferers—A bear's dinner—Mode in which Arctic rocks travel—The ice-belt.

On the abating of the great storm referred to in the last chapter, the hunters sought to free themselves from their snowy prison, and succeeded in burrowing, so to speak, upwards after severe labour, for the hut was buried in drift which the violence of the gale had rendered extremely compact.

O'Riley was the first to emerge into the upper world. Having dusted the snow from his garments, and shaken himself like a Newfoundland dog, he made sundry wry faces, and gazed round him with the look of a man that did not know very well what to do with himself.

"It's a quare place, it is, intirely," he remarked, with a shake of the head that betokened intense sagacity, while he seated himself on a mound of snow and watched his comrades as they busied themselves in dragging their sleeping-bags and cooking utensils from the cavern they had just quitted. O'Riley seemed to be in a contemplative mood, for he did not venture any further remark, although he looked unutterable things as he proceeded quietly to fill his little black pipe.

"Ho! O'Riley, lend a hand, you lazy fellow," cried Fred; "work first and play afterwards, you skulker."

"Sure that same is what I'm doin'," replied O'Riley with a bland smile, which he eclipsed in a cloud of smoke. "Haven't I bin workin' like a naagur for two hours to git out of that hole, and ain't I playin' a tune on me pipe now? But I won't be cross-grained. I'll lind ye a hand av ye behave yerself. It's a bad thing to be cross-grained," he continued, pocketing his pipe and assisting to arrange the sledge; "me owld grandmother always towld me that, and she wos wise, she wos, beyand ordn'r. More like Salomon nor anything else."

"She must have directed that remark specially to you, I think," said Fred—"(Let Dumps lead, West, he's tougher than the others)—did she not, O'Riley?"

"Be no manes. It wos to the pig she said it. Most of her conversation (and she had a power of it) wos wid the pig; and many's the word o'

119

good advice she gave it, as it sat in its usual place beside the fire fore-nint her. But it wos all thrown away, it wos, for there wosn't another pig in all the length o' Ireland as had sich a will o' its own; and it had a screech, too, when it wosn't plaazed, as bate all the steam whistles in the world, it did. I've often moralated on that same, and I've noticed that, as it is wid pigs, so it is wid men and women—some of them at laste—the more advice ye give them, the less they take."

"Down, Poker! quiet, good dog!" said West, as he endeavoured to restrain the ardour of the team, which, being fresh and full fed, could scarcely be held in by the united efforts of himself and Meetuck, while their companions lashed their provisions, etc., on the sledge.

"Hold on, lads!" cried Fred, as he fastened the last lashing. "We'll be ready in a second. Now, then, jump on, two of you! Catch hold of the tail-line, Meetuck! All right!"

"Hall right!" yelled the Esquimau, as he let go the dogs and sprang upon the sledge.

The team struggled and strained violently for a few seconds in their efforts to overcome the *vis inertiæ* of the sledge, and it seemed as if the traces would part; but they were made of tough walrus-hide, and held on bravely, while the heavy vehicle gradually fetched way, and at length flew over the floes at the rate of seven or eight miles an hour. Travelling, however, was not now quite so agreeable as it had been when they set out from the ship; for the floes were swept bare in some places by the gale, while in other places large drifts had collected, so that the sledge was either swaying to and fro on the smooth ice, and swinging the dogs almost off their feet, or it was plunging heavily through banks of soft snow.

As the wind was still blowing fresh, and would have been dead against them had they attempted to return by a direct route to the ship, they made for the shore, intending to avail themselves of the shelter afforded by the ice-belt. Meanwhile the carcass of the walrus—at least as much of it as could not be packed on the sledge—was buried in the hut, and a spear planted above it to mark the spot.

"Ha! an' it's cowld," said O'Riley, wrapping himself more closely in his fur jumper as they sped along. "I wish we wos out o' the wind, I do."

"You'll have your wish soon, then," answered West, "for that row of icebergs we're coming to will shelter us nearly all the way to the land."

"Surely you are taking us too much off to the right, Meetuck," said

Fred; "we are getting farther away from the ship."

No fee. De win' too 'trong. We turn hup 'long shore very quick, soon—
na!"

Meetuck accompanied each word with a violent nod of his head, at the same time opening and shutting his mouth and winking with both eyes, being apparently impressed with the conviction that such contortions of visage rendered his meaning more apparent.

Look! look! ho! Nannook, nannook!" (a bear, a bear!) whispered the Esquimau with sudden animation, just as they gained the lee of the first iceberg.

The words were unnecessary, however, for the whole party were looking ahead with the most intense eagerness at a bear which their sudden advent had aroused from a nap in the crevice of the iceberg. A little cub was discerned a moment after standing by her side, and gazing at the intruders with infantine astonishment. While the muskets were being loosened and drawn out, Meetuck let slip all the dogs, and in a few seconds they were engaged in active warfare with the enemy.

'Oh! musha! Dumps is gone intirely!" The quadruped referred to was tossed to a height of about thirty feet, and alighted senseless upon the ice. The bear seized him with her teeth and tossed him with an incredibly slight effort. The other dogs, nothing daunted by the fate of their comrade, attacked the couple in the rear, biting their heels, and so distracting their attention that they could not make an energetic attack in any direction. Another of the dogs, however, a young one, waxing reckless, ventured too near the old bear, and was seized by the back, and hurled high into the air, through which it wriggled violently, and descended with a sounding whack upon the ice. At the same moment a volley from the hunters sent several balls into the carcass of both mother and cub; but, although badly wounded, neither of them evinced any sign of pain or exhaustion as they continued to battle with the remaining dogs.

The dogs that had already fallen in the fray had not been used to bear-hunting; hence their signal defeat. But this was not the case with the others, all of which were old campaigners; and Poker especially, although not old in years, was a practical fighter, having been trained not to attack but to harass. The systematic and steady way in which they advanced before the bear, and retired, right and left, leading her into a profitless pursuit, was very interesting to witness. Another volley from the hunters caused them to make off more rapidly, and wounded the cub severely, so much so that in a few minutes it began to flag. Seeing this, the mother placed it in front of her, and urged it forward with her snout so quickly that it was with the utmost difficulty the men could keep up with them. A well-directed shot, however, from Fred Ellice brought the old bear to the ground; but she rose instantly, and again advanced, pushing her cub before her, while the dogs continued to embarrass her. They now began to fear that, in spite of dogs and men, the wounded bears would escape, when an opportune crack in the ice presented itself, into which they both tumbled, followed by the yelping, and we may add limping, dogs. Before they could scramble up on the other side, Meetuck and Fred, being light of foot, gained upon them sufficiently to make sure shots.

"There they go," cried Fred, as the she-bear bounced out of the crack with Poker hanging to her heels. Poker's audacity had at last outstripped his sagacity, and the next moment he was performing a tremendous somersault. Before he reached the ice, Meetuck and Fred fired simultaneously, and when the smoke cleared away the old bear was stretched out in death. Hitherto the cub had acted exclusively on the defensive, and intrusted itself entirely to the protection of its dam; but now it seemed to change its character entirely. It sprang upon its mother's body, and, assuming an attitude of extreme ferocity, kept the dogs at bay, snapping and snarling right and left until the hunters came up.

For the first time since the chase began a feeling, of intense pity touched Fred's heart, and he would have rejoiced at that moment had the mother risen up and made her escape with her cub. He steeled his heart, however, by reflecting that fresh provisions were much wanted on board the *Dolphin*; still, neither he nor his shipmates could bring themselves to shoot the gallant little animal, and it is possible that they might have made up their minds to allow it to escape after all, had not Meetuck quietly ended their difficulty by putting a ball through its heart.

"Ah! then, Meetuck," said O'Riley, shaking his head as they examined their prize, "ye're a hardhearted spalpeen, ye are, to kill a poor little baby like that in cowld blood. Well, well, it's yer natur', an' yer trade, so I s'pose it's all right."

The weight of this bear, which was not of the largest size, was afterwards found to be above five hundred pounds, and her length was eight feet nine inches. The cub weighed upwards of a hundred pounds, and was larger than a Newfoundland dog.

The operation of cutting out the entrails, preparatory to packing on the sledge, was now commenced by Meetuck, whose practised hand applied the knife with the skill, though not with the delicacy, of a surgeon.

"She has been a hungry bear, it seems," remarked Fred, as he watched the progress of the work, "if we may judge from the emptiness of her stomach."

"Och! but she's had a choice morsel, if it was a small wan," exclaimed O'Riley in surprise, as he picked up a plug of tobacco. On further examination being made, it was found that this bear had dined on raisins, tobacco, pork, and adhesive plaster! Such an extraordinary mixture of articles, of course, led the party to conclude that either she had helped herself to the stores of the *Dolphin* placed on Store Island, or that she had fallen in with those of some other vessel. This subject afforded food for thought and conversation during the next hour or two, as they drove towards the ship along the ice-belt of the shore.

The ice-belt referred to is a zone of ice which extends along the shore from the unknown regions of the North. To the south it breaks up in summer and disappears altogether, but in the latitude which our travellers had now reached, it was a permanent feature of the scenery all the year round, following the curvatures and indentations of bays and rivers, and increasing in winter or diminishing in summer, but never melting entirely away. The surface of this ice-belt was covered with immense masses of rock many tons in weight, which had fallen from the cliffs above. Pointing to one of these as they drove along, West remarked to Fred,—

"There is a mystery explained, sir. I have often wondered how huge, solitary stones, that no machinery of man's making could lift, have come to be placed on sandy shores where there were no other rocks of any kind within many miles of them. The ice must have done it, I see."

"True, West. The ice, if it could speak, would explain many things that now seem to us mysterious; and yonder goes a big rock on a journey that may perhaps terminate at a thousand miles to the south of this."

The rock referred to was a large mass that became detached from the cliffs and fell, as he spoke, with a tremendous crash upon the ice-belt, along which it rolled for fifty yards. There it would lie all winter, and in spring the mass of ice to which it was attached would probably break off and float away with it to the south, gradually melting until it allowed the rock to sink to the bottom of the sea, or depositing it, perchance, on some distant shore, where such rocks are not wont to lie—there to remain an object of speculation and wonderment to the unlearned of all future ages.

Some of the bergs close to which they passed on the journey were very fantastically formed, and many of them were more than a mile long, with clear, blue, glassy surfaces, indicating that they had been but recently thrown off from the great glacier of the North. Between two of these they drove for some time, before they found that they were going into a sort of blind alley.

"Sure the road's gittin' narrower," observed O'Riley, as he glanced up at the blue walls, which rose perpendicularly to a height of sixty feet on either hand. "Have a care, Meetuck, or ye'll jam us up, ye will."

"'Tis a pity we left the ice-belt," remarked Fred, "for this rough work among the bergs is bad for man and dog. How say you, Meetuck—shall we take to it again when we get through this place?"

"Faix, then, we'll nive'r git through," said O'Riley, pointing to the end of the chasm, where a third iceberg had entirely closed the opening.

The Esquimau pulled up, and after advancing on foot a short way to examine, returned with a rueful expression on his countenance.

"Ha! no passage, I suppose?" said Fred.

"Bad luck to ye!" cried O'Riley, "won't ye spaak?"

"No rod—muss go bock," replied Meetuck, turning the dogs in the direction whence they had come, and resuming his place on the sledge.

The party had to retrace their steps half-a-mile in consequence of this unfortunate interruption, and return to the level track of the ice-belt, which they had left for a time and taken to the sea-ice, in order to avoid the sinuosities of the land. To add to their misfortunes, the dogs began to flag, so that they were obliged to walk behind the sledge at a slow pace, and snow began to fall heavily. But they pressed forward manfully, and having regained the shore-ice, continued to make their way northward towards the ship, which was now spoken of by the endearing name of home.

CHAPTER XIV.

Departure of the sun—Effects of darkness on dogs—Winter arrangements in the interior of the "Dolphin."

It is sad to part with an old friend, especially if he be one of the oldest and best friends we ever had. When the day of departure arrives, it is of no avail that he tells us kindly he will come back again. That assurance is indeed a comfort after he is gone, and a sweet star of hope that shines brighter and brighter each day until he comes back; but it is poor consolation to us at the time of parting, when we are squeezing his hand for the last time, and trying to crush back the drops that *will* overflow.

The crew of the *Dolphin* had, in the course of that winter, to part with one of their best friends; one whom they regarded with the most devoted attachment; one who was not expected to return again till the following spring, and one, therefore, whom some of them might, perhaps, never see again.

Mivins became quite low-spirited about it, and said "as 'ow 'e'd 'ave a 'eavy 'eart for *h*ever and *h*ever, *h*amen," after he was gone. O'Riley remarked, in reference to his departure, that every man in the ship was about to lose a *son*! Yes, indeed he did; he perpetrated that atrocious pun, and wasn't a bit ashamed of it. O'Riley had perpetrated many a worse pun than that before; it's to be hoped for the credit of his country he has perpetrated a few better ones since!

Yes, the period at length arrived when the great source of light and heat was about to withdraw his face from these Arctic navigators for a long, long time, and leave them in unvarying night. It was a good while, however, before he went away altogether, and for many weeks after winter set in in all its intensity, he paid them a daily visit which grew gradually shorter and shorter, until that sad evening in which he finally bade them farewell.

About the middle of October the dark months overspread the Bay of Mercy, and the reign of perpetual night began. There was something terribly depressing at first in this uninterrupted gloom, and for some time after the sun ceased to show his disk above the horizon the men of the *Dolphin* used to come on deck at noon, and look out for the faint streak of light that indicated the presence of the life-giving luminary with all the earnestness and longing of Eastern fire-worshippers.

The dogs, too, became sensibly affected by the continued absence of light, and seemed to draw more sympathetically than ever to their human companions in banishment. A curious and touching instance of this feeling was exhibited when the pack were sent to sleep on Store Island. A warm kennel had been erected for them there, partly in order that the ship might be kept more thoroughly clean, and partly that the dogs might act as a guard over the stores, in case bears or wolves should take a fancy to examine them. But nothing would induce the poor animals to keep away from the ship and remain beyond the sound of human voices. They deserted their comfortable abode with one consent the first time they were sent to it, preferring to spend the night by the side of the ship upon the bare snow. Coaxing them was of no use. O'Riley tried it in vain.

"Ah! then," said he to Dumps with a wheedling air and expression of intense affection that would have taken by storm the heart of any civilized dog, "*won't* ye come now an' lay in yer own kennel? Sure it's a beautiful wan, an' as warm as the heart of an iceberg. Doo come now, avic, an' I'll show ye the way."

But Dumps's heart was marble; he wouldn't budge. By means of a piece of walrus, however, he was at length induced to go with the Irishman to the kennel, and was followed by the entire pack. Here O'Riley endeavoured to make them comfortable, and prevailed on them to lie down and go to sleep; but whenever he attempted to leave them, they were up and at his heels in a moment.

"Och! but ye're too fond o' me intirely, Doo lie down agin, and I'll sing ye a ditty?"

True to his word, O'Riley sat down by the dog-kennel, and gave vent to a howl which his "owld grandmother," he said, "used to sing to the pig;" and whether it was the effects of this lullaby, or of the cold, it is impossible to say, but O'Riley at length succeeded in slipping away and regaining the ship, unobserved by his canine friends. Half-an-hour later he went on deck to take a mouthful of fresh air before supper, and on looking over the side he saw the whole pack of dogs lying in a circle close to the ship, with Dumps comfortably asleep in the middle, and using Poker's back for a pillow.

"Faix, but ye must be fond of the cowld to lie there all night when ye've got a palace on Store Island."

"Fond of society, rather," observed Captain Guy, who came on deck at the moment; "the poor creatures cannot bear to be left alone. It is a strange quality in dogs which I have often observed before."

"Have ye, capting? Sure I thought it was all owin' to the bad manners o' that baste Dumps, which is for iver leadin' the other dogs into mischief."

"Supper's ready, sir," said Mivins, coming up the hatchway, and touching his cap.

"Look here, Mivins," said O'Riley, as the captain went below, "can you point out the mornin' star to me, lad?"

"The morning star?" said Mivins slowly, as he thrust his hands into the breast of his jumper, and gazed upwards into the dark sky, where the starry host blazed in Arctic majesty. "No, *ho*f course, I can't. Why, don't you know that there *hain't* no *morning* star when it's *night* all round?"

"Faix ye're right. I niver thought o' that."

Mivins was evidently a little puffed up with a feeling of satisfaction at the clever way in which he had got out of the difficulty, without displaying his ignorance of astronomy, and was even venturing, in the pride of his heart, to make some speculative and startling assertions in regard to the "'eavenly bodies" generally, when Buzzby put his head up the hatchway.

"Hallo! messmates, wot's ado now? Here's the supper awaitin', and the tea bilin' like blazes!"

Mivins instantly dived down below, as the sailors express it; and we may remark, in passing, that the expression, in this particular case, was not inappropriate, for Mivins, as we have elsewhere said, was remarkably agile and supple, and gave beholders a sort of impression that he went head-foremost at everything. O'Riley followed at a more reasonable rate, and in a few minutes the crew of the *Dolphin* were seated at supper in the cabin, eating with as much zest, and laughing and chatting as blithely, as if they were floating calmly on their ocean home in temperate climes. Sailors are proverbially light-hearted, and in their moments of comfort and social enjoyment they easily forget their troubles. The depression of spirits that followed the first disappearance of the sun soon wore off, and they went about their various avocations cheerfully by the light of the aurora borealis and the stars.

The cabin, in which they now all lived together, had undergone considerable alterations. After the return of Fred Ellice and the

128

hunting-party, whom we left on the ice-belt in the last chapter, the bulk-head, or partition, which separated the cabin from the hold had been taken down, and the whole was thrown into one large apartment, in order to secure a freer circulation of air and warmth. All round the walls inside of this apartment moss was piled to the depth of twelve inches to exclude the cold, and this object was further gained by the spreading of a layer of moss on the deck above. The cabin hatchway was closed, and the only entrance was at the farther end, through the hold, by means of a small doorway in the bulk-head, to which was attached a sort of porch, with a curtain of deer-skins hung in front of it. In the centre of the floor stood an iron cooking-stove, which served at once the purpose of preparing food and warming the cabin, which was lighted by several small oil lamps. These were kept burning perpetually, for there was no distinction between day and night in mid-winter, either in the cabin or out of doors.

In this snug-looking place the officers and men of the ship messed, and dwelt, and slept together; but, notwithstanding the *apparent* snugness, it was with the greatest difficulty they could keep themselves in a sufficient degree of warmth to maintain health and comfort. Whenever the fire was allowed to get low, the beams overhead became coated with hoar-frost; and even when the temperature was raised to the utmost possible pitch, it was cold enough, at the extreme ends of the apartment, to freeze a jug of water solid.

A large table occupied the upper end of the cabin between the stove and the stern, and round this the officers and crew were seated when O'Riley entered and took his place among them. Each individual had his appointed place at the mess-table, and with unvarying regularity these places were filled at the appointed hours.

"The dogs seem to be disobedient," remarked Amos Parr, as his comrade sat down; "they'd be the better of a taste o' Meetuck's cat, I think."

"It's truth ye're sayin'," replied O'Riley, commencing a violent assault on a walrus-steak; "they don't obey orders at all, at all. An' Dumps, the blaggard, is as cross-grained as me grandmother's owld pig—"

A general laugh here interrupted the speaker, for O'Riley could seldom institute a disparaging comparison without making emphatic allusion to the pig that once shared with him the hospitalities of his grandmother's cabin.

"Why, everything you speak of seems to be like that wonderful pig, messmate," said Peter Grim.

"Ye're wrong there intirely," retorted O'Riley. "I niver seed nothing like it in all me thravels except yerself, and that only in regard to its muzzle, which was black and all kivered over with bristles, it wos. I'll throuble you for another steak, messmate; that walrus is great livin'.—We owe ye thanks for killin' it, Mister Ellice."

"You're fishing for compliments, but I'm afraid I have none to give you. Your first harpoon, you know, was a little wide of the mark, if I recollect right, wasn't it?"

"Yis, it wos—about as wide as the first bullet. I mis-remember exactly who fired it—wos it you, Meetuck?"

Meetuck, being deeply engaged with a junk of fat meat at that moment, expressed all he had to say in a convulsive gasp without interrupting his supper.

"Try a bit of the bear," said Fred to Tom Singleton; "it's better than the walrus to my taste."

"I'd rather not," answered Tom, with a dubious shake of the head.

"It's a most unconscionable thing to eat a beast o' that sort," remarked Saunders gravely.

"Especially one who has been in the habit of living on raisins and sticking-plaster," said Bolton with a grin.

"I have been thinking about that," said Captain Guy, who had been for some time listening in silence to the conversation, "and I cannot help thinking that Esquimaux must have found a wreck somewhere in this neighbourhood and carried away her stores, which Bruin had managed to steal from them."

"May they not have got some of the stores of the brig we saw nipped some months ago?" suggested Singleton.

"Possibly they may."

"I dinna think that's likely," said Saunders, shaking his head. "Yon brig had been deserted long ago, and her stores must have been consumed, if they were taken out of her at all, before we thought o' comin' here."

For some time the party in the cabin ate in silence.

"We must wait patiently," resumed the captain, as if he were tired of following up a fruitless train of thought. "What of your theatricals, Fred? we must get them set a-going as soon as possible."

The captain spoke animatedly, for he felt that, with the prospect of a long dark winter before them, it was of the greatest importance that the spirits of the men should be kept up.

"I find it difficult to beat up recruits," answered Fred, laughing; "Peter Grim has flatly refused to act, and O'Riley says he could no more learn a part off by heart than—"

"His grandmother's pig could," interrupted David Mizzle, who, having concluded supper, now felt himself free to indulge in conversation.

"Och! ye spalpeen," whispered the Irishman.

"I have written out the half of a play which I hope to produce in a few days on the boards of our Arctic theatre with a talented company, but I must have one or two more men—one to act the part of a lady. Will you take that part, Buzzby?"

"Wot! *me?*" cried the individual referred to with a stare of amazement.

"Oh yes! *do*, Buzzby," cried several of the men with great delight. "You're just cut out for it."

"Blue eyes," said one.

"Fair hair," cried another.

"And plump," said a third.

"Wid cheeks like the hide of a walrus," cried O'Riley; "but, sure, it won't show wid a veil on."

"Come, now, you won't refuse."

But Buzzby did refuse; not, however, so determinedly but that he was induced at last to allow his name to be entered in Fred's note-book as a supernumerary.

"Hark!" cried the captain; "surely the dogs must have smelt a bear."

There was instantly a dead silence in the cabin, and a long, loud wail from the dogs was heard outside.

"It's not like their usual cry when game is near," said the second mate.

"Hand me my rifle, Mivins," said the captain, springing up and pulling forward the hood of his jumper, as he hurried on deck followed by the crew.

It was a bright, still, frosty night, and the air felt intensely sharp, as if needles were pricking the skin, while the men's breath issued from their lips in white clouds and settled in hoar-frost on the edges of their hoods. The dogs were seen galloping about the ice-hummocks as if in agitation, darting off to a considerable distance at times, and returning with low whines to the ship.

"It is very strange," remarked the captain. "Jump down on the ice, boys, and search for footprints. Extend as far as Store Island, and see that all is right there."

In a few seconds the men scattered themselves right and left, and were lost in the gloom, while the vessel was left in charge of Mivins and four men. A strict search was made in all directions, but no traces of animals could be found; the stores on the island were found undisturbed; and gradually the dogs ceased their agitated gyrations, and seemed inclined to resume their slumbers on the ice.

Seeing this, and supposing that they were merely restless, Captain Guy recalled his men, and not long after every man in the cabin of the *Dolphin* was buried in profound slumber.

CHAPTER XV.

Strangers appear on the scene—The Esquimaux are hospitably entertained by the sailors—A spirited, traffic—Thieving propensities and summary justice.

Dumps sat on the top of a hummock, about quarter of a mile from the ship, with an expression of subdued melancholy on his countenance, and thinking, evidently, about nothing at all. Poker sat in front of him gazing earnestly and solemnly right into his eyes with a look that said, as plain as if he had spoken, "What a tremendously stupid old fellow you are, to be sure!" Having sat thus for full five minutes, Dumps wagged his tail. Poker, observing the action, returned the compliment with his stump. Then Poker sprang up and barked savagely, as much as to say, "Play, won't you?" but Dumps wouldn't; so Poker endeavoured to relieve his mind by gambolling violently round him.

We would not have drawn your attention, reader, to the antics of our canine friends, were it not for the fact that these antics attracted the notice of a personage who merits particular description. This was no other than one of the Esquimau inhabitants of the land—a woman, and *such* a woman! Most people would have pronounced her a man, for she wore precisely the same dress—fur jumper and long boots—that was worn by the men of the *Dolphin*. Her lips were thick and her nose was blunt; she wore her hair turned up, and twisted into a knot on the top of her head; her hood was thrown back, and inside of this hood there was a baby—a small and a very fat baby! It was, so to speak, a conglomerate of dumplings. Its cheeks were two dumplings, and its arms were four dumplings—one above each elbow and one below. Its hands, also, were two smaller dumplings, with ten extremely little dumplings at the end of them. This baby had a nose, of course, but it was so small that it might as well have had none; and it had a mouth, too, but that was so capacious that the half of it would have been more than enough for a baby double the size. As for its eyes they were large and black—black as two coals—and devoid of all expression save that of astonishment.

Such were the pair that stood on the edge of the ice-belt gazing down upon Dumps and Poker. And no sooner did Dumps and Poker catch sight of them than they sprang hastily towards them, wagging their tails—or, more correctly speaking, their tail and a quarter. But on a nearer approach those sagacious animals discovered that the woman and her child were strangers, whereupon they set up a dismal howl, and fled towards the ship as fast as they could run.

Now, it so happened that, at this very time, the howl of the dogs fell upon the ears of two separate parties of travellers—the one was a band of Esquimaux who were moving about in search of seals and walruses, to which band this woman and her baby belonged; the other was a party of men under command of Buzzby, who were returning to the ship after an unsuccessful hunt. Neither party saw the other, for one approached from the east, the other from the west, and the ice-belt, on the point of which the woman stood, rose up between them.

"Hallo! what's yon?" exclaimed Peter Grim, who was first to observe the woman.

"Dun'no'," said Buzzby, halting; "it looks like a bear."

"Faix an' it is, then, it's got a young wan on its back," cried O'Riley.

"We had better advance and find out," remarked West, as he led the way, while several of the men threw up their arms in token of their friendly intentions. O'Riley capered somewhat extravagantly as he drew near, partly with the intention of expressing his feelings of good-will towards the unknown, and partly in order to relieve the excitement caused by the unexpected apparition.

These demonstrations, however, had the effect of terrifying the woman, who wheeled suddenly round and made off.

"Och! it *is* a man. Hooray, boys! give chase."

"Men don't usually carry babies on their backs and tie their hair up into top-knots," remarked Grim, as he darted past in pursuit.

A few seconds sufficed to enable Grim to overtake the woman, who fell on her knees the instant she felt the sailor's heavy hand on her shoulder.

"Don't be afeard, we won't hurt ye," said Buzzby in a soothing tone, patting the woman on the head and raising her up.

"No, avic, we's yer frinds; we'll not harm a hair o' yer beautiful head, we won't. Ah! then, it's a swate child, it is, bless its fat face," said O'Riley, stroking the baby's head tenderly with his big hand.

It was with difficulty that the poor creature's fears were calmed at first, but the genuine tenderness displayed by the men towards the baby, and the perfect complacency with which that conglomerate of dumplings received their caresses, soon relieved her mind, and she began to regard her captors with much curiosity, while they endeavoured by signs and words to converse with her. Unfortunately Meetuck was not with the party, he having been left on board ship to assist in a general cleaning of the cabin that had been instituted that day.

"Sure, now, ye don't know how to talk with a girl at all, ye don't; let *me* try," cried O'Riley, after several of the party had made numerous ineffectual attempts to convey their meaning. "Listen to *me*, darlint, and don't mind them stupid grampuses. Where have ye comed from, now? tell me, dear, *doo* now."

O'Riley accompanied the question with a smile of ineffable sweetness and a great deal of energetic pantomime, which, doubtless, explained much of his meaning to himself, but certainly to no one else.

"Ah! then, ye don't understand me? Well, well, now, isn't that strange? Look you, avic, have ye seen a brig or a brig's crew anywhere betune this and the north pole?—try, now, an' remember." He illustrated this question by holding up both arms straight above his head to represent the masts of a brig, and sticking his right leg straight out in front of him, to represent the bowsprit; but the woman gazed at him with an air of obtuse gravity that might have damped the hopes even of an Irishman. O'Riley prided himself, however, on not being easily beat, and despite his repeated failures, and the laughter of his messmates, was proceeding to make a third effort, when a loud shout from the cliffs caused the whole party to start and turn their eyes in that direction. The cry had been uttered by a figure whose costume bore so close a resemblance to that which they themselves wore, that they thought for a moment it was one of their own shipmates; but a second glance proved that they were mistaken, for the individual in question carried a spear, which he brandished with exceedingly fierce and warlike intentions.

"Faix it must be her husband," said O'Riley.

"Hallo! lads, there's more on 'em," cried Grim, as ten or twelve Esquimaux emerged from the rents and caverns, of the ice-belt, and scrambling to the top of surrounding hummocks and eminences, gazed towards the party of white men, while they threw about their arms and legs, and accompanied their uncouth and violent gesticulations with loud, excited cries. "I've a notion," he added, "that it was the scent o' them chaps set the dogs off after yon strange fashion t'other night."

It was evident that the Esquimaux were not only filled with unbounded astonishment at this Unexpected meeting With strangers, but were also greatly alarmed to see one of their own women in their power.

"Let's send the woman over to them," suggested one of the men.

"No, no; keep her as a hostage," said another.

"Look out, lads," cried Buzzby, hastily examining the priming of his musket, as additional numbers of the wild inhabitants of the North appeared on the scene, and crowned the ice-belt and the hummocks around them. "Let's show a bold front. Draw up in single line and hold on to the woman. West, put her in front."

The men instantly drew up in battle array, and threw forward their muskets; but as there were only a dozen of them, they presented a very insignificant group compared with the crowds of Esquimaux who appeared on the ice in front of them.

"Now, then, stand fast, men, and I'll show ye wot's the way to manage them chaps. Keep yer weather-eyes open, and don't let them git in rear of ye."

So saying, Buzzby took the Woman by the arm and led her out a few yards in front of his party, while the Esquimaux drew closer together, to prepare either to receive or make an attack, as the case might be. He then laid his musket down on the ice, and, still holding the woman by the arm, advanced boldly towards the natives unarmed. On approaching to within about twenty yards of them he halted, and raised both arms above his head as a sign of friendship. The signal was instantly understood, and one big fellow leaped boldly from his elevated position on a lump of ice, threw down his spear, and ran to meet the stranger.

In a few minutes Buzzby and the Esquimau leader came to a mutual understanding as to the friendly disposition of their respective parties, and the woman was delivered up to this big fellow, who turned out to be her husband after all, as O'Riley had correctly guessed. The other Esquimaux, seeing the amicable terms on which the leaders met, crowded in and surrounded them.

"Leave the half o' ye to guard the arms, and come on the rest of ye without 'em," shouted Buzzby.

The men obeyed, and in a few minutes the two parties mingled together with the utmost confidence. The sailors, however, deemed it prudent to get possession of their arms again as soon as possible; and after explaining as well as they could by signs that their home was only at a short distance, the whole band started off for the ship. The natives were in a most uproarious state of hilarity, and danced and yelled as they ambled along in their hairy dresses, evidently filled with delight at the prospect of forming a friendship with the white strangers, as they afterwards termed the crew of the *Dolphin*, although some of the said crew were, from exposure, only a few shades lighter than themselves.

Captain Guy was busily engaged with Fred Ellice and Tom Singleton in measuring and registering the state of the tide, when this riotous band turned the point of the ice-belt to the northward, and came suddenly into view.

"Jump down below, Fred, and fetch my rifle and sword; there are the natives!" cried the captain, seizing his telescope.—"Call all hands, Mivins, and let them arm; look alive!"

"All 'ands, *ahoy!*" shouted the steward, looking down the hatchway; "tumble up there, tumble up, 'ere come the Heskimows. Bring your harms with ye. Look alive!"

"Ay, ay!" shouted the men from below, and in a few minutes they crowded up the hatchway, pulling up their hoods and hauling on their mittens, for it was intensely cold.

"Why, captain, there are some of our men with them," exclaimed Tom Singleton, as he looked through his pocket-glass at them.

"So there are,—I see Buzzby and Grim. Come, that's fortunate, for they must have made friends with them, which it is not always easy to do. Hide your muskets, men, but keep on your cutlasses; it's as well to be prepared, though I don't expect to find those people troublesome. Is the soup in the coppers, David Mizzle?"

"Yes, sir, it is."

"Then put in an extra junk of pork, and fill it up to the brim."

While the cook went below to obey this order, the captain and half of the crew descended to the ice, and advanced unarmed to meet the natives. The remainder of the men stayed behind to guard the ship, and be ready to afford succour if need be. But the precaution was unnecessary, for the Esquimaux met the sailors in the most frank and confiding manner, and seemed quite to understand Captain Guy when he drew a line round the ship, and stationed sentries along it to prevent them from crossing. The natives had their dogs and sledges with them, and the former they picketed to the ice, while a few of their number, and the woman, whose name was Aninga, were taken on board and hospitably entertained.

t was exceedingly interesting and amusing to observe the feelings of amazement and delight expressed by those barbarous but good-humoured and intelligent people at everything they saw. While food was preparing for them, they were taken round the ship, on deck and below, and the sailors explained, in pantomime, the uses of everything. They laughed, and exclaimed, and shouted, and even roared with delight, and touched everything with their fingers, just as monkeys are wont to do when let loose. Captain Guy took Aninga and her tall husband, Awatok, to the cabin, where, through the medium of Meetuck, he explained the object of their expedition, and questioned the chief as to his knowledge of the country. Unfortunately Awatok and his band had travelled from the interior to the coast, and never having been more than twenty or thirty miles to the north of the Bay of Mercy, could give no information either in regard to the formation of the coast or the possibility of Europeans having wintered there. In fact, neither he nor his countrymen had ever seen Europeans before, and they were so much excited that it was difficult to obtain coherent answers to questions. The captain, therefore, postponed further inquiries until they had become somewhat accustomed to the novelty of their position.

Meanwhile, David Mizzle furnished them with a large supply of pea-soup, which they seemed to relish amazingly. Not so, however, the salt pork with which it had been made. They did, indeed, condescend to eat it, but they infinitely preferred a portion of raw walrus-flesh, which had been reserved as food for the dogs, and which they would speedily have consumed had it not been removed out of their reach. Having finished this, they were ordered to return to their camp on the ice beside the ship, and a vigorous barter was speedily begun.

First of all, however, a number of presents were made to them, and it would really have done your heart good, reader, to have witnessed the extravagant joy displayed by them on receiving such trifles as bits of hoop-iron, beads, knives, scissors, needles, etc. Iron is as precious among them as gold is among civilized people. The small quantities they possessed of it had been obtained from the few portions of wrecks that had drifted ashore in their ice-bound land. They used it for pointing their spear-heads and harpoons, which, in default of iron, were ingeniously made of ivory from the tusks of the walrus and the horn of the narwal. A bit of iron, therefore, was received with immense glee, and a penny looking-glass with shouts of delight.

But the present which drew forth the most uproarious applause was a Union Jack, which the captain gave to their chief, Awatok. He was in the cabin when it was presented to him. On seeing its gaudy colours unrolled, and being told that it was a gift to himself and his wife, he caught his breath, and stared, as if in doubt, alternately at the flag and the captain; then he gave vent to a tremendous shout, seized the flag, hugged it in his arms, and darted up on deck literally *roaring* with delight. The sympathetic hearts of the natives on the ice echoed the cry before they knew the cause of it; but when they beheld the prize, they yelled, and screamed, and danced, and tossed their arms in the air in the most violent manner.

"They're all mad, ivery mother's son o' them," exclaimed O'Riley, who for some time had been endeavouring to barter an old rusty knife for a pair of seal-skin boots.

"They looks like it," said Grim, who stood looking on with his legs apart and his arms crossed, and grinning from ear to ear.

To add to the confusion, the dogs became affected with the spirit of excitement that filled their masters, and gave vent to their feelings in loud and continuous howling which nothing could check. The imitative propensity of these singular people was brought rather oddly into play during the progress of traffic. Buzzby had produced a large roll of tobacco—which they knew the use of, having been already shown how to use a pipe—and cut off portions of it, which he gave in exchange for fox-skins, and deer-skins, and seal-skin boots. Observing this, a very sly, old Esquimau began to slice up a deer-skin into little pieces, which he intended to offer for the small pieces of tobacco! He was checked, however, before doing much harm to the skin, and the principles of exchange were more perfectly explained to him.

The skins and boots, besides walrus and seal flesh, which the crew were enabled to barter at this time, were of the utmost importance, for their fresh provisions had begun to get low, and their boots were almost worn out, so that the scene of barter was exceedingly animated. Davie Summers and his master, Mivins, shone conspicuous as bargain makers, and carried to their respective bunks a large assortment of native articles. Fred, and Tom Singleton, too, were extremely successful, and in a few hours a sufficient amount of skins were bartered to provide them with clothing for the winter. The quantity of fresh meat obtained, however, was not enough to last them a week, for the Esquimaux lived from hand to mouth, and the crew felt that they must depend on their own exertions in the hunt for this indispensable article of food, without which they could not hope to escape the assaults of the sailors' dread enemy, scurvy.

Meetuck's duties were not light upon this occasion, as you may suppose.

"Arrah! then, *don't* ye onderstand me?" cried O'Riley, in an excited tone, to a particularly obtuse and remarkably fat Esquimau, who was about as sharp at a bargain as himself.—"Hallo! Meetuck, come here, do, and tell this pork-faced spalpeen what I'm sayin'. Sure I couldn't spake plainer av I wos to try."

"I'll never get this fellow to understand," said Fred.—"Meetuck, my boy, come here and explain to him."

"Ho! Meetuck," shouted Peter Grim, "give this old blockhead a taste o' your lingo, I never met his match for stupidity."

"I do believe that this rascal wants the 'ole of this ball o' twine for the tusk of a sea-'oss.—Meetuck! w'ere's Meetuck? I say, give us a 'and 'ere, like a good fellow," cried Mivins; but Mivins cried in vain, for at that moment Saunders had violently collared the interpreter and dragged him towards an old Esquimau woman, whose knowledge of Scotch had not proved sufficient to enable her to understand the energetically-expressed words of the second mate.

During all this time the stars had been twinkling brightly in the sky, and the aurora shed a clear light upon the scene, while the air was still calm and cold; but a cloud or two now began to darken the horizon to the north-east, and a puff of wind blew occasionally over the icy plain, and struck with such chilling influence on the frames of the traffickers, that with one consent they closed their business for that day, and the Esquimaux prepared to return to their snow village, which was about ten miles to the southward, and which village had been erected by them only three days previous to their discovery of the ship.

"I'm sorry to find," remarked the captain to those who were standing near him, "that these poor creatures have stolen a few trifling articles from below. I don't like to break the harmonious feeling which now exists between us for the sake of a few worthless things, but I know that it does more harm than good to pass over an offence with the natives of these regions, for they attribute our forbearance to fear."

"Perhaps you had better tax them with the theft," suggested the surgeon; "they may confess it, if we don't look very angry."

A few more remarks were made by several of those who stood on the quarter-deck, suggesting a treatment of the Esquimaux which was not of the gentlest nature, for they felt indignant that their hospitality had been abused.

"No, no," replied the captain to such suggestions, "we must exercise forbearance. These poor fellows do not regard theft in the same light that we do; besides, it would be foolish to risk losing their friendship. Go down, Meetuck, and invite Awatok and his wife, and half-a-dozen of the chief men, into the cabin. Say I wish to have a talk with them."

The interpreter obeyed, and in a few minutes the officers of the ship and the chiefs of the Esquimaux were assembled in solemn conclave round the cabin table.

"Tell them, Meetuck," said the captain, "that I know they have stolen two pieces of hoop-iron and a tin kettle, and ask them why they were so ungrateful as to do it."

The Esquimaux, who were becoming rather alarmed at the stern looks of those around them, protested earnestly that they knew nothing about it, and that they had not taken the things referred to.

"Say that I do not believe them," answered the captain sternly. "It is an exceedingly wicked thing to steal and to tell lies. White men think those who are guilty of such conduct to be very bad."

"Ah, ye villain!" cried Saunders, seizing one of the Esquimaux named Oosuck by the shoulder, and drawing forth an iron spoon which he observed projecting from the end of his boot.

An exclamation of surprise and displeasure burst from the officers, but the Esquimaux gave vent to a loud laugh. They evidently thought stealing to be no sin, and were not the least ashamed of being detected. Awatok, however, was an exception. He looked grave and annoyed, but whether this was at being found out, or at the ingratitude of his people, they could not decide.

"Tell them," said the captain, "that I am much displeased. If they promise to return the stolen goods immediately, I will pass over their offence this time, and we will trade together, and live like brothers, and do each other good; but if not, and if any more articles are taken, I will punish them."

Having had this translated to them, the chiefs were dismissed, but the expression of indifference on some of their faces proved that no impression had been made upon them.

In a quarter of an hour the articles that had been mentioned as missing were returned; and in order to restore harmony, several plugs of tobacco and a few additional trinkets were returned by the messenger. Soon after, the dogs were harnessed, the sledges packed, and, with many protestations of good-will on both sides, the parties separated. A few cracks of their long whips, a few answering howls from the dogs, and the Esquimaux were off and out of sight, leaving the *Dolphin* in her former solitude under the shadow of the frowning cliffs.

"Fetch me the telescope, Mivins," said the captain, calling down the hatchway.

"Ay, ay, sir," answered the steward.

"Where's my hatchet?" cried Peter Grim, striding about the deck and looking into every corner in search of his missing implement. "It's my best one, and I can't get on without it, nohow."

The captain bit his lip, for he knew full well the cause of its absence.

"Please, sir," said the steward, coming on deck with a very perturbed expression of countenance, "the—the—a—"

"Speak out, man! what's the matter with you?"

"The glass ain't nowhere to be seen, sir."

"Turn up all hands!" shouted the captain, jumping down the hatchway. "Arm the men, Mr. Bolton, and order the largest sledge to be got ready instantly. This will never do. Harness the whole team."

Instantly the *Dolphin's* deck was a scene of bustling activity. Muskets were loaded, jumpers and mittens put on, dogs caught and harnessed, and every preparation made for a sudden chase.

"There, that will do," cried the Captain, hurrying on deck with a brace of pistols and a cutlass in his belt, "six men are enough; let twelve of the remainder follow on foot. Jump on the sledge, Grim and Buzzby; O'Riley, you go too. Have a Care, Fred; not too near the front. Now, Meetuck—"

One crack of the long whip terminated the sentence as if with a full stop, and in another moment the sledge was bounding over the snow like a feather at the tails of twelve dogs.

It was a long chase, for it was a "stern" one, but the Esquimaux never dreamed of-pursuit, and as their dogs were not too well fed they had progressed rather slowly. In less than two hours they were distinguished on the horizon far off to the southward, winding their way among the hummocks.

Now, Meetuck," said the captain, "drive like the wind, and lay me alongside of Awatok's sledge;—and be ready, men, to act."

Ay, ay, sir," Was the prompt reply, as the heavy whip fell on the flanks of the leaders.

A few minutes brought them up with Awatok's sledge, and Captain Guy, leaping upon it with a clasp-knife in his hand, cut the traces in a twinkling, set the dogs free, and turning round, seized the Esquimau by the collar. The big chief at first showed a disposition to resent this unceremonious treatment, but before he could move Grim seized his elbows in his iron grasp, and tied them adroitly together behind his back with a cord. At the same time poor Aninga and her baby were swiftly transferred to the sailors' sledge.

Seeing this, the whole band of natives turned back and rushed in a body to the rescue, flourishing their lances and yelling fiercely.

'Form line!" shouted the captain, handing Awatok and Aninga over to the care of O'Riley. "Three of you on the right fire over their heads, and let the rest reserve their fire. I will kill one of their dogs, for it won't do to let them fancy that nothing but noise comes out of our muskets. Ready—present!"

A rattling volley followed, and at the same moment one of the dogs fell with a death-yell on the ice, and dyed it with its blood.

"Forward!" shouted the captain.

The men advanced in a body at a smart run; but the terrified Esquimaux, who had never heard the report of fire-arms before, did not wait for them. They turned and fled precipitately, but not before Grim captured Oosuck, and dragged him forcibly to the rear, where he was pinioned and placed on the sledge with the others.

"Now, then, lads, that will do; get upon the sledge again. Away with you, Meetuck.—Look after Awatok, Grim; O'Riley will see that Aninga does not jump off."

"That he will, darlint," said the Irishman, patting the woman on the back.

"And I shall look after the baby," said Fred, chucking that series of dumplings under the chin—an act of familiarity that seemed to afford it immense satisfaction, for, notwithstanding the melancholy position of its father and mother as prisoners, it smiled on Fred benignly.

In five minutes the party were far on their way back to the ship, and in less than five hours after the Esquimaux had closed their barter and left for their village, four of their number, including the baby, were close prisoners in the *Dolphin's* hold. It was not Captain Guy's intention, however, to use unnecessarily harsh means for the recovery of the missing articles. His object was to impress the Esquimaux with a salutary sense of the power, promptitude, and courage of Europeans, and to check at the outset their propensity for thieving. Having succeeded in making two of their chief men prisoners, he felt assured that the lost telescope and hatchet would soon make their appearance; and in this he was not mistaken. Going to the hold where the prisoners sat with downcast looks, he addressed to them a lengthened speech as to the sin and meanness of stealing in general, and of stealing from those who had been kind to them in particular. He explained to them the utter hopelessness of their attempting to deceive or impose upon the white men in any way whatever, and assured them that if they tried that sort of thing again he would punish them severely; but that if they behaved well, and brought plenty of walrus-flesh to the ship, he would give them hoop-iron, beads, looking-glasses, etc. These remarks seemed to make a considerable impression on his uncouth hearers.

"And now," said the captain in conclusion, "I shall keep Awatok and his wife and child prisoners here, until my telescope and hatchet are returned [Awatok's visage fell, and his wife looked stolid], and I shall send Oosuck to his tribe [Oosuck's face lit up amazingly] to tell them what I have said."

In accordance with this resolve Oosuck was set free, and, making use of his opportunity, with prompt alacrity he sped away on foot over the ice to the southward, and was quickly lost to view.

CHAPTER XVI.

*The Arctic Theatre enlarged upon—Great success of the first play—
The Esquimaux submit, and become fast friends.*

The 1st of December was a great day on board the *Dolphin*, for on that day it was announced to the crew that "The Arctic Theatre" would be opened, under the able management of Mr. F. Ellice, with the play of "Blunderbore; or, the Arctic Giant." The bill, of which two copies were issued gratis to the crew, announced that the celebrated Peter Grim, Esq., who had so long trodden the boards of the *Dolphin,* with unparalleled success, had kindly consented to appear in the character of *Blunderbore* for one winter only. The other parts were as follows: —*Whackinta,* a beautiful Esquimau widow, who had been captured by two Polar bears, both of which were deeply in love with her, by Frederick Ellice, Esq. *First Bear,* a big one, by Terrence O'Riley, Esq. *Second Bear,* a little one, by David Summers, Esq. *Ben Bolt,* a brave British seaman, who had been wrecked in Blunderbore's desolate dominions, all the crew having perished except himself, by John Buzzby, Esq. These constituted the various characters of the piece, the name of which had been kept a profound secret from the crew until the morning of the day on which it was acted.

Fred's duties, as manager and author, upon this occasion were by no means light, for his troop, being unaccustomed to study, found the utmost difficulty in committing the simplest sentences to memory. O'Riley turned out to be the sharpest among them, but having agreed to impersonate the First Bear, and having to act his part in dumb show —bears not being supposed capable of speech—his powers of memory had not to be exerted. Grim was also pretty good; but Davie Summers could not be got to remember even the general arrangements of the piece; and as for Buzzby, he no sooner mastered a line than he forgot the one before it, and almost gave it up in despair. But by dint of much study and many rehearsals in secret, under the superintendence of Fred, and Tom Singleton, who undertook to assist, they succeeded at last in going through it with only a few mistakes.

On the morning of the 1st December, while the most of the crew were away at Red-Snow Valley cutting moss, Fred collected his *corps dramatique* for a last rehearsal in the forecastle, where they were secure from interruption, the place being so cold that no one would willingly go into it except under the force of necessity. A dim lantern lit up the apartment faintly.

"We must do it without a mistake this time," said Fred Ellice, opening his book, and calling upon Grim to begin.

"'Tis cold," began Grim.

"Stop, you're wrong."

"Oh! so I am," cried Grim, slapping his thigh, "I'll begin again."

It may be remarked here, that although Blunderbore was supposed to be an Esquimau monarch, he was compelled to speak English, being unfortunately ignorant—if we may so speak—of his native tongue!

"Oh! 'tis a dismal thing," began Grim again, "to dwell in solitude and cold! 'Tis very cold [Grim shuddered here tremendously], and—and—(what's next?)"

"Hunger," said Fred.

"Hunger gnaws my vitals. My name is Blunderbore. 'Twere better had I been born a Blunder*buss*, 'cause then I'd have *gone off* and dwelt in climes more shootable to my tender constitoosion. Ha! is that a bear I sees before me?"

"It's not *sees*," interrupted Fred.

At this moment a tremendous roar was heard, and O'Riley bounded from behind a top-sail, which represented an iceberg, dressed from head to foot in the skin of a white bear which had been killed a few days before.

"Stop, O'Riley," cried Fred; "you're too soon, man. *I* have to come on first as an Esquimau woman, and when Grim says to the woman he wishes he could see a bear, *then* you are to come."

"Och! whirra, but me brains is confuged intirely wid it all," said O'Riley, rising on his hind legs, and walking off with his tail, literally as well as figuratively, between his legs.

"Now, Buzzby, now; it's *your* time. When you hear the word 'misery,' come on and fight like a Trojan with the bears. The doctor will remind you."

Fred was remarkably patient and painstaking, and his pupils, though not apt scholars, were willing, so that the morning rehearsal was gone through with fewer mistakes than might have been expected; and

149

when the crew came back to dinner about mid-day, which, however, was as dark as midnight, their parts were sufficiently well got up, and nothing remained to be done but to arrange the stage and scenery for the evening's entertainment—it having been resolved that the performance should commence after supper. The stage was at the after part of the cabin, and raised about a foot above the deck; and its management had been intrusted to the doctor, who, assisted by Peter Grim, transformed that portion of the ship into a scene so romantically beautiful that the first sight of it petrified the crew with surprise. But until the curtain should rise all arrangements were carefully concealed from every one except the *dramatis personæ*. Even the captain and officers were forbidden to peep behind the sail that formed a curtain to the stage; and this secrecy, besides being necessary, was extremely useful, inasmuch as it excited the curiosity of the men, and afforded them food for converse and speculation for a week before the great day arrived.

The longed-for hour came at last. The cabin tables having been removed, and rows of seats placed in front of the stage, the men were admitted from the deck, to which they had been expelled an hour previous in order not to impede preliminary arrangements. There was great joking, of course, as they took their seats and criticised the fittings up. David Mizzle was of opinion that the foot-lights "wos oncommon grand," which was an unquestionable fact, for they consisted of six tin lamps filled with seal-oil, from the wicks of which rose a compound of yellow flame and smoke that had a singularly luminous effect. Amos Parr guessed that the curtain would be certain sure to get jammed at the first haul, and several of the others were convinced that O'Riley would stick his part in one way or another. However, an end was put to all remarks and expectation raised on tip-toe by the ringing of a small hand-bell, and immediately thereafter a violent pulling at the curtain which concealed the stage. But the curtain remained immovable (they always do on such occasions), and a loud whispering was heard behind the scenes.

"Clap on extra tackle and call all hands to hoist away," suggested one of the audience.

The laugh with which this advice was received was checked in the bud by the sudden rising of the curtain with such violence that the whole framework of the theatre shook again.

For a few seconds a dead silence reigned, for the men were stricken dumb with genuine amazement at the scene before them. The stage was covered with white sheets arranged in such a manner as to represent snow, and the more effectually to carry out the idea several huge blocks of real ice and a few patches of snow were introduced here and there, the cold in the after part of the cabin being too great to permit of their melting. A top-gallant-sail, on which were painted several blue cracks, and some strong white lights did duty for an iceberg, and filled up the whole back of the scene. In front of this, in the centre of the stage, on an extemporized hummock, sat Peter Grim, as the Giant Blunderbore. His colossal proportions were enhanced by the addition of an entire white bear-skin to his ordinary hairy dress, and which was thrown round his broad shoulders in the form of a tippet. A broad scarlet sash was tied round his waist, and a crown of brown paper painted in alternate diamonds of blue, red, and yellow sat upon his brow. Grim was in truth a magnificent-looking fellow, with his black beard and moustache; and the mock-heroic frown with which he gazed up (as one of the audience suggested) at the aurora borealis, while he grasped an enormous club in his right hand, became him well.

The first few seconds of dead silence with which this was received were succeeded by a long and loud burst of applause, the heartiness of which plainly showed that the scene far exceeded the expectations of the men.

"Bravo!" cried the captain, "excellent! nothing could be better."

"It beats natur', quite," said one.

"All to sticks," cried another.

"And wot a *tree*-mendous giant he makes. Three cheers for Peter Grim, lads!"

Three cheers were promptly given with right goodwill, but the giant did not move a muscle. He was far too deeply impressed with the importance of playing his part well to acknowledge the compliment. Having gazed long enough to enable the men to get rid of their first flow of enthusiasm, Blunderbore rose majestically, and coming forward to the foot-lights, looked straight over the heads of the men, and addressed himself to the opposite bulk-head.

"Oh! 'tis a dismal thing," he began, and continued to spout his part with flashing eyes and considerable energy, until he came to the word Blunderbuss, when, either from a mistaken notion as to when it was his time to go on, or nervous forgetfulness of the plan of the piece, the Little Bear sprang over the edge of the iceberg and alighted on the middle of the stage.

"Oh! bad luck to yees intirely," said the Big Bear from behind the scenes in an angry whisper, which was distinctly heard by the audience, "ye've gone and spoiled it all, ye have. Come off, will ye, and take yer turn at the right time, won't ye?"

In the midst of the shout of delight caused by this mistake, O'Riley, forgetting that he was a bear, rushed on the stage on his hind legs, seized the Little Bear by the fore leg, and dragged him off at the other side amid loud applause. Blunderbore, with admirable self-possession resumed his part the instant there was a calm, and carried it successfully to a close.

Just as he ended, Fred waddled on, in the guise of an Esquimau woman; and so well was he got up that the crew looked round to see i Aninga (who, with her husband, had been allowed to witness the play) was in her place. Fred had intentionally taken Aninga as his model, and had been very successful in imitating the top-knot of hair. The baby, too, was hit off to perfection, having been made by Mivins, who proved himself a genius in such matters. Its head was a ball of rags covered with brown leather, and two white bone buttons with black spots in the centre did duty for its eyes.

The first thing Whackinta did on coming forward was to deposit the baby on the snow with its head downwards by mistake, whereat it began to scream vociferously. This scream was accomplished by Davie Summers creeping below the stage and putting his mouth to a hole in the flooring close to which the baby's head lay. Davie's falsetto was uncommonly like to a child's voice, and the effect was quite startling. Of course Whackinta tried to soothe it, and failing in this she whipped it, which caused it to yell with tenfold violence. Thereafter losing all patience, she covered its face and stuffed its mouth with a quantity of snow, and laying it down on its back, placed a large block of ice on its head. This, as might be expected, had the desired effect, and the baby was silenced—not, however, until Whackinta had twice called down the hole in a hoarse whisper, "That'll do, Davie; stop, man, stop!" Then, sitting down on the hummock which Blunderbore had just left— and from behind which he was now eagerly watching her—she began to weep.

Having given full vent to her feelings in a series of convulsive sobs, Whackinta addressed a lengthened harangue, in a melancholy tone of voice, to the audience, the gist of which was that she was an unfortunate widow; that two bears had fallen in love with her, and

152

stolen her away from her happy home in Nova Zembla; and, although they allowed her to walk about as much as she chose, they watched her closely and prevented her escaping to her own country. Worst of all, they had told her that she must agree to become the wife of one or other of them, and if she did not make up her mind and give them an answer that very day, she was to be killed and eaten by both of them. In order the more strongly to impress the audience with her forlorn condition, Whackinta sang a tender and touching ditty, composed by herself expressly for the occasion, and sang it so well that it was encored twice.

To all this Blunderbore listened with apparent rapture, and at length ventured to advance and discover himself; but the instant Whackinta saw him she fell on her knees and trembled violently.

"Spare me, good king," she said; "do not slay me. I am a poor widow, and have been brought here by two bears against my will."

"Woman," said the giant, "my name is Blunderbore. I am, as you perceive by my crown, a king; and I am a lonely man. If I kill the two bears you speak of, will you marry me?"

"Oh, do not ask me, good Blunderbore! I cannot; it is impossible. I cannot love you—you are—forgive me for saying it—too big, and fierce, and ugly to love."

Blunderbore frowned angrily, and the audience applauded vociferously at this.

"You cannot love me! ha!" exclaimed the giant, glaring round with clenched teeth.

At this moment the Big Bear uttered an awful roar, Whackinta gave a piercing scream and fled, and Blunderbore hid himself hastily behind the hummock. The next moment the two bears bounded on the stage and began to gambol round it, tossing up their hind legs and roaring and leaping in a manner that drew forth repeated plaudits. At length the Little Bear discovered the baby, and, uttering a frantic roar of delight, took it in its fore paws and held it up. The Big Bear roared also, of course, and rushing forward caught the baby by the leg, and endeavoured to tear it away from the Little Bear, at which treatment the poor baby again commenced to cry passionately. In the struggle the baby's head came off, upon which the Little Bear put the head into its mouth and swallowed it. The Big Bear immediately did the same with the body; but its mouth was too small, and the body stuck fast and could not be finally disposed of until the Little Bear came to the rescue and pushed it forcibly down its throat. Having finished this delicate little morsel the two bears rose on their hind legs and danced a hornpipe together—Tom Singleton playing the tune for them on a flute behind the scenes. When this was done they danced off the stage, and immediately, as if in the distance, was heard the voice of a man singing. It came gradually nearer, and at last Buzzby, in the character of Ben Bolt, swaggered up to the foot-lights with his hands in his breeches pockets.

"I'm a jolly, jolly tar,
Wot has comed from afar,
An' it's all for to seek my fortin"—

sang Buzzby. "But I've not found it yit," he continued, breaking into prose, "and there don't seem much prospect o' findin' it here anyhow. Wot an 'orrible cold place it is, ugh!"

Buzzby was received with enthusiastic cheers, for he was dressed in the old familiar blue jacket, white ducks, pumps, and straw hat set jauntily on one side of his head—a costume which had not been seen for so many months by the crew of the *Dolphin*, that their hearts warmed to it as if it were an old friend.

Buzzby acted with great spirit, and was evidently a prime favourite. He could scarcely recollect a word of his part, but he remembered the general drift of it, and had ready wit enough to extemporize. Having explained that he was the only survivor of a shipwrecked crew, he proceeded to tell some of his adventures in foreign lands, and afterwards described part of his experiences in a song, to which the doctor played an accompaniment behind the scenes. The words were composed by himself, sung to the well-known Scotch air, "Corn Riggs," and ran as follows:—

THE JOLLY TAR.

My comrades, you must know
It was many years ago
I left my daddy's cottage in the greenwood O!
And I jined a man-o'-war
An' became a jolly tar,
An' fought for king and country on the high seas O!
Pull, boys, cheerily, our home is on the sea
Pull, boys, merrily and lightly O!
Pull, boys, cheerily, the wind is passing free
An' whirling up the foam an' water sky-high O!

There's been many a noble fight,
But Trafalgar was the sight
That beat the Greeks and Romans in their glory O!
For Britain's jolly sons
Worked the thunder-blazing guns,
And Nelson stood the bravest in the fore-front O!
Pull, boys, etc.

A roaring cannon shot
Came an' hit the very spot
Where my leg goes click-an'-jumble in the socket O!
And swept it overboard
With the precious little hoard
Of pipe an' tin an' baccy in the pocket O!
Pull, boys, etc.

They took me down below,
An' they laid me with a row
Of killed and wounded messmates on a table O!
Then up comes Dr. Keg,
An' says, Here's a livin' leg
I'll sew upon the stump if I am able O!
Pull, boys, etc.

This good and sturdy limb
Had belonged to fightin' Tim,
An' scarcely had they sewed it on the socket O!
When up the hatch I flew,
An' dashed among the crew,
An' sprang on board the Frenchman like a rocket O!
Pull, boys, etc.

'Twas this that gained the day,
For that leg it cleared the way—
And the battle raged like fury while it lasted O!
Then ceased the shot and shell
To fall upon the swell,
And the Union Jack went bravely to the mast-head O!'
Pull, boys, etc.

We need scarcely say that this song was enthusiastically encored, and that the chorus was done full justice to by the audience, who picked it up at once and sang it with lusty vehemence. At the last word Ben Bolt nodded familiarly, thrust his hands into his pockets, and swaggered off whistling "Yankee Doodle." It was a matter of uncertainty where he had swaggered off to, but it was conjectured that he had gone on his journey to anywhere that might turn up.

Meanwhile, Blunderbore had been bobbing his head up and down behind the hummock in amazement at what he heard and saw, and when Ben Bolt made his exit he came forward. This was the signal for the two bears to discover him and rush on with a terrific roar. Blunderbore instantly fetched them each a sounding whack on their skulls, leaped over both their backs, and bounded up the side of the iceberg, where he took refuge, and turned at bay on a little ice pinnacle constructed expressly for that purpose.

An awful fight now ensued between the giant and the two bears. The pinnacle on which Blunderbore stood was so low that the Big Bear, by standing up on its hind legs, could just scratch his toes, which caused the giant to jump about continually; but the sides of the iceberg were so smooth that the bears could not climb up it. This difficulty, indeed, constituted the great and amusing feature of the fight; for no sooner did the Little Bear creep up to the edge of the pinnacle, than the giant's tremendous club came violently down on its snout (which had been made of hard wood on purpose to resist the blows), and sent it sprawling back on the stage, where the Big Bear invariably chanced to be in the way, and always fell over it. Then they both rose, and, roaring fearfully, renewed the attack, while Blunderbore laid about him with the club ferociously. Fortune, however, did not on this occasion favour the brave. The Big Bear at last caught the giant by the heel and pulled him to the ground; the Little Bear instantly seized him by the throat; and, notwithstanding his awful yells and struggles, it would have gone ill with Blunderbore had not Ben Bolt opportunely arrived at that identical spot at that identical moment in the course of his travels.

Oh! it was a glorious thing to see the fear-nothing, dare-anything fashion in which, when he saw how matters stood, Ben Bolt threw down his stick and bundle, drew his cutlass, and attacked the two bears at once, single-handed, crying, "Come on," in a voice of thunder. And it was a satisfactory thing to behold the way in which he cut and slashed at their heads (the heads having been previously prepared for such treatment), and the agility he displayed in leaping over their backs and under their legs, and holding on by their tails, while they vainly endeavoured to catch him. The applause was frequent and prolonged, and the two Esquimau prisoners rolled about their burly figures and laughed till the tears ran down their fat cheeks. But when Ben Bolt suddenly caught the two bears by their tails, tied them together in a double knot, and fled behind a hummock, which the Big Bear passed on one side and the Little Bear on the other, and so, as a matter of course, stuck hard and fast, the laughter was excessive; and when the gallant British seaman again rushed forward, massacred the Big Bear with two terrific cuts, slew the Little Bear with one tremendous back-hander, and then sank down on one knee and pressed his hand to his brow as if he were exhausted, a cheer ran from stem to stern of the *Dolphin*, the like of which had not filled the hull of that good ship since she was launched upon her ocean home!

It was just at this moment that Whackinta chanced, curiously enough, to return to this spot in the course of *her* wanderings. She screamed in horror at the sight of the dead bears, which was quite proper and natural, and then she started at the sight of the exhausted Bolt, and smiled sweetly—which was also natural—as she hastened to assist and sympathize with him. Ben Bolt fell in love with her at once, and told her so off-hand, to the unutterable rage of Blunderbore, who recovered from his wounds at that moment, and seizing the sailor by the throat, vowed he would kill and quarter, and stew and boil, and roast and eat him in one minute if he didn't take care what he was about.

The audience felt some fears for Ben Bolt at this point, but their delight knew no bounds when, shading the giant off and springing backwards, he buttoned up his coat and roared, rather than said, that though he were all the Blunderbores and blunderbusses in the world rolled together and changed into one immortal blunder-*cannon*, he didn't care a pinch of bad snuff for him, and would knock all the teeth in his head down his throat. This valorous threat he followed up by shaking his fist close under the giant's nose and crying out, "Come on'"

But the giant did not come on. He fortunately recollected that he owed his life to the brave sailor; so he smiled, and saying he would be his friend through life, insisted on seizing him by the hand and shaking it violently. Thereafter he took Ben Bolt and Whackinta by their right hands, and leading them forward to the foot-lights, made them a long speech to the effect that he owed a debt of gratitude to the former for saving his life which he could never repay, and that he loved the latter too sincerely to stand in the way of her happiness. Then he joined their right hands, and they went down on one knee, and he placed his hands on their heads, and looked up at the audience with a benignant smile, and the curtain fell amid rapturous cheers.

In this play it seemed somewhat curious and unaccountable that Whackinta forgot to inquire for her demolished baby, and appeared to feel no anxiety whatever about it. It was also left a matter of uncertainty whether Ben Bolt and his Esquimau bride returned to live happily during the remainder of their lives in England, or took up their permanent abode with Blunderbore. But it is not our province to criticise; we merely chronicle events as they occurred.

The entertainments were to conclude with a hornpipe from Mivins; but just as that elastic individual had completed the first of a series of complicated evolutions, and was about to commence the second, a vociferous barking of the dogs was heard outside, accompanied by the sound of human voices. The benches were deserted in a moment, and the men rushed upon deck, catching up muskets and cutlasses, which always stood in readiness, as they went. The sounds proceeded from a party of about twenty Esquimaux who had been sent from the camp with the stolen property, and with a humble request that the offence might be forgiven, and their chief and his wife returned to them. They were all unarmed; and the sincerity of their repentance was further attested by the fact that they brought back, not only the hatchet and telescope, but a large assortment of minor articles that had not been missed.

Of course the apology was accepted; and, after speeches were delivered, and protestations of undying friendship made on both sides, the party were presented with a few trinkets and a plug of tobacco each, and sent back in a state of supreme happiness to their village, where for a week Awatok kept the men of his tribe, and Aninga the women, in a state of intense amazement by their minute descriptions of the remarkable doings of the white strangers.

The friendship thus begun between the Esquimaux and the *Dolphin's* crew was never once interrupted by any unpleasant collision during the months that they afterwards travelled and hunted in company. Strength of muscle and promptitude in action are qualities which all nations in a savage state understand and respect, and the sailors proved that they possessed these qualities in a higher degree than themselves during the hardships and dangers incident to Arctic life, while at the same time their seemingly endless resources and contrivances impressed the simple natives with the belief that white men could accomplish anything they chose to attempt.

CHAPTER XVII.

Expeditions on foot—Effects of darkness on dogs and men—The first death—Caught in a trap—The Esquimau camp.

"I don't know how it is, an' I can't tell wot it is, but so it is," remarked Buzzby to Grim, a week after the first night of the theatricals, "that that 'ere actin' has done us all a sight o' good. Here we are as merry as crickets every one, although we're short o' fresh meat, and symptoms o' scurvy are beginning to show on some of us."

"It's the mind havin' occupation, an' bein' prewented from broodin' over its misfortins," replied Grim, with the air of a philosopher.

Grim did not put this remark in turned commas, although he ought to have done so, seeing that it was quoted from a speech made by the captain to Singleton the day before.

"You see," continued Grim, "we've been actin' every night for a week past. Well, if we hadn't been actin', we should ha' been thinkin' an' sleepin'; too much of which, you see, ain't good for us, Buzzby, and would never pay."

Buzzby was not quite sure of this, but contented himself by saying, "Well, mayhap ye're right. I'm sorry it's to come to an end so soon; but there is no doubt that fresh meat is ondispensable. An' that reminds me, messmate, that I've not cleaned my musket for two days, an' it wouldn't do to go on a hunt with a foul piece, nohow. We start at ten o'clock, A.M., don't we?"

Grim admitted that they did—remarking that it might just as well be ten P.M. for all the difference the *sun* would make in it—and went below with Buzzby.

In the cabin active preparations were making for an extended hunting-expedition, which the empty state of the larder rendered absolutely necessary. For a week past the only fresh provisions they had procured were a white fox and a rabbit, notwithstanding the exertions of Meetuck, Fred, and the doctor, who with three separate parties had scoured the country for miles round the ship. Scurvy was now beginning to appear among them, and Captain Guy felt that although they had enough of salt provisions to last them the greater part of the winter, if used with economy, they could not possibly subsist on these alone. An extended expedition in search of seals and walruses was therefore projected.

It was determined that this should consist of two parties, the one to proceed north, the other to travel south in the tracks of the Esquimaux, who had left their temporary village in search of walruses, they also being reduced almost to a state of starvation.

The plan of the expedition was as follows:—

One party, consisting of ten men, under Bolton, the first mate, was to take the largest sledge, and the whole team of dogs, on which, with twelve days' provisions and their sleeping-bags, they were to proceed northward along the coast as far as possible; and, in the event of being unsuccessful, they were to turn homeward on the eighth day, and make the best of their way back on short allowance.

The other party, consisting of fifteen men, under Saunders, the second mate, was to set off to the southward on foot, dragging a smaller sledge behind them, and endeavour to find the Esquimaux, who, it was supposed, could not be far off, and would probably have fresh meat in their camp.

It was a clear, cold, and beautiful star-light day when the two parties started simultaneously on their separate journeys. The coruscations of the aurora were more than usually vivid, and the snow gave forth that sharp, dry, *crunching* sound, under the heels of the men as they moved about, that denotes intense frost.

"Mind that you hug the land, Mr. Bolton," said the captain at parting; "don't get farther out on the floes than you can help. To meet with a gale on the ice is no joke in these latitudes."

The first mate promised obedience; and the second mate having been also cautioned to hug the land, and not to use their small supply of spirits for any other purpose than that of lighting the lamp, except in cases of the most urgent need, they set off with three hearty cheers, which were returned by Captain Guy and those who remained with him in the ship. All the able and effective men were sent on these expeditions; those who remained behind were all more or less affected with scurvy, except the captain himself, whose energetic nature seemed invulnerable, and whose flow of spirits never failed. Indeed, it is probable that to this hearty and vigorous temperament, under God, he owed his immunity from disease; for, since provisions began to fail, he along with all his officers had fared precisely like the men—the few delicacies they possessed having been reserved for the sick.

Unfortunately, their stock of lime-juice was now getting low, and the crew had to be put on short allowance. As this acid is an excellent anti-scorbutic, or preventive of scurvy, as well as a cure, its rapid diminution was viewed with much concern by all on board. The long-continued absence of the sun, too, now began to tell more severely than ever on men and dogs. On the very day the expeditions took their departure one of the latter, which had been left behind on account of illness, was attacked with a strange disease, of which several of the team eventually died before the winter came to an end. It was seized with spasms, and, after a few wild paroxysms, lapsed into a lethargic state. In this condition the animal functions went on apparently as well as usual, the appetite continued not only good but voracious. The disease was clearly mental. It barked furiously at nothing, and walked in straight or curved lines perseveringly; or, at other times, it remained for hours in moody silence, and then started off howling as if pursued. In thirty-six hours after the first attack the poor animal died, and was buried in the snow on Store Island.

This was the first death that had occurred on board, and although it was only a dog, and not one of the favourites, its loss cast a gloom over the crew for several days. It was the first blow of the fell destroyer in the midst of their little community, which could ill spare the life even of one of the lower animals, and they felt as if the point of the wedge had now been entered, and might be driven farther home ere long.

The expressive delight of the poor dogs on being admitted to the light of the cabin showed how ardently they longed for the return of the sun. It was now the beginning of December, and the darkness was complete. Not the faintest vestige of twilight appeared even at noon. Midnight and noonday were alike. Except when the stars and aurora were bright, there was not light enough to distinguish a man's form at ten paces distant, and a blacker mass than the surrounding darkness alone indicated where the high cliffs encompassed the Bay of Mercy. When therefore any one came on deck, the first thing he felt on groping his way about was the cold noses of the dogs pushed against his hands, as they frisked and gambolled round him. They howled at the appearance of an accidental light, as if they hoped the sun, or at least the moon, were going to rise once more, and they rejoiced on being taken below, and leaped up in the men's faces for sympathy, and whined, and all but spoke with excess of satisfaction.

The effect of the monotony of long-continued darkness and the absence of novelty had much to do also with the indifferent health of many of the men. After the two expeditions were sent out, those who remained behind became much more low spirited, and the symptoms of scurvy increased. In these circumstances Captain Guy taxed his inventive genius to the utmost to keep up their spirits and engage their minds. He assumed an air of bustling activity, and attached a degree of importance to the regular performance of the light duties of the ship that they did not in reality possess apart from their influence as discipline. The cabin was swept and aired, the stove cleaned, the fittings dusted, the beds made, the tides, thermometers, and barometers registered; the logs posted up, clothes mended, food cooked, traps visited, etc., with the regularity of clockwork, and every possible plan adopted to occupy every waking hour, and to prevent the men from brooding over their position. When the labours of the day were over, plans were proposed for getting up a concert, or a new play, in order to surprise the absentees on their return. Stories were told over and over again, and enjoyed if good, or valued far beyond their worth if bad. When old stories failed, and old books were read, new stories were invented; and here the genius of some was drawn out, while the varied information of others became of great importance. Tom Singleton, in particular, entertained the men with songs and lively tunes on the flute, and told stories, as one of them remarked, "like a book." Joseph West, too, was an invaluable comrade in this respect. He had been a studious boy at school, and a lover of books of all kinds, especially books of travel and adventure. His memory was good, and his inventive powers excellent, so that he recalled wonderful and endless anecdotes from the unfathomable stores of his memory, strung them together into a sort of story, and told them in a soft, pleasant voice that captivated the ears of his audience; but poor West was in delicate health, and could not speak so long as his messmates would have wished. The rough life they led, and the frequent exposure to intense cold, had considerably weakened a frame which had never been robust, and an occasional cough, when he told a long story, sometimes warned him to desist. Games, too, were got up. "Hide and seek" was revived with all the enthusiasm of boyhood, and "fox-chase" was got up with tremendous energy. In all this the captain was the most earnest and vigorous, and in doing good to others he unconsciously did the greatest possible amount of good to himself; for his forgetfulness of self, and the activity of his mind in catering for the wants and amusements of his men, had the effect of imparting a cheerfulness to his manner, and a healthy tone to his mind, that tended powerfully to sustain and invigorate his body. But despite all this, the men grew worse, and a few of them showed such alarming symptoms that the doctor began to fear there would soon be a breach in their numbers.

Meanwhile Saunders and his fifteen men trudged steadily to the southward, dragging their sledge behind them. The ice-floes, however, turned out to be very rugged and hummocky, and retarded them so much that they made but slow progress until they passed the Red-Snow Valley, and doubled the point beyond it. Here they left the floes, and took to the natural highway afforded by the ice-belt, along which they sped more rapidly, and arrived at the Esquimau village in the course of about five hours.

Here all was deserted and silent. Bits of seal and walrus hide and bones and tusks were scattered about in all directions, but no voices issued from the dome-shaped huts of snow.

"They're the likest things to bee-skeps I ever saw," remarked Saunders, as he and his party stood contemplating the little group of huts. "And they don't seem to care much for big doors."

Saunders referred here to the low tunnels, varying from three to twelve feet, that formed the entrance to each hut.

"Mayhap there's some o' them asleep inside," suggested Tom Green, the carpenter's mate; "suppose we go in and see."

"I daresay ye're no far wrong," replied the second mate, to whom the idea seemed to be a new one. "Go in, Davie Summers, ye're a wee chap, and can bend your back better than the most o' us."

Davie laughed as he went down on his hands and knees, and creeping in at the mouth of one of the tunnels, which barely permitted him to enter in that position, disappeared.

Several of the party at the same time paid similar visits to the other huts, but they all returned with the same remark—"empty." The interiors were begrimed with lamp-black and filth, and from their appearance seemed to have been deserted only a short time before.

Buzzby, who formed one of the party, rubbed his nose for some time in great perplexity, until he drew from Davie Summers the remark that his proboscis was red enough by nature and didn't need rubbing. "It's odd," he remarked; "they seems to ha' bin here for some time, and yit they've niver looked near the ship but once. Wot's become on 'em / don't know."

"Don't you?" said Davie in a tone of surprise; "now that *is* odd. One would have thought that a fellow who keeps his weather-eye so constantly open should know everything."

"Don't chaff, boy, but lend a hand to undo the sled-lashings. I see that Mr. Saunders is agoin' to anchor here for the night."

The second mate, who had been taking a hasty glance at the various huts of the village, selected two of the largest as a lodging for his men, and having divided them into two gangs, ordered them to turn in and sleep as hard as possible.

"S'pose we may sup first?" said Summers in a whining tone of mock humility.

"In coorse you may," answered Tom Green, giving the lad a push that upset him in the snow.

"Come here, Buzzby, I want to speak to 'ee," said Saunders, leading him aside. "It seems to me that the Esquimaux canna be very far off, and I observe their tracks are quite fresh in the snow leadin' to the southward, so I mean to have a night march after them; but as the men seem pretty weel tired I'll only take two o' the strongest. Who d'ye think might go?"

"I'll go myself, sir."

"Very good; and who else, think 'ee? Amos Parr seems freshest."

"I think Tom Green's the man wot can do it. I seed him capsize Davie Summers jist now in the snow; an' when a man can skylark, I always know he's got lots o' wind in 'im."

"Very good. Then go, Buzzby, and order him to get ready, and look sharp about it."

"Ay, ay, sir," cried Buzzby, as he turned to prepare Green for the march.

In pursuance of this plan, an hour afterwards Saunders and his two followers left the camp with their sleeping-bags and a day's provisions on their shoulders, having instructed the men to follow with the sledge at the end of five hours, which period was deemed sufficient time for rest and refreshment.

For two hours the trio plodded silently onward over the ice-belt by the light of a clear, starry sky. At the end of that time clouds began to gather to the westward, rendering the way less distinct, but still leaving sufficient light to render travelling tolerably easy. Then they came to a part of the coast where the ice-belt clung close to a line of perpendicular cliffs of about three miles in extent. The ice-belt here was about twenty feet broad. On the left the cliffs referred to rose sheer up several hundred feet; on the right the ice-belt descended only about three feet to the floes. Here our three adventurous travellers were unexpectedly caught in a trap. The tide rose so high that it raised the sea-ice to a level with the ice-belt, and, welling up between the two, completely overflowed the latter.

The travellers pushed on as quickly as possible, for the precipices on their left forbade all hope of escape in that direction, while the gap between the ice-belt and the floes, which was filled with a gurgling mixture of ice and water, equally hemmed them in on the right. Worse than all, the tide continued to rise, and when it reached half-way to their knees, they found it dangerous to advance for fear of stepping into rents and fissures which were no longer visible.

"What's to be done noo?" inquired Saunders, coming to a full stop, and turning to Buzzby with a look of blank despair.

"Dun'no'," replied Buzzby, with an equally blank look of despair; as he stood with his legs apart and his arms hanging down by his side—the very personification of imbecility. "If I wos a fly I'd know wot to do. I'd walk up the side o' that cliff till I got to a dry bit, and then I'd stick on. But, not bein' a fly, in coorse I can't."

Buzzby said this in a recklessly facetious tone, and Tom Green followed it up with a remark to the effect that "he'd be blowed if he ever wos in sich a fix in his life;" intimating his belief, at the same time, that his "toes wos freezin'."

"No fear o' that," said the second mate; "they'll no freeze as lang as they're in the water. We'll just have to stand here till the tide goes doon."

Saunders said this in a dogged tone, and immediately put his plan in force by crossing his arms and planting his feet firmly on the submerged ice and wide apart. Buzzby and Green, however, adopted the wiser plan of moving constantly about within a small circle, and after Saunders had argued for half-an-hour as to the advantages of his plan, he followed their example. The tide rose above their knees, but they had fortunately on boots made by the Esquimaux, which were perfectly waterproof; their feet, therefore, although very cold, were quite dry. In an hour and three-quarters the ice-belt was again uncovered, and the half-frozen travellers resumed their march with the utmost energy.

Two hours later and they came to a wide expanse of level ground at the foot of the high cliffs, where a group of Esquimau huts, similar to those they had left, was descried.

"They're all deserted too," remarked Buzzby.

But Buzzby was wrong, for at that moment a very small and particularly fat little boy in a fox-skin dress appeared at the mouth of one of the low tunnels that formed the entrance to the nearest hut. This boy looked exactly like a lady's muff with a hairy head above it and a pair of feet below. The instant he observed the strangers he threw up his arms, uttered a shrill cry of amazement, and disappeared in the tunnel. Next instant a legion of dogs rushed out of the huts barking furiously, and on their heels came the entire population, creeping on their hands and knees out of the tunnel mouths like dark hairy monsters issuing from their holes. They had spears and knives of ivory with them; but a glance showed the two parties that they were friends, and in a few moments Awatok and his comrades were chattering vociferously round the sailors, and endeavouring by word and sign to make themselves understood.

The Esquimaux received the three visitors and the rest of the sledge party, who came up a few hours later, with the utmost hospitality. But we have not space to tell of how they dragged them into their smoky huts of snow; and how they offered them raw seal-flesh to eat; and how, on the sailors expressing disgust, they laughed, and added moss mixed with oil to their lamps to enable them to cook their food, and how they managed by signs and otherwise to understand that the strangers had come in search of food, at which they (the Esquimaux) were not surprised; and how they assured their visitors (also by means of signs) that they would go a-hunting with them on the following day, whereat they (the sailors) were delighted, and shook hands all round. Neither have we space to tell of how the visitors were obliged to conform to custom, and sleep in the same huts with men, women, children, and dogs, and how they felt thankful to be able to sleep anywhere and anyhow without being frozen. All this, and a great deal more, we are compelled to skip over here, and leave it, unwillingly, to the vivid imagination of our reader.

CHAPTER XVIII.

The hunting-party—Reckless driving—A desperate encounter with a walrus, etc.

Late in the day, by the bright light of the stars, the sailors and the Esquimaux left the snow-huts of the village, and travelling out to seaward on the floes, with dogs and sledges, lances and spears, advanced to do battle with the walrus.

The northern lights were more vivid than usual, making the sky quite luminous; and there was a sharp freshness in the air, which, while it induced the hunters to pull their hoods more tightly round their faces, also sent their blood careering more briskly through their veins, as the drove swiftly over the ice in the Esquimau sledges.

"Did ye ever see walruses afore, Davie?" inquired Buzzby, who sat beside Summers on the leading sledge.

"None but what I've seed on this voyage."

"They're remarkable creeturs," rejoined Buzzby, slapping his hand on his thigh. "I've seed many a one in my time, an' I can tell ye, lad, thcy're ugly customers. They fight like good uns, and give the Esquimaux a deal o' trouble to kill them—they do."

"Tell me a story about 'em, Buzzby—do, like a good chap," said Davie Summers, burying his nose in the skirts of his hairy garment to keep it warm. "You're a capital hand at a yarn; now, fire away."

"A story, lad; I don't know as how I can exactly tell ye a story, but I'll give ye wot they calls a hanecdote. It wos about five years ago, more or less, I wos out in Baffin's Bay, becalmed off one o' the Esquimau settlements, when we wos lookin' over the side at the lumps of ice floatin' past, up got a walrus not very far off shore, and out went half-a-dozen kayaks, as they call the Esquimau men's boats, and they all sot on the beast at once. Well, it wos one o' the brown walruses, which is always the fiercest; and the moment he got the first harpoon he went slap at the man that threw it. But the fellow backed out; and then a cry was raised to let it alone, as it wos a brown walrus. One young Esquimau, howsiver, would have another slap at it, and went so close that the brute charged, upset the kayak, and ripped the man up with his tusks. Seein' this, the other Esquimaux made a dash at it, and wounded it badly; but the upshot wos that the walrus put them all to flight and made off, clear away, with six harpoons fast in its hide."

"Busby's tellin' ye gammon," roared Tom Green, who rode on the second sledge in rear of that on which Davie Summers sat. "What is't all about?"

"About gammon, of coorse," retorted Davie. "Keep yer mouth shut for fear your teeth freeze."

"Can't ye lead us a better road?" shouted Saunders, who rode on the third sledge; "my bones are rattlin' about inside o' me like a bag o' ninepins."

"Give the dogs a cut, old fellow," said Buzzby, with a chuckle and a motion of his arm to the Esquimau who drove his sledge.

The Esquimau did not understand the words, but he quite understood the sly chuckle and the motion of the arm, so he sent the lash of the heavy whip with a loud crack over the backs of the team.

"Hold on for life!" cried Davie, as the dogs sprang forward with a bound.

The part they were about to pass over was exceedingly rough and broken, and Buzzby resolved to give his shipmates a shake. The pace was tremendous. The powerful dogs drew their loads after them with successive bounds, which caused a succession of crashes, as the sledges sprang from lump to lump of ice, and the men's teeth snapped in a truly savage manner.

"B-a-ck ye-r t-to-p-sails, will ye?" shouted Amos Parr.

But the delighted Esquimau leader, who entered quite into the joke, had no intention whatever of backing his top-sails; he administered another crack to the team, which yelled madly, and, bounding over a wide chasm in the ice, came down with a crash, which snapped the line of the leading dog and set it free. Here Buzzby caused the driver to pull up.

"Stop, ye varmint. Come to an anchor," said he. "Is that a way to drive the poor dogs?"

"Ye might have stopped him sooner, I think," cried the second mate in wrath.

"Hai!" shouted the band of Esquimaux, pointing to a hummock of ice a few hundred yards in advance of the spot on which they stood.

Instantly all were silent, and gazing intently ahead at a dark object that burst upwards through the ice.

"A walrus!" whispered Buzzby.

"So it is," answered Amos Parr.

"I've my doobts on that point," remarked Saunders.

Before the doubts of the second mate could be resolved, the Esquimaux uttered another exclamation, and pointed to another dark object a quarter of a mile to the right. It was soon found that there were several of these ocean elephants sporting about in the neighbourhood, and bursting up the young ice that had formed on several holes, by using their huge heads as battering-rams. It was quickly arranged that the party should divide into three, and while a few remained behind to watch and restrain the dogs, the remainder were to advance on foot to the attack.

Saunders, Buzzby, Amos Parr, Davie Summers, and Awatok formed one party, and advanced with two muskets and several spears towards the walrus that had been first seen, the sailors taking care to keep in rear of Awatok in order to follow his lead, for they were as yet ignorant of the proper mode of attack.

Awatok led the party stealthily towards a hummock, behind which he caused them to crouch until the walrus should dive. This it did in a few minutes, and then they all rushed from their place of concealment towards another hummock that lay about fifty yards from, the hole. Just as they reached it and crouched, the walrus rose, snorting the brine from its shaggy muzzle, and lashing the water into foam with its flippers.

"Losh, what a big un!" exclaimed Saunders in amazement; and well he might, for this was an unusually large animal, more like an elephant in size than anything else.

It had two enormous ivory tusks, with which it tore and pounded large fragments from the ice-tables, while it barked like a gigantic dog, and rolled its heavy form about in sport.

Awatok now whispered to his comrades, and attempted to get them to understand that they must follow him as fast as possible at the next run. Suddenly the walrus dived. Awatok rushed forward, and in another instant stood at the edge of the hole with his spear in readiness in his right hand and the coil of line in his left. The others joined him instantly, and they had scarcely come up when the huge monster again rose to the surface.

Saunders and Buzzby fired at his head the moment it appeared above water, and Awatok at the same time planted a spear in his breast, and ran back with the coil. The others danced about in an excited state, throwing their spears and missing their mark, although it was a big one, frequently.

"Give him a lance-thrust, Amos," cried Saunders, reloading his piece.

But Amos could not manage it, for the creature lashed about so furiously that, although he made repeated attempts, he failed to do more than prick its tough sides and render it still more savage. Buzzby, too, made several daring efforts to lance it, but failed, and nearly slipped into the hole in his recklessness. It was a wild scene of confusion—the spray was dashed over the ice round the hole, and the men, as they ran about in extreme excitement, slipped and occasionally tumbled in their haste; while the maddened brute glared at them like a fiend, and bellowed in its anger and pain.

Suddenly it dived, leaving the men staring at each other. The sudden cessation of noise and turmoil had a very strange effect.

"Is't away?" inquired Saunders, with a look of chagrin.

He was answered almost instantly by the walrus reappearing, and making furious efforts by means of its flippers and tusks to draw itself out upon the ice, while it roared with redoubled energy. The shot that was instantly fired seemed to have no effect, and the well-directed harpoon of Awatok was utterly disregarded by it. Amos Parr, however, gave it a lance-thrust that caused it to howl vehemently, and dyed the foam with its blood.

"Hand me a spear, Buzzby," cried Saunders; "the musket-balls seem to hurt him as little as peas. Oot o' my gait."

The second mate made a rush so tremendous that something awful would infallibly have resulted, had he not struck his foot against a bit of ice and fallen violently on his breast. The impetus with which he had started shot him forward till his head was within a foot of the walrus's grim muzzle. For one moment the animal looked at the man, as if it were surprised at his audacity, and then it recommenced its frantic struggles, snorting blood, and foam, and water into Saunders's face as he scrambled out of its way. Immediately after, Awatok fixed another harpoon in its side, and it dived again.

The struggle that ensued was tremendous, and the result seemed for a long time to be doubtful. Again and again shots were fired and spear-thrusts made with effect, but the huge creature seemed invulnerable. Its ferocity and strength remained unabated, while the men—sailors and Esquimau alike—were nearly exhausted. The battle had now lasted three hours; the men were panting from exertion; the walrus, still bellowing, was clinging to the edge of the ice, which for several yards round the hole was covered with blood and foam.

"Wot a brute it is!" said Buzzby, sitting down on a lump of ice and looking at it in despair.

"We might have killed it lang ago had I not wet my gun," growled Saunders, regarding his weapon, which was completely drenched, with a look of contempt.

"Give it another poke, Awatok," cried Amos Parr; "you'll know best whereabouts its life lies; I can make nothin' o't."

Awatok obeyed, and gave it a thrust under the left flipper that seemed to reach its heart, for it fell back into the water and struggled violently. At the same moment Davie Summers mounted to the top of a hummock, part of which overhung the pool, and launched a harpoon down upon its back. This latter blow seemed to revive its ferocity, for it again essayed to clamber out on the ice, and looked up at Davie with a glance of seeming indignation; while Buzzby, who had approached, fell backward as he retreated from before it. At the same time Saunders succeeded in getting his musket to go off. The ball struck it in the eye, and entering the brain, caused instant death, a result which was greeted with three enthusiastic cheers.

The getting of this enormous creature out of the water would have been a matter of no small difficulty had there not been such a large party present. Even as it was it took them a considerable time to accomplish this feat, and to cut it up and pack it on the sledges.

While the battle above described was going on, two smaller walruses had been killed and secured, and the Esquimaux were in a state of great glee, for previous to the arrival of the sailors they had been unsuccessful in their hunts, and had been living on short allowance. On returning home there was a general feasting and merrymaking, and Saunders felt that if he remained there long they would not only eat up their own meat, but his also. He therefore resolved to return immediately to the ship with his prize, and leave part of his men behind to continue the hunt until he should return with the sledge.

But he was prevented from putting this intention into practice by a hurricane which burst over the Arctic Regions with inconceivable bitterness, and for two days kept all the inhabitants of the snow-village confined to their huts. This hurricane was the fiercest that had swept over these bleak regions of ice since the arrival of the *Dolphin*. The wind shrieked as it swept round the cliffs, and down the ravines, and out upon the frozen sea, as if a legion of evil spirits were embodied and concentrated in each succeeding blast. The snow-drift rose in solid masses, whirled madly round for a few seconds, and then was caught by the blast and swept away like sheets of white flame. The thermometer stood at 25° below zero, a temperature that was mild compared with what it usually had been of late, but the fierce wind abstracted heat from everything exposed to it so rapidly that neither man nor beast could face it for a moment. Buzzby got a little bit of his chin frozen while he merely put his head out at the door of the hut to see how the weather looked; and Davie Summers had one of his fingers slightly frozen while in the act of carrying in one of the muskets that had been left outside by mistake.

As for the Esquimaux, they recked not of the weather. Their snow-huts were warm, and their mouths were full, so like wise men and women they waited patiently within doors till the storm should blow itself out. The doings of these poor people were very curious. They ate voraciously, and evidently preferred their meat raw. But when the sailors showed disgust at this, they at once made a small fire of moss mingled with blubber, over which they half-cooked their food.

Their mode of procuring fire was curious. Two small stones were take —one a piece of white quartz, the other a piece of iron-stone—and struck together smartly. The few sparks that flew out were thrown upon a kind of white down, found on the willows, under which was placed a lump of dried moss. It was usually a considerable time before they succeeded in catching a spark; but, once caught, they had no difficulty in blowing it into a flame.

They had also an ingenious contrivance for melting snow. This was a flat stone, supported by two other stones, and inclined slightly at one end. Upon this flat stone a lump of snow was placed, and below it was kindled a small fire of moss and blubber. When the stone became heated, the snow melted and flowed down the incline into a small seal skin cup placed there to catch it.

During the continuance of the storm the sailors shared the food and lodging of these Esquimaux. They were a fat, oily, hospitable, dirty race, and vied with each other in showing kindness to those who had been thus thrown into their society. As Davie Summers expressed it, "they were regular trumps;" and according to Buzzby's opinion, "they wos the jolliest set o' human walruses wot he had ever comed across in all his travels; and he ought to know, for he had always kep' his weather-eye open, he had, and wouldn't give in on that p'int, he wouldn't, to no man livin'."

CHAPTER XIX.

The northern party—A narrow escape, and a great discovery—
Esquimaux again, and a joyful surprise.

It is interesting to meditate, sometimes, on the deviousness of the paths by which men are led in earthly affairs—even when the starting-point and the object of pursuit are the same. The two parties which left the *Dolphin* had for their object the procuring of fresh food. The one went south and the other north; but their field was the same—the surface of the frozen sea and the margin of the ice-girt shore. Yet how different their experiences and results were the sequel will show.

As we have already said, the northern party was in command of Bolton, the first mate, and consisted of ten men, among whom were our hero, Fred, Peter Grim, O'Riley, and Meetuck, with the whole team of dogs and the large sledge.

Being fine weather when they set out, they travelled rapidly, making twenty miles, as near as they could calculate, in the first six hours. The dogs pulled famously, and the men stepped out well at first, being cheered and invigorated mentally by the prospect of an adventurous excursion and fresh meat. At the end of the second day they buried part of their stock of provisions at the foot of a conspicuous cliff, intending to pick it up on their return; and thus lightened, they advanced more rapidly, keeping farther out on the floes, in hopes of falling in with walruses or seals.

Their hopes, however, were doomed to disappointment. They got only one seal, and that was a small one—scarcely sufficient to afford a couple of meals to the dogs.

They were "misfortunate entirely," as O'Riley remarked; and to add to their misfortunes, the floe-ice became so rugged that they could scarcely advance at all.

"Things grow worse and worse," remarked Grim, as the sledge, for the twentieth time that day, plunged into a crack in the ice, and had to be unloaded ere it could be got out. "The sledge won't stand much o' sich work, and if it breaks—good-bye to it, for it won't mend without wood, and there's none here."

"No fear of it," cried Bolton encouragingly; "it's made of material as tough as your own sinews, Grim, and won't give way easily, as the thumps it has withstood already prove.—Has it never struck you, Fred," he continued, turning to our hero who was plodding forward in silence—"has it never struck you that when things in this world get very bad, and we begin to feel inclined to give up, they somehow or other begin to get better?"

"Why, yes, I have noticed that; but I have a vague sort of feeling just now that things are not going to get better. I don't know whether it's this long-continued darkness, or the want of good food, but I feel more downcast than I ever was in my life before."

Bolton's remark had been intended to cheer, but Fred's answer proved that a discussion of the merits of the question was not likely to have a good effect on the men, whose spirits were evidently very much cast down, so he changed the subject.

Fortunately, at that time an incident occurred which effected the mate's purpose better than any efforts man could have made. It has frequently happened that when Arctic voyagers have, from sickness and long confinement during a monotonous winter, become so depressed in spirits that games and amusements of every kind bailed to rouse them from their lethargic despondency, sudden danger has given to their minds the needful impulse, and effected a salutary change, for a time at least, in their spirits. Such was the case at the present time. The men were so worn with hard travel and the want of fresh food, and depressed by disappointment and long-continued darkness, that they failed in their attempts to cheer each other, and at length relapsed into moody silence. Fred's thoughts turned constantly to his father, and he ceased to remark cheerfully, as was his wont, on passing objects. Even O'Riley's jests became few and far between, and at last ceased altogether. Bolton alone kept up his spirits, and sought to cheer his men, the feeling of responsibility being, probably, the secret of his superiority over them in this respect. But even Bolton's spirits began to sink at last.

While they were thus groping sadly along among the hummocks, a large fragment of ice was observed to break off from a berg just over their heads.

"Look out! follow me, quick!" shouted the first mate in a loud, sharp voice of alarm, at the same time darting in towards the side of the berg.

The startled men obeyed the order just in time, for they had barely reached the side of the berg when the enormous pinnacle fell, and was shattered into a thousand fragments on the spot they had just left. A rebounding emotion sent the blood in a crimson flood to Fred's forehead, and this was followed by a feeling of gratitude to the Almighty for the preservation of himself and the party. Leaving the dangerous vicinity of the bergs, they afterwards kept more in-shore.

"What can yonder mound be?" said Fred, pointing to an object that was faintly seen at a short distance off upon the bleak shore.

"An Esquimau hut, maybe," replied Grim.—"What think'ee, Meetuck?"

Meetuck shook his head and looked grave, but made no reply.

"Why don't you answer?" said Bolton. "But come along, we'll soon see."

Meetuck now made various ineffectual attempts to dissuade the party from examining the mound, which turned out to be composed of stones heaped upon each other; but as all the conversation of which he was capable failed to enlighten his companions as to what the pile was, they instantly set to work to open a passage into the interior, believing that it might contain fresh provisions, as the Esquimaux were in the habit of thus preserving their superabundant food from bears and wolves. In half-an-hour a hole, large enough for a man to creep through, was formed, and Fred entered, but started back with an exclamation of horror on finding himself in the presence of a human skeleton, which was seated on the ground in the centre of this strange tomb, with its head and arms resting on the knees.

"It must be an Esquimau grave," said Fred, as he retreated hastily; "that must be the reason why Meetuck tried to hinder us."

"I should like to see it," said Grim, stooping and thrusting his head and shoulders into the hole.

"What have you got there?" asked Bolton, as Grim drew back and held up something in his hand.

"Don't know exactly. It's like a bit o' cloth." On examination the article was found to be a shred of coarse cloth, of a blue or black colour; and being an unexpected substance to meet with in such a place, Bolton turned round with it to Meetuck in the hope of obtaining some information. But Meetuck was gone. While the sailors were breaking into the grave, Meetuck had stood aloof with a displeased expression of countenance, as if he were angry at the rude desecration of a countryman's tomb; but the moment his eye fell on the shred of cloth an expression of mingled surprise and curiosity crossed his countenance, and, without uttering a word, he slipped noiselessly into the hole, from which he almost immediately issued bearing several articles in his hand. These he held up to view, and with animated words and gesticulations explained that this was the grave of a white man, not of a native.

The articles he brought out were a pewter plate and a silver table-spoon.

"There's a name of some kind written here," said Bolton, as he carefully scrutinized the spoon. "Look here, Fred, your eyes are better than mine, see if you can make it out."

Fred took it with a trembling hand, for a strange feeling of dread had seized possession of his heart, and he could scarcely bring himself to look upon it. He summoned up courage, however; but at the first glance his hand fell down by his side, and a dimness came over his eyes, for the word *"POLE STAR"* was engraven on the handle. He would have fallen to the ground had not Bolton caught him.

"Don't give way, lad, the ship may be all right. Perhaps this is one o' the crew that died."

Fred did not answer, but recovering himself with a strong effort, he said, "Pull down the stones, men."

The men obeyed in silence, and the poor boy sat down on a rock to await the result in trembling anxiety. A few minutes sufficed to disentomb the skeleton, for the men sympathized with their young comrade, and worked with all their energies.

"Cheer up, Fred," said Bolton, coming and laying his hand on the youth's shoulder; "it's *not* your father. There is a bit of *black* hair sticking to the scalp."

With a fervent expression of thankfulness Fred rose and examined the skeleton, which had been placed in a sort of sack of skin, but was destitute of clothing. It was quite dry, and must have been there a long time. Nothing else was found, but from the appearance of the skull and the presence of the plate and spoon, there could be no doubt that it was that of one of the *Pole Star's* crew.

It was now resolved that they should proceed along the coast and examine every creek and bay for traces of the lost vessel.

"O Bolton! my heart misgives me," said Fred, as they drove along; "I fear that they have all perished."

"Niver a bit, sir," said O'Riley, in a sympathizing tone; "yon chap must have died and been buried here be the crew as they wint past."

"You forget that sailors don't bury men under mounds of stone, with pewter plates and spoons beside them."

O'Riley was silenced, for the remark was unanswerable.

"He may ha' bin left or lost on the shore, and been found by the Esquimaux," suggested Peter Grim.

"Is that not another tomb?" inquired one of the men, pointing towards an object which stood on the end of a point or cape towards which they were approaching.

Ere any one could reply, their ears were saluted by the well-known bark of a pack of Esquimau dogs. In another moment they dashed into the midst of a snow village, and were immediately surrounded by the excited natives. For some time no information could be gleaned from their interpreter, who was too excited to make use of his meagre amount of English. They observed, however, that the natives, although much excited, did not seem to be so much surprised at the appearance of white men amongst them as those were whom they had first met with near the ship. In a short time Meetuck, apparently, had expended all he had to say to his friends, and turned to make explanations to Bolton in a very excited tone; but little more could be made out than that what he said had some reference to white men. At length, in desperation, he pointed to a large hut, which seemed to be the principal one of the village, and dragging the mate towards it, made signs to him to enter.

Bolton hesitated an instant.

"He wants you to see the chief of the tribe, no doubt," said Fred; "you'd better go in at once."

A loud voice shouted something in the Esquimau language from within the hut. At the sound Fred's heart beat violently, and pushing past the mate he crept through the tunnelled entrance and stood within. There was little furniture in this rude dwelling. A dull flame flickered in a stone lamp which hung from the roof, and revealed the figure of a large Esquimau reclining on a couch of skins at the raised side of the hut.

The man looked up hastily as Fred entered, and uttered a few unintelligible words.

"Father!" cried Fred, gasping for breath, and springing forward.

Captain Ellice, for it was indeed he, started with apparent difficulty and pain into a sitting posture, and throwing back his hood revealed a face whose open, hearty, benignant expression shone through a coat of dark brown which long months of toil and exposure had imprinted on it. It was thin, however, and careworn, and wore an expression that seemed to be the result of long-continued suffering.

"Father!" he exclaimed in an earnest tone; "who calls me father?"

"Don't you know me, father?—don't you remember Fred?—look at—"

Fred checked himself, for the wild look of his father frightened him.

"Ah! these dreams," murmured the old man; "I wish they did not come so—"

Placing his hand on his forehead, he fell backwards in a state of insensibility into the arms of his son.

CHAPTER XX.

*Keeping it down—Mutual explanations—The true comforter—Death—
New-Year's day.*

It need scarcely be said that the sailors outside did not remain long in
ignorance of the unexpected and happy discovery related in the last
chapter. Bolton, who had crept in after Fred, with proper delicacy of
feeling retired the moment he found how matters stood, and left father
and son to expend, in the privacy of that chamber of snow, those
feelings and emotions which can be better imagined than described.

The first impulse of the men was to give three cheers, but Bolton
checked them in the bud.

"No, no, lads. Ye must hold on," he said, in an eager but subdued
voice. "Doubtless it would be pleasant to vent our feelings in a hearty
cheer, but it would startle the old gentleman inside. Get along with you,
and let us get ready a good supper."

"O morther!" exclaimed O'Riley, holding on to his sides as if he
believed what he said, "me biler'll bust av ye don't let me screech."

"Squeeze down the safety-valve a bit longer, then," cried Bolton, as
they hurried along with the whole population to the outskirts of the
village. "Now, then, ye may fire away, they won't hear ye—huzza!"

A long enthusiastic cheer instantly burst from the sailors, and was
immediately followed by a howl of delight from the Esquimaux, who
capered round their visitors with uncouth gestures and grinning faces.

Entering one of the largest huts, preparations for supper were promptly
begun. The Esquimaux happened to be well supplied with walrus-
flesh, so the lamps were replenished, and the hiss of the frying steaks
and dropping fat speedily rose above all other sounds.

Meanwhile, Fred and his father, having mutually recovered somewhat
of their wonted composure, began to tell each other the details of their
adventures since they last met, while the former prepared a cup of
coffee and a steak for their mutual comfort.

"But, father," said Fred, busying himself at the lamp, "you have not yet
told me how you came here, and what has become of the *Pole Star*,
and how it was that one of your men came to be buried in the

185

Esquimau fashion, and how you got your leg broken."

"Truly, Fred, I have not told you all that, and to give it you all in detail will afford us many a long hour of converse hereafter, if it please God, whose tenderness and watchful care of me has never failed. But I can give you a brief outline of it thus:—

"I got into Baffin's Bay and made a good fishing of it the first year, but was beset in the ice, and compelled to spend two winters in these regions. The third year we were liberated, and had almost got fairly on our homeward voyage when a storm blew us to the north and carried us up here. Then our good brig was nipped and went to the bottom, and all the crew were lost except myself and one man. We succeeded in leaping from one piece of loose ice to another until we reached the solid floe and gained the land, where we were kindly received by the Esquimaux. But poor Wilson did not survive long. His constitution had never been robust, and he died of consumption a week after we landed. The Esquimaux buried him after their own fashion, and, as I afterwards found, had buried a plate and a spoon along with him. These, with several other articles, had been washed ashore from the wreck. Since then I have been living the life of an Esquimau, awaiting an opportunity of escape either by a ship making its appearance or a tribe of natives travelling south. I soon picked up their language, and was living in comparative comfort, when, during a sharp fight I chanced to have with a Polar bear, I fell and broke my leg. I have lain here for many months, and have suffered much, Fred; but, thank God, I am now almost well, and can walk a little, though not yet without pain."

"Dear father," said Fred, "how terribly you must have felt the want of kind hands to nurse you during those dreary months, and how lonely you must have been!"

"Nay, boy, not quite so lonely as you think. I have learned the truth of these words, 'I will never leave thee, nor forsake thee'—'Call upon Me in the time of trouble, and I will deliver thee.' This, Fred, has been my chief comfort during the long hours of sickness."

Captain Ellice drew forth a soiled pocket Bible from his breast as he spoke.

"It was your beloved mother's, Fred, and is the only thing I brought with me from the wreck; but it was the only thing in the brig I would not have exchanged for anything else on earth. Blessed Bible! It tells of Him whose goodness I once, in my ignorance, thought I knew, but whose love I have since been taught 'passeth knowledge.' It has been a glorious sun to me, which has never set in all the course of this long Arctic night. It has been a companion in my solitude, a comfort in my sorrows, and even now is an increase to my joy; for it tells me that if I commit my way unto the Lord, he will bring it to pass, and already I see the beginning of the end fulfilled."

Fred's eyes filled with tears as his father spoke; but he remained silent, for he knew that of late he had begun to neglect God's blessed Word, and his conscience smote him.

It were impossible here to enter minutely into the details of all that Captain Ellice related to Fred during the next few days, while they remained together in the Esquimau village. To tell of the dangers, the adventures, and the hair-breadth escapes that the crew of the *Pole Star* went through before the vessel finally went down, would require a whole volume. We must pass it all over, and also the account of the few days that followed, during which sundry walruses were captured, and return to the *Dolphin*, to which Captain Ellice had been conveyed on the sledge, carefully wrapped up in deer-skins, and tended by Fred.

A party of the Esquimaux accompanied them, and as a number of the natives from the other village had returned with Saunders and his men to the ship, the scene she presented, when all parties were united, was exceedingly curious and animated.

The Esquimaux soon built quite a little town of snow-huts all round the *Dolphin*, and the noise of traffic and intercourse was peculiarly refreshing to the ears of those who had long been accustomed to the death-like stillness of an Arctic winter. The beneficial effect of the change on men and dogs was instantaneous. Their spirits rose at once, and this, with the ample supply of fresh meat that had been procured, soon began to drive scurvy away.

There was one dark spot, however, in this otherwise pleasant scene—one impending event that cast a gloom over all. In his narrow berth in the cabin Joseph West lay dying. Scurvy had acted more rapidly on his delicate frame than had been expected. Despite Tom Singleton's utmost efforts and skill, the fell disease gained the mastery, and it soon became evident that this hearty and excellent man was to be taken away from them.

During the last days of his illness, Captain Ellice was his greatest comfort and his constant companion. He read the Bible to him, and when doubts and fears arose, as they sometimes did, he pointed him to Jesus, and spoke of that love from which nothing could separate him.

It was on Christmas day that West died.

"O sir," said he to Captain Ellice just an hour before he breathed his last, "how much I regret the time that I have lost! How I wish now that had devoted more of my precious time to the study of the Word and to prayer! How many opportunities of speaking a word for Jesus I have neglected. Once, everything seemed of importance; now, but *one* thing is worthy of a thought."

"True," answered the captain, "'the one thing needful.' It is strange that we will scarce permit ourselves to think or speak of *that* till we come to die. But you have thought on Jesus long ere now, have you not?"

"Yes," answered West faintly, "I have; but I take no comfort from that thought. When I think of my past life it is only with regret. My hope is in the Lord. What I have been, or might have been, is nothing. One thing I know—I *am* a sinner; and this I also know—'Christ Jesus came into the world to save sinners!'"

These were the last words the dying man spoke. Shortly after, he fell asleep.

Next day the body of Joseph West was put in a plain deal coffin, and conveyed to Store Island, where it was placed on the ground. They had no instruments that could penetrate the hard rock, so were obliged to construct a tomb of stones, after the manner of the Esquimaux, under which the coffin was laid and left in solitude.

New-Year's day came, and preparations were made to celebrate the day with the usual festivities. But the recent death had affected the crew too deeply to allow them to indulge in the unrestrained hilarity of that season. Prayers were read in the morning, and both Captain Guy and Captain Ellice addressed the men feelingly in allusion to their late shipmate's death and their own present position. A good dinner was also prepared, and several luxuries served out, among which were the materials for the construction of a large plum-pudding. But no grog was allowed, and they needed it not. As the afternoon advanced, stories were told, and even songs were sung; but these were of a quiet kind, and the men seemed, from an innate feeling of propriety, to suit them to the occasion. Old friends were recalled, and old familiar scenes described. The hearths of home were spoken of with a depth of feeling that showed how intense was the longing to be seated round them again, and future prospects were canvassed with keen interest and with hopeful voices. New-Year's day came and went, and when it was gone the men of the *Dolphin* did not say, "what a jolly day it was." They *said* little or nothing, but long after they *thought* of it as a bright spot in their dreary winter in the Bay of Mercy—as a day in which they had enjoyed earnest, glad, and sober communings of heart.

CHAPTER XXI.

First gleam of light—Trip to welcome the sun—Bears and strange discoveries—O'Riley is reckless—First view of the sun.

The wisest of men has told us that "it is a pleasant thing for the eyes to behold the sun," but only those who spend a winter in the Arctic Regions can fully appreciate the import of that inspired saying. It is absolutely essential to existence that the bright beams of the great luminary should fall on animal as well as plant. Most of the poor dogs died for want of this blessed light, and had it been much longer withheld, doubtless our navigators would have sunk also.

About the 20th of January a faint gleam of light on the horizon told of the coming day. It was hailed with rapture, and long before the bright sun himself appeared on the southern horizon the most of the men made daily excursions to the neighbouring hilltops to catch sight of as much as possible of his faint rays. Day by day those rays expanded, and at last a sort of *dawn* enlightened a distant portion of their earth, which, faint though it was at first, had much the appearance in their eyes of a bright day. But time wore on, and *real* day appeared. The red sun rose in all its glory, showed a rim of its glowing disk above the frozen sea, and then sank, leaving a long gladsome smile of twilight behind. This great event happened on the 19th of February, and would have occurred sooner, but for the high cliffs to the southward which intervened between the ship and the horizon.

On the day referred to, a large party was formed to go to the top of the cliffs at Red-Snow Valley to welcome back the sun.

"There's scarce a man left behind," remarked Captain Guy, as they started on this truly joyous expedition.

"Only Mizzle, sir," said Buzzby, slapping his hands together, for the cold was intense; "he said as how he'd stop and have dinner ready agin our return."

There was a general laugh from the men, who knew that the worthy cook had other reasons for not going—namely, his shortness of wind, and his inveterate dislike to ascend hills.

"Come, Fred," cried Captain Ellice, who had completely recovered from his accident, "I shall be quite jealous of your friend Singleton if you bestow so much of your company on him. Walk with me, sirrah, I command you, as I wish to have a chat."

"You are unjust to me," replied Fred, taking his father's arm, and falling with him a little to the rear of the party; "Tom complains that I have quite given him up of late."

"Och! isn't it a purty sight," remarked O'Riley to Mivins, "to see us all goin' out like good little childers to see the sun rise of a beautiful mornin' like this?"

"So it *his*," answered Mivins; "but I wish it wasn't quite so cold."

It was indeed cold—so cold that the men had to beat their hands together, and stamp their feet, and rush about like real children, in order to keep their bodies warm. This month of February was the coldest they had yet experienced. Several times the thermometer fell to the unexampled temperature of 75° below zero, or 107° below the freezing-point of water. When we remind our young readers that the thermometer in England seldom falls so low as zero, except in what we term weather of the utmost severity, they may imagine—or rather, they may try to imagine—what 75° *below* zero must have been.

It was not quite so cold as that upon this occasion, otherwise the men could not have shown face to it.

"Let's have leap-frog," shouted Davie; "we can jump along as well as walk along. Hooray! *hup!*"

The "hup" was rather an exclamation of necessity than of delight, inasmuch as that it was caused by Davie coming suddenly down flat on the ice in the act of vainly attempting to go leap-frog over Mivins's head.

"That's your sort," cried Amos Parr; "down with you, Buzzby."

Buzzby obeyed, and Amos, being heavy and past the agile time of life, leaped upon, instead of over, his back, and there stuck.

"Not so high, lads," cried Captain Guy. "Come, Mr. Saunders, give us a back."

"Faix he'd better go on his hands an' knees."

"That's it! over you go! hurrah, lads!"

In five minutes nearly the whole crew were panting from their violent exertions, and those who did not or could not join panted as much rom laughter. The desired result, however, was speedily gained. They vere all soon in a glow of heat, and bade defiance to the frost.

\n hour's sharp climb brought the party almost to the brow of the hill, rom which they hoped to see the sun rise for the first time for nearly ive months. Just as they were about to pass over a ridge in the cliffs, Captain Guy, who had pushed on in advance with Tom Singleton, was obserbved to pause abruptly and make signals for the men to advance vith caution. He evidently saw something unusual, for he crouched behind a rock and peeped over it. Hastening up as silently as possible, hey discovered that a group of Polar bears were amusing themselves on the other side of the cliffs, within long gunshot. Unfortunately not one of the party had brought fire-arms. Intent only on catching a sight of the sun, they had hurried off unmindful of the possibility of their catching sight of anything else. They had not even a spear; and the ew oak cudgels that some carried, however effectual they might have proved at Donnybrook, were utterly worthless there.

There were four large bears and a young one, and the gambols they performed were of the most startling as well as amusing kind. But that vhich interested and surprised the crew most was the fact that these bears were playing with barrels, and casks, and tent-poles, and sails. They were engaged in a regular frolic with these articles, tossing them up in the air, pawing them about, and leaping over them like kittens. In these movements they displayed their enormous strength several times. Their leaps, although performed with the utmost ease, were so great as to prove the iron nature of their muscles. They tossed the heavy casks, too, high into the air like tennis-balls, and in two instances, while the crew were watching them, dashed a cask in pieces with a slight blow of their paws. The tough canvas yielded before them like sheets of paper, and the havoc they committed was wonderful to behold.

'Most extraordinary!' exclaimed Captain Guy, after watching them for some time in silence. "I cannot imagine where these creatures can have got hold of such things. Were not the goods at Store Island all right this morning, Mr. Bolton?"

"Yes, sir, they were."

"Nothing missing from the ship?"

"No, sir, nothing."

"It's most unaccountable."

"Captain Guy," said O'Riley, addressing his commander with a solemn face, "haven't ye more nor wance towld me o' the queer thing in the deserts they calls the *mirage*?"

"I have," answered the captain, with a puzzled look.

"An' didn't ye say there was somethin' like it in the Polar Seas, that made ye see flags, an' ships, an' things o' that sort when there was no sich things there at all?"

"True, O'Riley, I did."

"Faix, then, it's my opinion that yon bears is a *mirage*, an' the sooner we git out o' their way the better."

A smothered laugh greeted this solution of the difficulty.

"I think I can give a better explanation—begging your pardon, O'Riley," said Captain Ellice, who had hitherto looked on with a sly smile. "More than a year ago, when I was driven past this place to the northward, I took advantage of a calm to land a supply of food, and a few stores and medicines, to be a stand-by in case my ship should be wrecked to the northward. Ever since the wreck actually took place I have looked forward to this *cache* of provisions as a point of refuge on my way south. As I have already told you, I have never been able to commence the southward journey; and now I don't require these things, which is lucky, for the bears seem to have appropriated them entirely."

"Had I known of them sooner, captain," said Captain Guy, "the bears should not have had a chance."

"That accounts for the supply of tobacco and sticking-plaster we found in the bear's stomach," remarked Fred, laughing.

"True, boy; yet it surprises me that they succeeded in breaking into my *cache*, for it was made of heavy masses of stone, many of which required two and three men to lift them, even with the aid of handspikes."

"What's wrong with O'Riley?" said Fred, pointing to that eccentric individual, who was gazing intently at the bears, muttering between his teeth, and clinching his cudgel nervously.

"Sure it's a cryin' shame," he soliloquized in an undertone, quite unconscious that he was observed, "that ye should escape, ye villains. Av I only had a musket now—but I han't. Arrah! av it was only a spear. Be the mortial! I think I could crack the skull o' the small wan! Faix,

194

then, I'll try!"

At the last word, before any one was aware of his intentions, this son of Erin, whose blood was now up, sprang down the cliffs towards the bears, flourishing his stick, and shouting wildly as he went. The bears instantly paused in their game, but showed no disposition to retreat.

"Come back, you madman!" shouted the captain; but the captain shouted in vain.

"Stop! halt! come back!" chorused the crew.

But O'Riley was deaf. He had advanced to within a few yards of the bears, and was rushing forward to make a vigorous attack on the little one.

"He'll be killed!" exclaimed Fred in dismay.

"Follow me, men," shouted the captain, as he leaped the ridge: "make all the noise you can."

In a moment the surrounding cliffs were reverberating with the loud halloos and frantic yells of the men, as they burst suddenly over the ridge, and poured down upon the bears like a torrent of maniacs.

Bold though they were, they couldn't stand this. They turned tail and fled, followed by the disappointed howls of O'Riley, and also by his cudgel, which he hurled violently after them as he pulled up.

Having thus triumphantly put the enemy to flight, the party continued their ascent of the hill, and soon gained the summit.

"There it is!" shouted Fred, who, in company with Mivins, first crossed the ridge, and tossed his arms in the air.

The men cheered loudly as they hurried up and one by one emerged into a red glow of sunshine. It could not be termed *warm*, for it had no power in that frosty atmosphere, and only a small portion of the sun's disk was visible. But his *light* was on every crag and peak around; and as the men sat down in groups, and, as it were, bathed in the sunshine, winking at the bright gleam of light with half-closed eyes, they declared that it *felt* warm, and wouldn't hear anything to the contrary, although Saunders, true to his nature, endeavoured to prove to them that the infinitely small degree of heat imparted by such feeble rays could not by any possibility be *felt* except in imagination. But Saunders was outvoted. Indeed, under the circumstances, he had not a chance of proving his point; for the more warm the dispute became, the greater was the amount of animal heat that was created, to be placed, falsely, to the credit of the sun.

Patience, however, is a virtue which is sure to meet with a reward. The point which Saunders failed to prove by argument, was pretty well proved to every one (though not admitted) by the agency of John Frost. That remarkably bitter individual nestled round the men as they sat sunning themselves, and soon compelled them to leap up and apply to other sources for heat. They danced about vigorously, and again took to leap-frog. Then they tried their powers at the old familiar games of home. Hop-step-and-jump raised the animal thermometer considerably, and the standing leap, running leap, and high leap sent it up many degrees. But a general race brought them almost to a summer temperature, and at the same time, most unexpectedly, secured to them a hare! This little creature, of which very few had yet been procured, darted in an evil hour out from behind a rock right in front of the men, who, having begun the race for sport, now continued it energetically for profit. A dozen sticks were hurled at the luckless hare, and one of these felled it to the ground.

After this they returned home in triumph, keeping up all the way an animated dispute as to the amount of heat shed upon them by the sun, and upon that knotty question, "Who killed the hare?"

Neither point was settled when they reached the *Dolphin*, and, we may add, for the sake of the curious reader, neither point is settled yet.

CHAPTER XXII.

The "Arctic Sun"—Rats! rats! rats!—A hunting-party—Out on the floes —Hardships.

Among the many schemes that were planned and carried out for lightening the long hours of confinement to their wooden home in the Arctic Regions, was the newspaper started by Fred Ellice, and named, as we have already mentioned, the *Arctic Sun*.

It was so named because, as Fred stated in his first leading article, it was intended to throw light on many things at a time when there was no other sun to cheer them. We cannot help regretting that it is not in our power to present a copy of this well-thumbed periodical to our readers; but being of opinion that *something* is better than *nothing*, we transcribe the following extract as a specimen of the contributions from the forecastle. It was entitled—

JOHN BUZZBY'S OPPINYUNS O' THINGS IN GIN'RAL.

Mr. Editer,—As you was so good as to ax from me a contribootion to your waluable peeryoddical, I beg heer to stait that this heer article is intended as a gin'ral summery o' the noos wots agoin'. Your reeders will be glad to no that of late the wether's bin gittin' colder, but they'll be better pleased to no that before the middle o' nixt sumer it's likely to git a, long chawk warmer. There's a gin'ral complaint heer that Mivins has bin eatin' the shuger in the pantry, an' that's wots makin' it needfull to put us on short allowance. Davie Summers sais he seed him at it, an' it's a dooty the guvermint owes to the publik to have the matter investigated. It's gin'rally expected, howsever, that the guvermint won't trubble its hed with the matter. There's bin an onusual swarmin' o' rats in the ship of late, an' Davie Summers has had a riglar hunt after them. The lad has becum more than ornar expert with his bow an' arrow, for he niver misses now—exceptin', always, when he dusn't hit—an' for the most part takes them on the pint on the snowt with his blunt-heded arow, which he drives in—the snowt, not the arow. There's a gin'ral wish among the crew to no whether the north pole *is* a pole or a dot. Mizzle sais it's a dot, and O'Riley swears (no, he don't do that, for we've gin up swearin' in the fog-sail), but he sais that it's a real post, 'bout as thick again as the main-mast, an' nine or ten times as hy. Grim sais it's nother wun thing nor anuther, but a hydeear that *is* sumhow or other a fact, but yit don't exist at all. Tom Green wants to no if there's any conexshun between it an' the pole that's conected with elections. In fact, we're all at sea, in a riglar muz abut this, an' as Dr. Singleton's a syentiffick man, praps he'll give us a leadin' article in your nixt—so no more at present from— Yours to command,

JOHN BUZZBY.

This contribution was accompanied with an outline illustration of Mivins eating sugar with a ladle in the pantry, and Davie Summers peeping in at the door—both likenesses being excellent.

Some of the articles in the *Arctic Sun* were grave and some were gay, but all of them were profitable, for Fred took care that they should be charged either with matter of interest or matter provocative of mirth. And, assuredly, no newspaper of similar calibre was ever looked forward to with such expectation, or read and re-read with such avidity. It was one of the expedients that lasted longest in keeping up the spirits of the men.

The rat-hunting referred to in the foregoing "summary" was not a mere fiction of Buzzby's brain. It was a veritable fact. Notwithstanding the extreme cold of this inhospitable climate, the rats in the ship increased to such a degree that at last they became a perfect nuisance. Nothing was safe from their attacks—whether substances were edible or not, they were gnawed through and ruined—and their impudence, which seemed to increase with their numbers, at last exceeded all belief. They swarmed everywhere—under the stove, about the beds, in the lockers, between the sofa cushions, amongst the moss round the walls, and inside the boots and mittens (when empty) of the men. And they became so accustomed to having missiles thrown at them, that they acquired to perfection that art which Buzzby described as "keeping one's weather-eye open."

You couldn't hit one if you tried. If your hand moved towards an object with which you intended to deal swift destruction, the intruder paused, and turned his sharp eyes towards you, as if to say, "What! going to try it again?—come, then, here's a chance for you." But when you threw, at best you could only hit the empty space it had occupied the moment before. Or, if you seized a stick, and rushed at the enemy in wrath, it grinned fiercely, showed its long white teeth, and then vanished with a fling of its tail that could be construed into nothing but an expression of contempt.

At last an expedient was hit upon for destroying these disagreeable inmates. Small bows and arrows were made, the latter having heavy, blunt heads, and with these the men slaughtered hundreds. Whenever any one was inclined for a little sport, he took up his bow and arrows, and retiring to a dark corner of the cabin, watched for a shot. Davie Summers acquired the title of Nimrod in consequence of his success in this peculiar field.

At first the rats proved a capital addition to the dogs' meals, but at length some of the men were glad to eat them, especially when fresh meat failed altogether, and scurvy began its assaults. White or Arctic foxes, too, came about the ship sometimes in great numbers, and proved an acceptable addition to their fresh provisions; but at one period all these sources failed, and the crew were reduced to the utmost extremity, having nothing to eat except salt provisions. Notwithstanding the cheering influence of the sun, the spirits of the men fell as their bodily energies failed. Nearly two-thirds of the ship's company were confined to their berths. The officers retained much of their wonted health and vigour, partly in consequence, no doubt, of their unwearied exertions in behalf of others. They changed places with the men at last, owing to the force of circumstances—ministering to their wants, drawing water, fetching fuel, and cooking their food—carrying out, in short, the divine command, "By love serve one another."

During the worst period of their distress a party was formed to go out upon the floes in search of walruses.

"If we don't get speedy relief," remarked Captain Guy to Tom Singletor in reference to this party, "some of us will die. I feel certain of that. Poor Buzzby seems on his last legs, and Mivins is reduced to a shadow."

The doctor was silent, for the captain's remark was too true.

"You must get up your party at once, and set off after breakfast, Mr. Bolton," he added, turning to the first mate. "Who can accompany you?"

"There's Peter Grim, sir; he's tough yet, and not much affected by scurvy. And Mr. Saunders, I think, may—"

"No," interrupted the doctor, "Saunders must not go. He does not look very ill, and I hope is not, but I don't like some of his symptoms."

"Well, doctor, we can do without him. There's Tom Green and O'Riley. Nothing seems able to bring down O'Riley. Then there's—"

"There's Fred Ellice," cried Fred himself, joining the group; "I'll go with you if you'll take me."

"Most happy to have you, sir. Our healthy hands are very short, but we can muster sufficient, I think."

The captain suggested Amos Parr and two or three more men, and then dismissed his first mate to get ready for an immediate start.

"I don't half like your going, Fred," said his father. "You've not been well lately, and hunting on the floes, I know from experience, is hard work."

"Don't fear for me, father; I've quite recovered from my recent attack, which was but slight after all, and I know full well that those who are well must work as long as they can stand."

"Ho, lads! look alive there! are you ready?" shouted the first mate down the hatchway.

"Ay, ay, sir," replied Grim, and in a few minutes the party were assembled on the ice beside the small sledge with their shoulder-belts on, for most of the dogs were either dead or dying of that strange complaint to which allusion has been made in a previous chapter.

They set out silently, but ere they had got a dozen yards from the ship Captain Guy felt the impropriety of permitting them thus to depart.

"Up, lads, and give them three cheers!" he cried, mounting the ship's side and setting the example.

A hearty, generous spirit, when vigorously displayed, always finds a ready response from human hearts. The few sailors who were on deck at the time, and one or two of the sick men who chanced to put their heads up the hatchway, rushed to the side, waved their mittens—in default of caps—and gave vent to three hearty British cheers. The effect on the drooping spirits of the hunting-party was electrical. They pricked up like chargers that had felt the spur, wheeled round, and returned the cheer with interest. It was an apparently trifling incident, but it served to lighten the way and make it seem less dreary for many a long mile.

"I'm tired of it intirely," cried O'Riley, sitting down on a hummock, on the evening of the second day after setting out on the hunt; "here we is, two days out, an' not a sign o' life nowhere."

"Come, don't give in," said Bolton cheerfully; "we're sure to fall in with a walrus to-day."

"I think so," cried Fred; "we have come so far out upon the floes that there must be open water near."

"Come on, then," cried Peter Grim; "don't waste time talking."

Thus urged O'Riley rose, and throwing his sledge-strap over his shoulder, plodded on wearily with the rest.

Their provisions were getting low now, and it was felt that if they did not soon fall in with walruses or bears they must return as quickly as possible to the ship in order to avoid starving. It was therefore a matter of no small satisfaction that, on turning the edge of an iceberg, they discovered a large bear walking leisurely towards them. To drop their sledge-lines and seize their muskets was the work of a moment. But, unfortunately, long travelling had filled the pans with snow, and it required some time to pick the touch-holes clear. In this extremity Peter Grim seized a hatchet and ran towards the bear, while O'Riley charged it with a spear. Grim delivered a tremendous blow at its head with his weapon; but his intention was better than his aim, for he missed the bear and smashed the corner of a hummock of ice. O'Riley was more successful. He thrust the spear into the animal's shoulder; but the shoulder-blade turned the head of the weapon, and caused it to run along at least three feet just under the skin. The wound, although not fatal, was so painful that Bruin uttered a loud roar of disapproval, wheeled round, and ran away!—an act of cowardice so unusual on the part of a Polar bear that the whole party were taken by surprise. Several shots were fired after him, but he soon disappeared among the ice-hummocks, having fairly made off with O'Riley's spear.

The disappointment caused by this was great, but they had little time to think of it, for soon after a stiff breeze of wind sprang up, which freshened into a gale, compelling them to seek the shelter of a cluster of icebergs, in the midst of which they built a snow-hut. Before night a terrific storm was raging, with the thermometer 40° below zero. The sky became black as ink, drift whirled round them in horrid turmoil, and the wild blast came direct from the north, over the frozen sea, shrieking and howling in its strength and fury.

All that night and the next day it continued. Then it ceased, and for the first time that winter a thaw set in, so that ere morning their sleeping-bags and socks were thoroughly wetted. This was of short duration, however. In a few hours the frost set in again as intense as ever, converting all their wet garments and bedding into hard cakes of ice. To add to their misfortunes their provisions ran out, and they were obliged to abandon the hut and push forward towards the ship with the utmost speed. Night came on them while they were slowly toiling through the deep drifts that the late gale had raised, and to their horror they found they had wandered out of their way, and were still but a short distance from their snow-hut. In despair they returned to pass the night in it, and spreading their frozen sleeping-bags on the snow, they lay down, silent and supperless, to rest till morning.

CHAPTER XXIII.

Unexpected arrivals—The rescue party—Lost and found—Return to the ship.

The sixth night after the hunting-party had left the ship, Grim and Fred Ellice suddenly made their appearance on board. It was quite dark, and the few of the ship's company who were able to quit their berths were seated round the cabin at their meagre evening meal.

"Hallo, Fred!" exclaimed Captain Ellice, as his son staggered rather than walked in and sank down on a locker. "What's wrong, boy? where are the rest of you?"

Fred could not answer; neither he nor Grim was able to utter a word at first. It was evident that they laboured under extreme exhaustion and hunger. A mouthful of hot soup administered by Tom Singleton rallied them a little, however.

"Our comrades are lost, I fear."

"Lost!" exclaimed Captain Guy. "How so? Speak, my boy; but hold, take another mouthful before you speak. Where did you leave them, say you?"

Fred looked at the captain with a vacant stare. "Out upon the ice to the north; but, I say, what a comical dream I've had!" Here he burst into a loud laugh. Poor Fred's head was evidently affected, so his father and Tom carried him to his berth.

All this time Grim had remained seated on a locker swaying to and fro like a drunken man, and paying no attention to the numerous questions that were put to him by Saunders and his comrades.

"This is bad!" exclaimed Captain Guy, pressing his hand on his forehead.

"A search must be made," suggested Captain Ellice. "It's evident that the party have broken down out on the floes, and Fred and Grim have been sent to let us know."

"I know it," answered Captain Guy. "A search must be made, and that instantly, if it is to be of any use; but in which direction are we to go is the question. These poor fellows cannot tell us. 'Out on the ice to the north' is a wide word.—Fred, Fred, can you not tell us in which direction we ought to go to search for them?"

"Yes, far out on the floes—among hummocks—far out," murmured Fred, half unconsciously.

"We must be satisfied with that. Now, Mr. Saunders, assist me to get the small sledge fitted out. I'll go to look after them myself."

"An' I'll go with 'ee, sir," said the second mate promptly.

"I fear you are hardly able."

"No fear o' me, sir. I'm better than 'ee think."

"I must go too," added Captain Ellice; "it is quite evident that you cannot muster a party without me."

"That's impossible," interrupted the doctor. "Your leg is not strong enough nearly for such a trip; besides, my dear sir, you must stay behind to perform my duties, for the ship can't do without a doctor, and I shall go with Captain Guy, if he will allow me."

"That he won't," cried the captain. "You say truly the ship cannot be left without a doctor. Neither you nor my friend Ellice shall leave the ship with my permission. But don't let us waste time talking.—Come, Summers and Mizzle, you are well enough to join, and, Meetuck, you must be our guide. Look alive and get yourselves ready."

In less than half-an-hour the rescue party were equipped and on their way over the floes. They were six in all—one of the freshest among the crew having volunteered to join those already mentioned.

It was a very dark night, and bitterly cold; but they took nothing with them except the clothes on their backs, a supply of provisions for their lost comrades, their sleeping-bags, and a small leather tent. The captain also took care to carry with them a flask of brandy.

The colossal bergs, which stretched like well-known land-marks over the sea, were their guides at first; but after travelling ten hours without halting, they had passed the greater number of those with which they were familiar, and entered upon an unknown region. Here it became necessary to use the utmost caution. They knew that the lost men must be within twenty miles of them, but they had no means of knowing the exact spot, and any footprints that had been made were now obliterated. In these circumstances Captain Guy had to depend very much on his own sagacity.

Clambering to the top of a hummock, he observed a long stretch of level floe to the northward.

"I think it likely," he remarked to Saunders, who had accompanied him, "that they may have gone in that direction. It seems an attractive road among this chaos of ice-heaps."

"I'm no sure o' that," objected Saunders; "yonder's a pretty clear road away to the west, maybe they took that."

"Perhaps they did, but as Fred said they had gone far out on the ice *to the north*, I think it likely they've gone in *that* direction."

"Maybe ye're right, sir, and maybe ye're wrang," answered Saunders, as they returned to the party. As this was the second mate's method of intimating that he *felt* that he ought to give in (though he didn't give in, and never would give in *absolutely*), the captain felt more confidence in his own opinion.

"Now, Meetuck, keep your eyes open," he added, as they resumed their rapid march.

After journeying on for a considerable distance, the men were ordered to spread out over the neighbouring ice-fields, in order to multiply the chances of discovering tracks; but there seemed to be some irresistible power of attraction which drew them gradually together again, however earnestly they might try to keep separate. In fact, they were beginning to be affected by the long-continued march and the extremity of the cold.

This last was so great that constant motion was absolutely necessary in order to prevent them from freezing. There was no time allowed for rest—life and death were in the scale. Their only hope lay in a continuous and rapid advance, so as to reach the lost men ere they should freeze or die of starvation.

"Holo! look 'eer!" shouted Meetuck, as he halted and went down on his knees to examine some marks on the snow.

"These are tracks!" cried Captain Guy eagerly. "What think you, Saunders?"

"They look like it"

"Follow them up, Meetuck. Go in advance, my lad, and let the rest of you scatter again."

In a few minutes there was a cry heard, and as the party hastened towards the spot whence it came, they found Davie Summers pointing eagerly to a little snow-hut in the midst of a group of bergs.

With hasty steps they advanced towards it, and the captain, with a terrible misgiving at heart, crept in.

"Ah! then, is it yerself, darlint?" were the first words that greeted him.

A loud cheer from those without told that they heard and recognized the words. Immediately two of them crept in, and striking a light, kindled a lamp, which revealed the care-worn forms of their lost comrades stretched on the ground in their sleeping-bags. They were almost exhausted for want of food, but otherwise they were uninjured.

The first congratulations over, the rescue party immediately proceeded to make arrangements for passing the night. They were themselves little better than those whom they had come to save, having performed an uninterrupted march of eighteen hours without food or drink.

It was touching to see the tears of joy and gratitude that filled the eyes of the poor fellows, who had given themselves up for lost, as they watched the movements of their comrades while they prepared food for them; and the broken, fitful conversation was mingled strangely with alternate touches of fun and deep feeling, indicating the conflicting emotions that struggled in their breasts.

"I knowed ye would come, captain; bless you, sir," said Amos Parr, in an unsteady voice.

"Come! Av coorse ye knowed it," cried O'Riley energetically. "Och, but don't be long wid the mate, darlints, me stummik's shut up intirely."

"There won't be room for us all here, I'm afraid," remarked Bolton.

This was true. The hut was constructed to hold six, and it was impossible that ten could *sleep* in it, although they managed to squeeze in.

"Never mind that," cried the captain. "Here, take a drop of soup; gently, not too much at a time."

"Ah, then, it's cruel of ye, it is, to give me sich a small taste."

It was necessary, however, to give men in their condition a "small taste" at first, so O'Riley had to rest content. Meanwhile, the rescue party supped heartily, and after a little more food had been administered to the half-starved men, preparations were made for spending the night. The tent was pitched, and the sleeping-bags spread out on the snow. Then Captain Guy offered up fervent thanks to God for his protection thus far, and prayed shortly but earnestly for deliverance from their dangerous situation; after which they all lay down and slept soundly till morning—or at least as soundly as could be expected with a temperature at 55° below zero.

Next morning they prepared to set out on their return to the ship. But this was no easy task. The exhausted men had to be wrapped up carefully in their blankets, which were sewed closely round their limbs, then packed in their sleeping-bags and covered completely up, only a small hole being left opposite their mouths to breathe through, and after that they were lashed side by side on the small sledge. The larger sledge, with the muskets, ammunition, and spare blankets, had to be abandoned. Then the rescue party put their shoulders to the tracking-belts, and away they went briskly over the floes.

But the drag was a fearfully heavy one for men who, besides having walked so long and so far on the previous day, were, most of them, much weakened by illness, and very unfit for such laborious work. The floes, too, were so rugged that they had frequently to lift the heavy sledge and its living load over deep rents and chasms which, in circumstances less desperate, they would have scarcely ventured to do. Work as they would, however, they could not make more than a mile an hour, and night overtook them ere they reached the level floes. But it was of the utmost importance that they should continue to advance, so they pushed forward until a breeze sprang up that pierced them through and through.

Fortunately there was a bright moon in the sky, which enabled them to pick their way among the hummocks. Suddenly, without warning, the whole party felt an alarming failure of their energies. Captain Guy, who was aware of the imminent danger of giving way to this feeling, cheered the men to greater exertion by word and voice, but failed to rouse them. They seemed like men walking in their sleep.

"Come, Saunders, cheer up, man!" cried the captain, shaking the mate by the arm; but Saunders stood still, swaying to and fro like a drunken man. Mizzle begged to be allowed to sleep, if it were only for two minutes, and poor Davie Summers deliberately threw himself down on the snow, from which, had he been left, he would never more have risen.

The case was now desperate. In vain the captain shook and buffeted the men. They protested that they did not feel cold—"they were quite warm, and only wanted a little sleep." He saw that it was useless to contend with them, so there was nothing left for it but to pitch the tent.

This was done as quickly as possible, though with much difficulty, and the men were unlashed from the sledge and placed within the tent. The others then crowded in, and falling down beside each other were asleep in an instant. The excessive crowding of the little tent was an advantage at this time, as it tended to increase their animal heat. Captain Guy allowed them to sleep only two hours, and then roused them in order to continue the journey; but short though the period of rest was, it proved sufficient to enable the men to pursue their journey with some degree of spirit. Still it was evident that their energies had been overtaxed; for when they neared the ship next day, Tom Singleton, who had been on the look-out, and advanced to meet them, found that they were almost in a state of stupor, and talked incoherently—sometimes giving utterance to sentiments of the most absurd nature with expressions of the utmost gravity.

Meanwhile, good news was brought them from the ship. Two bears and a walrus had been purchased from the Esquimaux, a party of whom—sleek, fat, oily, good-humoured, and hairy—were encamped on the lee side of the *Dolphin*, and were busily engaged in their principal and favourite occupation—eating!

CHAPTER XXIV.

Winter ends—The first insect—Preparations for departure—Narrow escape—Cutting out—Once more afloat—Ship on fire—Crew take to the boats.

Winter passed away, with its darkness and its frost, and, happily, with its sorrows; and summer—bright, glowing summer—came at last, to gladden the heart of man and beast in the Polar Regions.

We have purposely omitted to make mention of spring, for there is no such season, properly so called, within the Arctic Circle. Winter usually terminates with a gushing thaw, and summer then begins with a blaze of fervent heat. Not that the heat is really so intense as compared with that of southern climes, but the contrast is so great that it *seems* as though the Torrid Zones had rushed towards the Pole.

About the beginning of June there were indications of the coming heat. Fresh water began to trickle from the rocks, and streamlets commenced to run down the icebergs. Soon everything became moist, and a marked change took place in the appearance of the ice-belt, owing to the pools that collected on it everywhere and overflowed.

Seals now became more numerous in the neighbourhood, and were frequently killed near the *atluks*, or holes, so that fresh meat was secured in abundance, and the scurvy received a decided check. Reindeer, rabbits, and ptarmigan, too, began to frequent the bay, so that the larder was constantly full, and the mess-table presented a pleasing variety—rats being no longer the solitary dish of fresh meat at every meal. A few small birds made their appearance from the southward, and these were hailed as harbingers of the coming summer.

One day O'Riley sat on the taffrail, basking in the warm sun, and drinking in health and gladness from its beams. He had been ill, and was now convalescent. Buzzby stood beside him.

"I've bin thinkin'," said Buzzby, "that we don't half know the blessin's that are given to us in this here world till we've had 'em taken away. Look, now, how we're enjoyin' the sun an' the heat, just as if it wos so much gold!"

"Goold!" echoed O'Riley, in a tone of contempt; "faix I niver thought so little o' goold before, let me tell ye. Goold can buy many a thing, it can, but it can't buy sunshine. Hallo! what's this?"

O'Riley accompanied the question with a sudden snatch of his hand.

"Look here, Buzzby! Have a care, now! jist watch the openin' o' my fist."

"Wot is it?" inquired Buzzby, approaching, and looking earnestly at his comrade's clinched hand with some curiosity.

"There he comes! Now, then, not so fast, ye spalpeen!"

As he spoke, a small fly, which had been captured, crept out from between his fingers, and sought to escape. It was the first that had visited these frozen regions for many, many months, and the whole crew were summoned on deck to meet it as if it were an old and valued friend.

"Let it go, poor thing!" cried half-a-dozen of the men, gazing at the little prisoner with a degree of interest that cannot be thoroughly understood by those who have not passed through experiences similar to those of our Arctic voyagers.

"Ay, don't hurt it, poor thing! You're squeezin' it too hard!" cried Amos Parr.

"Squaazing it! no, then, I'm not. Go, avic, an' me blessin' go wid ye."

The big, rough hand opened, and the tiny insect, spreading its gossamer wings, buzzed away into the bright atmosphere, where it was soon lost to view.

"Rig up the ice-saws, Mr. Bolton; set all hands at them, and get out the powder-canisters," cried Captain Guy, coming hastily on deck.

"Ay, ay, sir," responded the mate. "All hands to the ice-saws! Look alive, boys! Ho! Mr. Saunders! Where's Mr. Saunders?"

"Here 'am," answered the worthy second mate in a quiet voice.

"Oh, you're there! Get up some powder, Mr. Saunders, and a few canisters."

There was a heartiness in the tone and action with which these orders were given and obeyed that proved they were possessed of more than ordinary interest; as, indeed, they were, for the time had now come for making preparations for cutting the ship out of winter-quarters, and getting ready to take advantage of any favourable opening in the ice that might occur.

"Do you hope to effect much?" inquired Captain Ellice of Captain Guy, who stood at the gangway watching the men as they leaped over the side and began to cut holes with ice-chisels preparatory to fixing the saws and powder-canisters.

"Not much," replied the captain; "but a *little* in these latitudes is worth fighting hard for, as you are well aware. Many a time have I seen a ship's crew strain and heave on warps and cables for hours together, and only gain a yard by all their efforts; but many a time, also, have I seen a single yard of headway save a ship from destruction."

"True," rejoined Captain Ellice; "I have seen a little of it myself. There is no spot on earth, I think, equal to the Polar Regions for bringing out into bold relief two great and *apparently* antagonistic truth's—namely, man's urgent need of all his powers to accomplish the work of his own deliverance, and man's utter helplessness and entire dependence on the sovereign will of God."

"When shall we sink the canisters, sir?" asked Bolton, coming up and touching his hat.

"In an hour, Mr. Bolton; the tide will be full then, and we shall try what effect a blast will have."

"My opeenion is," remarked Saunders, who passed at the moment with two large bags of gunpowder under his arms, "that it'll have no effect at a'. It'll just loosen the ice roond the ship."

The captain smiled as he said, "*That* is all the effect I hope for, Mr. Saunders. Should the outward ice give way soon, we shall then be in a better position to avail ourselves of it."

As Saunders predicted, the effect of powder and saws was merely to loosen and rend the ice-tables in which the *Dolphin* was imbedded; but deliverance was coming sooner than any of those on board expected. That night a storm arose, which, for intensity of violence, equalled, if it did not surpass, the severest gales they had yet experienced. It set the great bergs of the Polar Seas in motion, and these moving mountains of ice slowly and majestically began their voyage to southern climes, crashing through the floes, overturning the hummocks, and ripping up the ice-tables with quiet but irresistible momentum. For two days the war of ice continued to rage, and sometimes the contending forces, in the shape of huge tongues and corners of bergs, were forced into the Bay of Mercy, and threatened swift destruction to the little craft, which was a mere atom that might have been crushed and sunk and scarcely missed in such a wild scene.

213

At one time a table of ice was forced out of the water and reared up, like a sloping wall of glass, close to the stern of the *Dolphin*, where all the crew were assembled with ice-poles ready to do their utmost; but their feeble efforts could have availed them nothing had the slowly-moving mass continued its onward progress.

"Lower away the quarter-boat," cried the captain, as the sheet of ice six feet thick came grinding down towards the starboard quarter.

Buzzby, Grim, and several others sprang to obey, but before they could let go the fall-tackles, the mass of ice rose suddenly high above the deck, over which it projected several feet, and caught the boat. In another moment the timbers yielded, the thwarts sprang out or were broken across, and slowly, yet forcibly, as a strong hand might crush an egg-shell, the boat was squeezed flat against the ship's side.

"Shove, lads! if it comes on we're lost," cried the captain, seizing one of the long poles with which the men were vainly straining every nerve and muscle. They might as well have tried to arrest the progress of a berg. On it came, and crushed in the starboard quarter bulwarks. Providentially at that moment it grounded and remained fast; but the projecting point that overhung them broke off and fell on the deck with a crash that shook the good ship from stem to stern. Several of the men were thrown violently down, but none were seriously hurt in this catastrophe.

When the storm ceased the ice out in the strait was all in motion, and that round the ship had loosened so much that it seemed as if the *Dolphin* might soon get out into open water, and once more float upon its natural element. Every preparation, therefore, was made. The stores were re-shipped from Store Island; the sails were shaken out, and those of them that had been taken down were bent on to the yards; tackle was overhauled; and, in short, everything was done that was possible under the circumstances. But a week passed away ere they succeeded in finally warping out of the bay into the open sea beyond.

It was a lovely morning when this happy event was accomplished. Before the tide was quite full, and while they were waiting until the command to heave on the warps should be given, Captain Guy assembled the crew for morning prayers in the cabin. Having concluded, he said:—

"My lads, through the great mercy of God we have been all, except one, spared through the trials and anxieties of a long and dreary winter, and are now, I trust, about to make our escape from the ice that has held us fast so long. It becomes me at such a time to tell you that, if I am spared to return home, I shall be able to report that every man in this ship has done his duty. You have never flinched in the hour of danger, and never grumbled in the hour of trial. Only one man—our late brave and warm-hearted comrade, Joseph West—has fallen in the struggle. For the mercies that have never failed us, and for our success in rescuing my gallant friend, Captain Ellice, we ought to feel the deepest gratitude to the Almighty. We have need, however, to pray for a blessing on the labours that are yet before us, for you are well aware that we shall probably have many a struggle with the ice before we are once more afloat on blue water. And now, lads, away with you on deck, and man the capstan, for the tide is about full."

The capstan was manned, and the hawsers were hove taut. Inch by inch the tide rose, and the *Dolphin* floated. Then a lusty cheer was given, and Amos Parr struck up one of those hearty songs intermingled with "Ho!" and "Yo heave ho!" that seem to be the life and marrow of all nautical exertion. At last the good ship forged ahead, and, *boring* through the loose ice, passed slowly out of the Bay of Mercy.

"Do you know I feel quite sad at quitting this dreary spot?" said Fred to his father, as they stood gazing backward over the taffrail. "I could not have believed that I should have become so much attached to it."

"We become attached to any spot, Fred, in which incidents have occurred to call forth frequently our deeper feelings. These rocks and stones are intimately associated with many events that have caused you joy and sorrow, hope and fear, pain and happiness. Men cherish the memory of such feelings, and love the spots of earth with which they are associated."

"Ah, father, yonder stands one stone, at least, that calls forth feelings of sorrow."

Fred pointed as he spoke to Store Island, which was just passing out of view. On this lonely spot the men had raised a large stone over the grave of Joseph West. O'Riley, whose enthusiastic temperament had caused him to mourn over his comrade more, perhaps, than any other man in the ship, had carved the name and date of his death in rude characters on the stone. It was a conspicuous object on the low island, and every eye in the *Dolphin* was fixed on it as they passed. Soon the point of rock that had sheltered them so long from many a westerly gale intervened and shut it out from view for ever.

When man's prospects are at the worst, it often happens that some unexpected success breaks on his path like a bright sunbeam. Alas! it often happens, also, that when his hopes are high and his prospects brightest, a dark cloud overspreads him like a funeral pall. We might learn a lesson from this—the lesson of dependence on that Saviour who *careth* for us, and of trust in that blessed assurance that "*all* things work together for good to them that love God."

A week of uninterrupted fair wind and weather had carried the *Dolphin* far to the south of their dreary wintering ground, and all was going well, when the worst of all disasters befell the ship—she caught fire! How it happened no one could tell. The smoke was first seen rising suddenly from the hold. Instantly the alarm was spread.

"Firemen, to your posts!" shouted the captain. "Man the water-buckets! Steady, men; no hurry. Keep order."

"Ay, ay, sir," was the short, prompt response, and the most perfect order *was* kept. Every command was obeyed instantly with a degree of vigour that is seldom exhibited save in cases of life and death.

Buzzby was at the starboard and Peter Grim at the larboard gangway, while the men stood in two rows, extending from each to the main hatch, up which ever thickening clouds of dark smoke were rolling. Bucket after bucket of water was passed along and dashed into the hold, and everything that could be done was done, but without effect. The fire increased. Suddenly a long tongue of flame issued from the smoking cavern, and lapped round the mast and rigging with greedy eagerness.

"There's no hope," said Captain Ellice in a low voice, laying his hand gently on Captain Guy's shoulder.

The captain did not reply, but gazed with an expression of the deepest regret, for one moment, at the work of destruction.

Next instant he sprang to the falls of the larboard quarter-boat.

"Now, lads," he cried energetically, "get out the boats. Bring up provisions, Mr. Bolton, and a couple of spare sails.—Mr. Saunders, see to the ammunition and muskets. Quick, men. The cabin will soon be too hot to hold you."

Setting the example, the captain sprang below, followed by Fred and Tom Singleton, who secured the charts, a compass, chronometer, and quadrant; also the log-book and the various journals and records of the voyage. Captain Ellice also did active service, and being cool and selfossessed he recollected and secured several articles which were afterwards of the greatest use, and which, but for him, would in such a trying moment have probably been forgotten.

Meanwhile, the two largest boats in the ship were lowered. Provisions, masts, sails, and oars, etc., were thrown in. The few remaining dogs, among whom were Dumps and Poker, were also embarked; and the crew hastily leaping in pushed off. They were not a moment too soon. The fire had reached the place where the gunpowder was kept, and although there was not a great quantity of it, there was enough when it exploded to burst open the deck. The wind, having free ingress, fanned the fire into a furious blaze, and in a few moments the *Dolphin* was wrapped in flames from stem to stern. It was a little after sunset when the fire was discovered. In two hours later the good ship was burned to the water's edge. Then the waves swept in, and while they extinguished the fire they sank the blackened hull, leaving the two crowded boats floating in darkness on the bosom of the ice-laden sea.

CHAPTER XXV.

Escape to Upernavik—Letter from home—Meetuck's grandmother—Dumps and Poker again.

For three long weeks the shipwrecked mariners were buffeted by winds and waves in open boats, but at last they were guided in safety through all their dangers and vicissitudes to the colony of Upernavik. Here they found several vessels on the point of setting out for Europe, one of which was bound for England, and in this vessel the crew of the *Dolphin* resolved to ship.

Nothing of particular interest occurred at this solitary settlement except *one* thing, but that one thing was a great event, and deserves very special notice. It was nothing less than the receipt of a letter by Fred from his cousin Isobel! Fred and Isobel, having been brought up for several years together, felt towards each other like brother and sister.

Fred received the letter from the pastor of the settlement shortly after landing, while his father and the captain were on board the English brig making arrangements for their passage home. He could scarcely believe his eyes when he beheld the well-known hand; but having at last come to realize the fact that he actually held a real letter in his hand, he darted behind one of the curious, primitive cottages to read it. Here he was met by a squad of inquisitive natives, so with a gesture of impatience he rushed to another spot; but he was observed and followed by half-a-dozen Esquimau boys, and in despair he sought refuge in the small church near which he chanced to be. He had not been there a second, however, when two old women came in, and, approaching him, began to scan him with critical eyes. This was too much, so Fred thrust the letter into his bosom, darted out, and was instantly surrounded by a band of natives, who began to question him in an unknown tongue. Seeing that there was no other resource, Fred turned round and fled towards the mountains at a pace that defied pursuit, and, coming to a halt in the midst of a rocky gorge that might have served as an illustration of what chaos was, he sat down behind a big rock to peruse Isobel's letter.

Having read it, he re-read it; having re-read it, he read it over again. Having read it over again, he meditated a little, exclaiming several times emphatically, "My *darling* Isobel," and then he read bits of it here and there; having done which, he read the *other* bits, and so got through it again. As the letter was a pretty long one, it took him a considerable time to do all this. Then it suddenly occurred to him that he had been thus selfishly keeping it all to himself instead of sharing it with his father; so he started up and hastened back to the village, where he found Captain Ellice in earnest confabulation with the pastor of the place. Seizing his parent by the arm, Fred led him into a room in the pastor's house, and, looking round to make sure that it was empty, he sought to bolt the door. But the door was a primitive one and had no bolt, so Fred placed a huge old-fashioned chair against it, and sitting down therein, while his father took a seat opposite, he unfolded the letter, and yet once again read it through.

The letter was about twelve months old, and ran thus:—

GRAYTON, *25th July.*

MY DARLING FRED,—It is now two months since you left us, and it seems to me two years. Oh, how I *do* wish that you were back! When I think of the terrible dangers that you may be exposed to amongst the ice my heart sinks, and I sometimes fear that we shall never see you or your dear father again. But you are in the hands of our Father in heaven, dear Fred, and I never cease to pray that you may be successful and return to us in safety. Dear, good old Mr. Singleton told me yesterday that he had an opportunity of sending to the Danish settlements in Greenland, so I resolved to write, though I very much doubt whether this will ever find you in such a wild far-offland.

Oh, when I think of where you are, all the romantic stories I have ever read of Polar Regions spring up before me, and *you* seem to be the hero of them all. But I must not waste my paper thus; I know you will be anxious for news. I have very little to give you, however. Good old Mr. Singleton has been *very* kind to us since you went away. He comes constantly to see us, and comforts dear mamma very much. Your friend, Dr. Singleton, will be glad to hear that he is well and strong. Tell my friend Buzzby that his wife sends her 'compliments!' I laugh while I write the word. Yes, she actually sends her 'compliments' to her husband. She is a very stern but a really excellent woman. Mamma and I visit her frequently when we chance to be in the village. Her two boys are the finest little fellows I ever saw. They are both so like each other that we cannot tell which is which when they are apart, and both are so like their father that we can almost fancy we see him when looking at either of them.

"The last day we were there, however, they were in disgrace, for Johnny had pushed Freddy into the washing-tub, and Freddy, in revenge, had poured a jug of treacle over Johnny's head! I am quite sure that Mrs. Buzzby is tired of being a widow—as she calls herself—and will be very glad when her husband comes back. But I must reserve chit-chat to the end of my letter, and first give you a minute account of all your friends."

Here followed six pages of closely-written quarto, which, however interesting they might be to those concerned, cannot be expected to afford much entertainment to our readers, so we will cut Isobel's letter short at this point.

"Cap'n's ready to go aboord, sir," said O'Riley, touching his cap to Captain Ellice while he was yet engaged in discussing the letter with his son.

"Very good."

"An', plaze sir, av ye'll take the throuble to look in at Mrs. Meetuck in passin', it'll do yer heart good, it will."

"Very well, we'll look in," replied the captain as he quitted the house of the worthy pastor.

The personage whom O'Riley chose to style Mrs. Meetuck was Meetuck's grandmother. That old lady was an Esquimau, whose age might be algebraically expressed as an *unknown quantity*. She lived in a boat turned upside down, with a small window in the bottom of it, and a hole in the side for a door. When Captain Ellice and Fred looked in, the old woman, who was a mere mass of bones and wrinkles, was seated on a heap of moss beside a fire, the only chimney to which was a hole in the bottom of the boat. In front of her sat her grandson Meetuck, and on a cloth spread out at her feet were displayed all the presents with which that good hunter had been loaded by his comrades of the *Dolphin*. Meetuck's mother had died many years before, and all the affection in his naturally warm heart was transferred to, and centred upon, his old grandmother. Meetuck's chief delight in the gifts he received was in sharing them, as far as possible, with the old woman. We say *as far as possible*, because some things could not be shared with her, such as a splendid new rifle and a silver-mounted hunting-knife and powder-horn, all of which had been presented to him by Captain Guy over and above his wages, as a reward for his valuable services. But the trinkets of every kind which had been given to him by the men were laid at the feet of the old woman, who looked at everything in blank amazement, yet with a smile on her wrinkled visage that betokened much satisfaction. Meetuck's oily countenance beamed with delight as he sat puffing his pipe in his grandmother's face. This little attention, we may remark, was paid designedly, for the old woman liked it, and the youth knew that.

"They have enough to make them happy for the winter," said Captain Ellice, as he turned to leave the hut.

"Faix they have. There's only two things wantin' to make it complate."

"What are they?" inquired Fred.

"Murphies and a pig, sure. That's all they need."

"Wot's come o' Dumps and Poker?" inquired Buzzby, as they reached the boat.

"Oh, I quite forgot them!" cried Fred. "Stay a minute, I'll run up and find them. They can't be far off."

For some time Fred searched in vain. At last he bethought him of Meetuck's hut as being a likely spot in which to find them. On entering he found the couple as he had left them, the only difference being that the poor old woman seemed to be growing sleepy over her joys.

"Have you seen Dumps or Poker anywhere?" inquired Fred.

Meetuck nodded, and pointed to a corner, where, comfortably rolled up on a mound of dry moss, lay Dumps; Poker, as usual, making use of him as a pillow.

"Thems is go bed," said Meetuck.

"Thems must get up then and come aboard," cried Fred, whistling.

At first the dogs, being sleepy, seemed indisposed to move; but at last they consented, and following Fred to the beach, were soon conveyed aboard the ship.

Next day Captain Guy and his men bade Meetuck and the kind, hospitable people of Upernavik farewell, and spreading their canvas to a fair breeze, set sail for England.

CHAPTER XXVI.

The return—The surprise—Buzzby's sayings and doings—The narrative—Fighting battles o'er again—Conclusion.

Once again we are on the end of the quay at Grayton. As Fred stands there, all that has occurred during the past year seems to him but a vivid dream.

Captain Guy is there, and Captain Ellice, and Buzzby, and Mrs. Buzzby too, and the two little Buzzbys also, and Mrs. Bright, and Isobel, and Tom Singleton, and old Mr. Singleton, and the crew of the wrecked *Dolphin*, and, in short, the "whole world"—of that part of the country.

It was a great day for Grayton that. It was a wonderful day—quite an indescribable day; but there were also some things about it that made Captain Ellice feel, somehow, that it was a mysterious day, for, while there were hearty congratulations, and much sobbing for joy, on the part of Mrs. Bright, there were also whisperings which puzzled him a good deal.

"Come with me, brother," said Mrs. Bright, at length, taking him by the arm, "I have to tell you something."

Isobel, who was on the watch, joined them, and Fred also went with them towards the cottage.

"Dear brother," said Mrs. Bright, "I—I—O Isobel, tell him. *I* cannot."

"What means all this mystery?" said the captain in an earnest tone, for he felt that they had something serious to communicate.

"Dear uncle," said Isobel, "you remember the time when the pirates attacked—"

She paused, for her uncle's look frightened her.

"Go on, Isobel," he said quickly.

"Your dear wife, uncle, *was not lost at that time*—"

Captain Ellice turned pale. "What mean you, girl? How came you to know this?" Then a thought flashed across him. Seizing Isobel by the shoulder he gasped, rather than said, "Speak quick—is—is she alive?"

"Yes, dear uncle, she—"

The captain heard no more. He would have fallen to the ground had not Fred, who was almost as much overpowered as his father, supported him. In a few minutes he recovered, and he was told that Alice was alive—in England—*in the cottage*. This was said as they approached the door. Alice was aware of her husband's arrival. In another moment husband and wife and son were reunited.

Scenes of intense joy cannot be adequately described, and there are meetings in this world which ought not to be too closely touched upon. Such was the present. We will therefore leave Captain Ellice and his wife and son to pour out the deep feelings of their hearts to each other, and follow the footsteps of honest John Buzzby, as he sailed down the village with his wife and children, and a host of admiring friends in tow.

Buzzby's feelings had been rather powerfully stirred up by the joy of all around, and a tear *would* occasionally tumble over his weather-beaten cheek, and hang at the point of his sunburnt and oft frost-bitten nose, despite his utmost efforts to subdue such outrageous demonstrations.

"Sit down, John dear," said Mrs. Buzzby in kind but commanding tones, when she got her husband fairly into his cottage, the little parlour of which was instantly crowded to excess. "Sit down, John dear, and tell us all about it."

"Wot! begin to spin the whole yarn o' the Voyage afore I've had time to say, 'How d'ye do?'" exclaimed Buzzby, at the same time grasping his two uproarious sons, who had, the instant he sat down, rushed at his legs like two miniature midshipmen, climbed up them as if they had been two masts, and settled on his knees as if they had been their own favourite cross-trees!

"No, John, not the yarn of the voyage," replied his wife, while she spread the board before him with bread and cheese and beer, "but tell us how you found old Captain Ellice and where, and what's comed of the crew."

"Werry good! then here goes."

Buzzby was a man of action. He screwed up his weather-eye (the one next his wife, *of course*, that being the quarter from which squalls might be expected). and began a yarn which lasted the better part of two hours.

It is not to be supposed that Buzzby spun it off without interruption. Besides the questions that broke in upon him from all quarters, the two

225

Buzzbys junior scrambled, as far as was possible, into his pockets, pulled his whiskers as if they had been hoisting a main-sail therewith, and, generally, behaved in such an obstreperous manner as to render coherent discourse all but impracticable. He got through with it, however; and then Mrs. Buzzby intimated her wish, pretty strongly, that the neighbours should vacate the premises, which they did laughingly, pronouncing Buzzby to be "a trump," and his better half "a true blue."

"Good day, old chap," said the last who made his exit; "tiller's fixed agin—nailed amid-ships, eh?"

"Hard and fast," replied Buzzby, with a broad grin, as he shut the door and returned to the bosom of his family.

Two days later a grand feast was given at Mrs. Bright's cottage, to which all the friends of the family were invited to meet with Captain Ellice and those who had returned from their long and perilous voyage. It was a joyful gathering that, and glad and grateful hearts were there.

Two days later still, and another feast was given. On this occasion Buzzby was the host, and Buzzby's cottage was the scene. It was a joyful meeting, too, and a jolly one to boot, for O'Riley was there, and Peter Grim, and Amos Parr, and David Mizzle, and Mivins—in short, the entire crew of the lost *Dolphin*—captain, mates, surgeon, and all. Fred and his father were also there, and old Mr. Singleton, and a number of other friends, so that all the rooms in the house had to be thrown open, and even then Mrs. Buzzby had barely room to move. It was on this occasion that Buzzby related to his shipmates how Mrs. Ellice had escaped from drowning on the night they were attacked by pirates on board the West Indiaman. He took occasion to relate the circumstances just before the "people from the house" arrived, and as the reader may perhaps prefer Buzzby's account to ours, we give it as it was delivered.

"You see, it happened this way," began Buzzby.

"Hand us a coal, Buzzby, to light my pipe, before ye begin," said Peter Grim.

"Ah! then, howld yer tongue, Blunderbore," cried O'Riley, handing the glowing coal demanded, with as much nonchalance as if his fingers were made of cast-iron.

"Well, ye see," resumed Buzzby, "when poor Mrs. Ellice wos pitched overboard, as I seed her with my own two eyes—"

"Stop, Buzzby," said Mivins; "'ow was 'er 'ead at the time?"

"Shut up, Mivins," cried several of the men; "go on, Buzzby."

"Well, I think her 'ead wos sou'-west, if it warn't nor'-east. Anyhow it wos pintin' somewhere or other round the compass. But, as I wos sayin', when Mrs. Ellice struck the water (an' she told me all about it herself, ye must know) she sank, and then she comed up, and didn't know how it wos, but she caught hold of an oar that wos floatin' close beside her, and screamed for help; but no help came, for it wos dark, and the ship had disappeared, so she gave herself up for lost. But in a little the oar struck agin a big piece o' the wreck o' the pirate's boat, and she managed to clamber upon it, and lay there, a'most dead with cold, till mornin'. The first thing she saw when day broke forth wos a big ship, bearin' right down on her, and she wos jist about run down when one o' the men observed her from the bow.

"'Hard a-port!' roared the man.

"'Port it is,' cried the man at the wheel, an' round went the ship like a duck, jist missin' the bit of wreck as she passed. A boat wos lowered, and Mrs. Ellice wos took aboard. Well, she found that the ship wos bound for the Sandwich Islands, and as they didn't mean to touch at any port in passin', Mrs. Ellice had to go on with her. Misfortins don't come single, howsiver. The ship wos wrecked on a coral reef, and the crew had to take to their boats, which they did, an' got safe to land; but the land they got to wos an out-o'-the-way island among the Feejees, and a spot where ships never come, so they had to make up their minds to stop there."

"I thought," said Amos Parr, "that the Feejees were cannibals, and that whoever was wrecked or cast ashore on their coasts was killed and roasted, and eat up at once."

"So ye're right," rejoined Buzzby; "but Providence sent the crew to one o' the islands that had bin visited by a native Christian missionary from one o' the other islands, and the people had gin up some o' their worst practices, and wos thinkin' o' turnin' over a new leaf altogether. So the crew wos spared, and took to livin' among the natives, quite comfortable like. But they soon got tired and took to their boats agin, and left. Mrs. Ellice, however, determined to remain and help the native Christians, till a ship should pass that way. For three years nothin' but canoes hove in sight o' that lonesome island; then, at last, a brig came, and cast anchor off shore. It wos an Australian trader that had been blown out o' her course on her way to England, so they took poor Mrs. Ellice aboard, and brought her home—and that's how it wos."

Buzzby's outline, although meagre, is so comprehensive that we do not think it necessary to add a word. Soon after he had concluded, the guests of the evening came in, and the conversation became general.

"Buzzby's jollification," as it was called in the village, was long remembered as one of the most interesting events that had occurred for many years. One of the chief amusements of the evening was the spinning of long yarns about the incidents of the late voyage, by men who could spin them well.

Their battles in the Polar Seas were all fought over again. The wondering listeners were told how Esquimaux were chased and captured; how walruses were lanced and harpooned; how bears were speared and shot; how long and weary journeys were undertaken on foot over immeasurable fields of ice and snow; how icebergs had crashed around their ship, and chains had been snapped asunder, and tough anchors had been torn from the ground or lost; how schools had been set agoing and a theatre got up; and how, provisions having failed, rats were eaten—and eaten, too, with gusto. All this and a great deal more was told on that celebrated night—sometimes by one, sometimes by another, and sometimes, to the confusion of the audience, by two or three at once, and, not unfrequently, to the still greater confusion of story-tellers and audience alike, the whole proceedings were interrupted by the outrageous yells and turmoil of the two indomitable young Buzzbys, as they romped in reckless joviality with Dumps and Poker. But at length the morning light broke up the party, and stories of the World of Ice came to an end.

And now, reader, our tale is told. But we cannot close without a parting word in regard to those with whom we have held intercourse so long.

It must not be supposed that from this date everything in the affairs of our various friends flowed on in a tranquil, uninterrupted course. This world is a battle-field, on which no warrior finds rest until he dies; and yet, to the Christian warrior on that field, the hour of death is the hour of victory. "Change" is written in broad letters on everything connected with Time; and he who would do his duty well, and enjoy the greatest possible amount of happiness here, must seek to prepare himself for every change. Men cannot escape the general law. The current of their particular stream may long run smooth, but sooner or later the rugged channel and the precipice will come. Some streams run quietly for many a league, and only at the last are troubled. Others burst from their very birth on rocks of difficulty, and rush, throughout their course, n tortuous, broken channels.

So was it with the actors in our story. Our hero's course was smooth. Having fallen in love with his friend Tom Singleton's profession, he studied medicine and surgery, became an M.D., and returned to practise in Grayton, which was a flourishing sea-port, and, during the course of Fred's career, extended considerably. Fred also fell in love with a pretty young girl in a neighbouring town, and married her. Tom Singleton also took up his abode in Grayton, there being, as he said, room for two." Ever since Tom had seen Isobel on the end of the quay, on the day when the *Dolphin* set sail for the Polar Regions, his heart had been taken prisoner. Isobel refused to give it back unless he, Tom, should return the heart which he had stolen from her. This he could not do, so it was agreed that the two hearts should be tied together, and they two should be constituted joint guardians of both. In short, they were married, and took Mrs. Bright to live with them, not far from the residence of old Mr. Singleton, who was the fattest and jolliest old gentleman in the place, and the very idol of dogs and boys, who loved him to distraction.

Captain Ellice, having had, as he said, "more than his share of the sea," resolved to live on shore, and, being possessed of a moderately comfortable income, he purchased Mrs. Bright's cottage on the green hill that overlooked the harbour and the sea. Here he became celebrated for his benevolence, and for the energy with which he entered into all the schemes that were devised for the benefit of the town of Grayton. Like Tom Singleton and Fred, he became deeply interested in the condition of the poor, and had a special weakness for *poor old women,* which he exhibited by searching up, and doing good to, every poor old woman in the parish. Captain Ellice was also celebrated for his garden, which was a remarkably fine one; for his flagstaff, which was a remarkably tall and magnificent one; and for his telescope, which constantly protruded from his drawingroom window, and pointed in the direction of the sea.

As for the others—Captain Guy continued his career at sea as commander of an East Indiaman. He remained stout and true-hearted to the last, like one of the oak timbers of his own good ship.

Bolton, Saunders, Mivins, Peter Grim, Amos Parr, and the rest of them, were scattered in a few years, as sailors usually are, to the four quarters of the globe. O'Riley alone was heard of again. He wrote to Buzzby "by manes of the ritin' he had larn'd aboord the *Dolfin*," informing him that he had forsaken the "say" and become a small farmer near Cork. He had plenty of murphies and also a pig—the latter "bein'" he said, "so like the wan that belonged to his owld grandmother that he thought it must be the same wan corned alive agin, or its darter."

And Buzzby—poor Buzzby—he also gave up the sea, much against his will, by command of his wife, and took to miscellaneous work, of which there was plenty for an active man in a sea-port like Grayton. His rudder, poor man, was again (and this time permanently) lashed amid-ships, and whatever breeze Mrs. Buzzby chanced to blow, his business was to sail *right before it.* The two little Buzzbys were the joy of their father's heart. They were genuine little true-blues, both of them, and went to sea the moment their legs were long enough, and came home, voyage after voyage, with gifts of curiosities and gifts of money to their worthy parents.

Dumps resided during the remainder of his days with Captain Ellice, and Poker dwelt with Buzzby. These truly remarkable dogs kept up their attachment to each other to the end. Indeed, as time passed by, they drew closer and closer together, for Poker became more sedate, and, consequently, a more suitable companion for his ancient friend. The dogs formed a connecting link between the Buzzby and Ellice families—constantly reminding each of the other's existence by the daily interchange of visits.

Fred and Tom soon came to be known as the best doctors with which that part of the country had ever been blessed. And the secret of their success lay in this, that while they ministered to the diseased bodies of men, they also ministered to their diseased souls. With skilful hands they sought to arrest the progress of decay; but when all their remedies failed, they did not merely cease their efforts and retire— they turned to the pages of divine truth, and directed the gaze of the dying sufferers to Jesus Christ, the Great Physician of souls. When death had done its work, they did not quit the mourning household as if they were needed there no longer, but kneeling down with the bereaved, they prayed to Him who alone can bind up the broken heart, and besought the Holy Spirit to comfort the stricken ones in their deep affliction.

Thus Fred and his friend went hand in hand together, respected and blessed by all who knew them—each year as it passed cementing closer and closer that undying friendship which had first started into being in the gay season of boyhood, and had bloomed and ripened amid the adventures, dangers, and vicissitudes of the World of Ice.

Lightning Source UK Ltd.
Milton Keynes UK
UKHW010758060223
416537UK00008B/1872

9 783734 093334